Let the Breeze Blow

Let the Breeze Blow

Eralides E. Cabrera

authorHOUSE®

AuthorHouse™
1663 Liberty Drive
Bloomington, IN 47403
www.authorhouse.com
Phone: 1-800-839-8640

First published by AuthorHouse 10/21/2011

ISBN: 978-1-4567-9927-4 (sc)
ISBN: 978-1-4567-9925-0 (e)

Library of Congress Control Number: 2011915745

Printed in the United States of America

Farewell, my happy country, beloved Eden!
Where'er the fates in their fury shall cast me,
Your sweet name shall be like flattery in my ear.
—"On Parting," Gertrudis Gómez de Avellaneda, 1836

Chapter One

It happened a long time ago, before cell phones or the Internet. The memories still haunted Carlos Garcia, a Cuban immigrant who had left his native island as a young teen. They say hardship can only be measured in terms of relativity, and Carlos was well aware of that saying. But in the end it did not matter if the events were not as horrible as the Holocaust. If they happened and they ruined your night's sleep, they were just as bad, even if you couldn't say it, and that was how Carlos came to deal with it. People may have thought him strange because of the grudges he held, but he had learned to deal with his experiences the best way he could. He would never say he had been the most horribly treated kid or that he had gone through hell, but sometimes, when he was with old friends who wanted to talk about the old days, the story always came up.

"And how did you get here? What happened?" the man standing next to him at the counter asked as he savored a cup of espresso in a local Miami restaurant.

Carlos seemed aloof, staring at the fading brown eyes of Francisco Peña, an old Cuban man he had befriended in his daily stops at this restaurant who was standing next to him at his other side. The two had become quite close. Peña watched Carlos with interest as he answered.

"I left when I was thirteen. I went to live in Spain."

"Oh, that must have been nice. Did your parents have relatives there?"

"My parents did not come with me. I traveled alone."

"Were you one of those Peter Pan kids?"

"No, not quite. By the way, do you know how the Peter Pan program worked?"

"I don't know the details, but I remember vaguely those kids leaving the airport with signs."

"Father Bryan O. Walsh, a priest here in Miami, started it. Around 1960, I think. People suspected that the Cuban government was going to kidnap children and brainwash them. That priest would find visas for the kids and a place to stay once they got here. I wasn't one of them. I left Cuba in the mid-sixties, but pretty much under the same conditions.

"There was this other priest, Father Camiña, in Spain. He would pick up children at the airport and take them to a refugee camp, feed us, and give us a place to sleep. No relatives met us at the airport, and we were thousands of miles from home. I'm not sure if Camiña was a Spaniard. He could have been a Cuban priest who picked up the Spanish accent. But in any event, I think about him daily. He saved so many children, you know. He did it all for the sake of charity."

"Whatever happened to him? Where is he now?"

"Once I came to the States I never heard from him again. I don't know if he's still alive, perhaps still living in Madrid."

"We Cubans have so many stories to tell," Peña said, cutting in. "Our suffering never ends. When I left my town, I was young, and my wife and two children came with me. We missed the October missile crisis by about one week. My children were lucky because they were small, four and five at the time, so they learned the language fast. But imagine that in another week we would have gotten stuck in Cuba for who knows how long. It was fate.

"Today my children are middle-aged and they have their own families. They made good on the opportunity they got. I'm happy for them and how I was able to give them a better life. Me and my wife, we just speak broken English, as you know. There was never any time in our lives to go to school and improve our education. It was always, work and work. And then we just got used to it. The routine, you know. The espresso coffee, the *guarapo*, ah, after a while you just realize that it all comes down to one thing—family. Well, family and culture. The money helps, yes, if you have it. But it's not worth killing yourself for it. What matters the most is to be happy, whatever makes you feel happy to be alive. And for me it's just that, the family, the culture, those things are irreplaceable. We couldn't have it if we had stayed in Cuba. So in your case, Carlos, you may have been separated from your family but look how far you've come. Here you are in Miami, a successful businessman. You think you could have all this if you were in Cuba?"

Peña stepped back and made a sweeping gesture with his right hand that arched away from Carlos's shoulder, as if to accentuate Carlos's wealth. Carlos felt intrigued to the point that he was tempted to turn around and look. Perhaps there was something back there he was missing. His car, a 2007 Mercedes, was parked half a block away and could not have been the object of Peña's point. Carlos winked at the gentleman, who had by now finished his cup of coffee, and turned to Peña.

"Peña, you should be proud of your own accomplishments and stop advertising me," Carlos said. "Like you just mentioned, money isn't everything. So what if you don't own a hotel? One does not have to have a new car or a new house to be happy. Success can be measured in many ways and not just by wealth. Listen, do you want your cup of coffee? You haven't had one yet. I'll treat."

"All right. And a cigar. One does not go without the other."

"Of course."

Now Peña squeezed himself between Carlos and the other man at the restaurant's counter. Inside were the regular customers sitting before glass tables, surrounded by large illuminated posters of Cuba.

Peña leaned his elbow on the counter. "Let me have two espressos," he said to the pretty brunette waitress wearing the long white *guayavera* and red bandanna, typical uniform of the restaurant.

"And a cigar," Peña added. "Let me pick it from the package."

The other man chuckled and bid them farewell.

"What a character, right?" another man said behind them.

He could not have been older than thirty, and he wore a white Armani zipper tee shirt that seemed a size too small for him. He moved next to Carlos at the other side, replacing the other man.

"What's amazing is his spirit," the stranger said. "Doesn't ever let up."

"So you know him."

"Who doesn't know Peña? He's spent half his lifetime in this cafeteria. Now that he's retired and has lots of time, he spends the day here drinking coffee and telling stories— which all have to do with Cuba, by the way."

The man extended his hand to Carlos.

"I'm José Cardona, at your service," he said.

Carlos shook his hand and couldn't help but glance at the man's chest that held a wide, eighteen-carat gold chain, from which hung a large, meticulously carved medallion of our Lady of Charity.

"I've had that all my life," José said, referring to his medallion. "Wouldn't go anywhere without it. It has protected me all these years."

"Good that you believe."

"José is a fisherman," Peña said. "And I mean a real fisherman. I've never seen anyone catch fish so big. I went on one of his trips and although I don't fish, I had the best of times just watching him and his pals bringing in the lines. What a skill those men have!"

"Oh, yeah? I do some fishing too. Where do you go?"

"I go around the Keys. How about you? You ever venture into Cuban waters?"

Cardona had a mischievous look about him.

"No, that's the last place I want to venture into. Unless perhaps they let me bring a missile launcher in case I run into some Cuban patrol. But with the Feds, you know, you're automatically classified as a terrorist if you do something like that and they throw you in jail for life. So I stay away."

"You're missing the best fish. They are in Cuban waters," Cardona said, smiling.

Carlos got the feeling Cardona was hiding something that he was desperate to tell.

"Would you like another coffee?" Carlos offered Peña. "It seems like you're out of it."

"No, too much of it gets you too fidgety. In fact, I think I'm gonna have a *guarapo* to water down the other one I had."

"Hey, miss, can I have a *guarapo* for here?" Carlos said, raising his hand to the waitress. "What do you do for a living, José?"

"I fish, like Peña said. I fish in Cuban waters and not just for fish."

"What do you mean?"

"You have family in Cuba?"

"I have cousins I have never met. I have an uncle who is over seventy and has many health problems. I send him medicines and money every once in a while. But besides them, no, I have nobody else. Everyone in my family is now here."

"Ever gone back?"

"No, never."

"Why not? Do you realize what you're missing? The beauty of the island."

"For as long as Castro is in power, I have no interest in going."

"You have an interest in going. Everyone who has Cuban roots does. You may refuse to accept that as the truth it is. You're held back by stubbornness and perhaps even fear of facing the past, but you're missing something you want very much, perhaps more than anything else, and that is to see your homeland, the place where you were born and had the best time of your life. Don't tell me it's not true."

"It's probably true. But I just won't go while that SOB is in power. He ruined my childhood and the lives of so many people. Why should I give him the satisfaction of returning when they practically kicked me out of there?"

"They didn't kick you out. They didn't kick anyone out. That's how they see it. You did not have to leave. All you had to do was agree with him and go along with the system. You could have done that and lived a halfway decent life in your homeland. You weren't forced to leave."

"Yeah? Stay and think like them. That sure sounds like tyranny to me."

"Okay, well, still, that's not forcing you to leave. It's called 'weaving,' as they see it. You know, they weave the bad weeds, like a gardener, and instead of pulling them by the roots or killing them, they give them the opportunity to leave. That's so. It's actually pretty smart on their part when you think about it."

By then the waitress had returned with an icy glass of *guarapo*, which she placed on the counter and almost touched the man's hand as she slid it on the surface. She gave him a dirty look that said a million words.

"See," José continued, "here in Miami, in the USA, we're supposed to be free, free to say what we want, and yet you cannot say certain things because people will mind it very much. They don't want you telling the truth as you see it. They want you to think like them, be a robot. How's that different than being in Cuba? So what I think you should do, my friend, and forgive me for telling you what to do, is do what your heart tells you. Satisfy yourself and take a trip to your island. Visit your family, and if you have to turn a deaf ear to some guard who wants to tell you about the wonders of Castro's revolution, go along with it. It's really no different than being here in Miami where you have to listen to the rightist mentality of our Cuban population. It's just the other extreme. You want to see Cuba in a different way, travel by sea. You'll never forget the busy coastline and sparkling white beaches. It's true what they say about the beaches, by the way, and I don't know how much you know about them, but they are really God-sent. I was in *Varadero* not too long ago. I just stood there mesmerized for a few minutes just admiring the sand, man. It's like something cosmic. There's no sand like that anywhere in the world."

"You know," Carlos said. "It's funny that you mention this topic in such detail. Right now I'm going through a heated debate in my house about traveling to Cuba. I've been here for forty-five years. I've never been back and do not intend to ever go back while Castro is there. But my wife, who was born in Cuba, and my daughter who was born here, are driving me nuts to go. It's pretty much come down to the two of them having to make the trip alone. I will not go. My wife keeps putting pressure on me, keeps saying she doesn't want to go without me, but my daughter cries because she wants to see the island. She wants to see where her parents came from, and my wife keeps saying she doesn't want to deprive her of that right. I keep telling them that it's even against the law if you're American-born like my daughter. Who knows what the consequences might be in the future, especially to a young woman like my daughter? But the debate gets hotter and hotter each day. My daughter is resolute about going, and my wife is giving in. I don't know what else to do."

"Let them go, Carlos. Don't worry about the law, man. What law? You know that as they say, 'Those who invented the law invented the trap too'—that is, how to circumvent the law. People do it all the time. If you wanna get there any kind of way, however you like, ask me. I'll get you there. It won't cost you much. Wanna bring something out of Cuba? Ask me too. Whatever it is, I'll get it here for you."

He gulped down his *guarapo* as the old man let out deep puffs of tobacco smoke behind him. Then he slipped him a business card under his left arm like a professional card player at a casino and took another drink of *guarapo*. The waitress passed near him inside the small working area and sneered at him. Carlos took the card.

"And what do you do?" Cardona asked casually.

"I run a couple of supermarkets in the city."

"A couple? Just a couple? Aren't you associated with that line, Prado's? I swear I've seen a dozen of those things all over town."

"Not that many. I handle three." Carlos answered rather naively, without realizing Cardona had known the names even before he told him.

"Prado's is doing okay. Maybe not like the Supreme

markets, but still good." Cardona added. "And I don't mean the group—you know what I mean?"

"I know what you mean. On the subject of the Supremes, they were great. The Supremes, I mean. I'm a music freak. I have a music background, and I recognize good music when I hear it. You know, the thing that always strikes me about the Supremes was their background voices. It wasn't Diana Ross doing the lead, which, by the way, not to take anything from her, she was great, but the background voices, man, I don't think there was another group of that era, male or female, that could make that type of background vocals like those girls did. It was Mary and Flo who did it for me. Those girls could wrap up their voices and make sounds that no one else was making. They made the Supremes."

"I never quite noticed that, but now that you say it, yeah, I guess that's right."

"You know why you never noticed it? It's because their voices are molded into the song. They're what make the song and your mind subconsciously gets attracted to the melody without knowing the technical reason why. But if you look deep, you'll see it. It's there. It's ingenuity in the vocals. You know, sometimes those who are supposed to follow actually lead. That's what happened with them. The background singers really carried the songs, much to the chagrin of that conceited Diana who eventually thought she was the Supremes all by herself, and still does today."

"Yeah. She's gotten in trouble a couple of times."

"Of course. Arrogance is the worst of human traits. Well, Mr. Cardona, it's been a pleasure. I have to get going. Let me see if Peña is going to need a ride. Peña?"

He turned towards Peña who was still working on his cigar quietly.

"What do you think?" he said. "I don't have any other way to get home."

9

Carlos placed a ten-dollar bill on the counter and pointed to the waitress. He was known at the restaurant for his generous tips.

"I can give you a ride too, if you want one," Cardona said to Peña.

"No, it's all right," Peña replied. "I've already bothered you many times. I'll go with Carlos."

"I'll see you around," Carlos said, shaking his hand. "Gotta get home at some point."

"Well, you just remember what I said, Carlos, and if you need me, you have my business card."

"Thank you, Mr. Cardona. I'll keep you in mind."

Those were Carlos's famous farewell words to salesmen who came tapping at his door. Yeah, yeah, your product is great, call you later. That's how he thought of José Cardona as he stepped into the parking lot into his E-250 black Mercedes, followed by Peña, still spewing blue smoke from his cigar.

"Shall I dispose of my cigar out here? You don't want me to stink up your car, right?"

"It's all right. It doesn't bother me."

"Nahh. I'll get rid of it. Lucia will scream when she smells it. It'll be all over your clothes."

"My wife doesn't care. Just get in and let's go."

"*Ayayay*, this is some car!"

"This is one of the smallest models of the Mercedes series, Peña," Carlos said. "You just noticed that it's a Mercedes?"

"People like that are like insurance companies," Peña suddenly said as the car got underway. "You don't want them, but you need them."

Carlos stopped at the light. They were on Fortieth Street, a busy section of South Miami that had been flocked by restaurants and utility stores of every imaginable kind. The traffic subsided a little at night, but the rush never stopped.

As soon as the light switched, the car behind them blew its horn.

"What, are you in a rush?" Mr. Peña shouted out as if he were speaking to the driver behind them.

Carlos laughed and pressed on the accelerator, making the short sports-model car take off smoothly from the intersection.

"Remember, Peña, we're in Miami."

"You know what I used to tell people like that when I drove? I would yell at them from the driver's window, 'Go over my roof if you're in such a hurry.' What's the point, *chico*? What do they want you to do, run a red light?"

"It's the lifestyle, Peña. It's got nothing to do with being in a hurry. That driver back there, whoever he is, probably has nowhere to go. He has all the time in the world."

"Everybody is darned conceited around here. That's what it is."

"Anyway, Peña, who's this José Cardona? Where do you know him from?"

"He's a peddler, Carlos. He gets people out of Cuba for money. That's how he makes his living. He's a true worm in the Cuban definition of the term, you know what I mean? And yet I have to admit, much to my regret, that I myself have used him a couple of times. I had him deliver some things to Cuba for my older brother, who's still there. It's like I said, an evil that you need. You know how much I paid him to deliver some medicines and some clothes to my family? Just for the delivery he charged me fifteen hundred dollars. Can you imagine? And yet I did it. I had too. My poor brother has diabetes real bad and there's very little medication available to him down there. And these are all prescribed medications here that I've sent him. They are hard to get. You can't send them by regular mail because they'll never make it through, plus you can only send five pounds anyway. So I used him, and I got everything through. No questions asked. I got nephews who I never met. One is a doctor. He can't even get a medical gown for himself. He drives a bicycle to work. Can you imagine? So I sent him two beautiful white medical gowns with his name sewn on the left breast pocket. Just beautiful, very professional, like it ought to be. And then I sent clothes for the rest of the family. What else am I gonna do, you know? I've done that a couple of times already with this guy, and the stuff gets delivered without a problem, no questions asked."

"How does he do it?"

"I don't know. All I know is he gets the stuff through for you. And he gets people out of Cuba too. Give him the cash, and he'll get them here. I don't know how, but he does it."

"Does he actually go to Cuba?"

"You know, I try not to ask any questions about this stuff because I feel ashamed that we have our own people doing things like this. It's people like this guy who keep Castro going. It's our own people who are our worst enemies sometimes."

"You know, Peña, right now this is a big controversy at my house. My wife is going to go to Cuba with my daughter. Between you and me, I would love to go back there and see the town where I came from, but I think like you. I would never go as long as Castro is in power."

"I have never gone back for that very reason. I've lost my mother and later my father, and I never went back. Now I have my brother who I haven't seen for more than forty years, and I still refuse to go. I feel like I'm aiding Castro if I go back. But the pressure is growing on me. I don't know if I can outlast it, honestly. My brother is getting sick and begs me to go see him. What am I gonna do? Keep waiting? Till when? I could drop dead tomorrow or so could my brother and then it would be all over. I'll die or live without the satisfaction of ever having seen my brother again. And it's like he says, 'All for what? Pride?' He doesn't understand. People in Cuba don't understand that because we are a family oriented people. We care about families first, then politics. That's why the people down there have a hard time understanding people like me who refuse to visit Cuba because they can't conceive that someone would sacrifice not seeing their families just because they don't want to return to Cuba while Castro is in power."

"Why doesn't your brother come here?"

Peña hesitated as Carlos sped into the super highway that led into Miami Beach. Peña lived in one of the adult communities near the downtown area on the way to the beach, and this was the fastest way to get there. Carlos could not decide whether the old man was frightened by his hasty driving or if he was pondering over his answer.

"You know, Carlos, to be honest with you, Castro has caused so much damage that we will never be able to recover. He has destroyed families, broken up marriages, separated children, done every conceivable thing. Between you and me, my brother was in favor of the Castro government. He is retired from being an agent for the State. He didn't want to come here for all those years for the same reason I won't go there. He believed in all that communist crap, so we were not seeing eye-to-eye for a while. Now that he's retired, we have reconciled, and he would like to come but is too ill to travel. Besides, he's got children who work in government. If he came here, their jobs would probably be affected. He's afraid, and I can't say I blame him. No, the ball is in my court. I'm the one who lives in a free country. I could go back now if I wanted and nobody would say a darn thing to me here. But that is because we are in the United States. Cuba is a prison."

"So you're actually thinking about going, eh?"

"I don't know if I can work up the nerve to go. My son says I should, and I'm thinking about it."

"Younger people always think it's easier because they haven't experienced what we have. I have that same problem."

"What were you telling me about your family?"

"Well, my seventeen-year-old daughter has been yearning to go for years. She wants to see where her parents come from. She has begged me to take her, but I've held out. But my wife thinks I'm silly. She thinks we should all go. I told her, 'You go. Take our daughter.' At first she did not want to. She wanted us all to go. She said she wouldn't go without me, and that's the way it's been for years, but now my daughter is set on going. She was planning to go with some group of students, but her mother won't have that."

"I can't say I blame her."

"No. I did not want her to go either, so what I did was convince my wife to go. I told her to take our daughter. I'll stay. And that's where we are now. She argues with me because she thinks I don't have the right to deprive our daughter of the right to see Cuba. We argue about this all the time. She thinks I'm stubborn and proud, like you said about your brother. But it's not that at all. This is the way I think of it. I left when I was a kid but was old enough to remember. I remember being in school and seeing the look in the teachers' faces—how they despised me once they knew I was leaving. Some people would not even say goodbye to me. That, I'll never forget."

"I know how you feel, but look, sooner or later you're gonna have to give in. And I know you'd want to protect them and not let them go alone, but you have only two choices, my friend. You either go with them, or let them go alone. I think it's safe for your daughter and wife there. Look, that government cares only about money right now. They treat tourists better than they treat their own people. Nothing is gonna happen to them."

"So what do you think about this guy Cardona? You think he could help me set up the trip for them?"

"Oh yeah, he could. The question is whether you would need him. Your daughter was born here, right?"

"That's one reason I don't want her to go. It could hurt her in the future. She's young, and who knows if someday she will want to work for the government or hold a job where she will need security clearance. Having been to Cuba could affect her. That's why if she ends up going with my wife, at least I'd like her to go through a third country where there will be no trace of her traveling. That's why I was asking you about this guy. Maybe we could use him."

"You can. He can get them there without a trace. He does it all the time."

"Hmmm."

The car exited the expressway. Carlos turned right at the end of the ramp and drove into one of the three high apartment buildings reserved for senior citizens that sat a couple of blocks from the highway intersection. He had dropped Peña here on many other occasions. He and the old man had developed a friendship that grew from daily encounters at the cafeteria where Carlos would stop on the early evenings for a drink of *guarapo* and a chat. Peña spent a good two hours every day hanging out at the restaurant, drinking espresso, and making conversation with anyone he met. Tonight Carlos felt a need not to let him go, as if somehow the old man could bring him luck in the decision he was about to make. His wife, Lucia, was sure to be home by now, waiting for him to engage him in a discussion of the trip their daughter insisted on taking. Perhaps Peña could take his place tonight. These old Cuban men were stubborn, but they were savvy. They had, after all, pursued the American dream at a later age and found it. They believed deeply in an American system that seemed now to be under attack by a long list of countries throughout the world. It was strange, he thought, but the old Cuban émigrés were the most faithful allies America had and did not know it. Despite all the empty promises of help in getting rid of Castro and the politicians' lip service that "Castro was out," men like Peña believed feverishly in America and had an unwavering faith in its government. Who better than a man like him to reason with Lucia and his daughter, Alicia?

"I'll talk to him for you," Peña said as he got out of the car. "He'll give me special consideration. He owes me."

"He owes you?"

Peña looked amused. He shut the passenger door and came confidently around the front of the car as if he knew Carlos would not move until he was safely inside the main door of the building. Recently there had been a mugging right in the parking lot of one of the buildings. Peña came to stand by the driver's door and spoke to Carlos through the half-open window.

"Listen, Carlos, go home and don't argue with your wife about the trip. Don't argue about anything that has to do with Castro. It's not worth it. Anything that has to do with that devil is not worth talking about. Like a bad weed, he'll be there much after we're gone, and if not him, his legacy, unfortunately. So make your family happy and don't listen to anyone. Do what's good for them and you and forget the rest. If you can't handle going back, then let your daughter and wife go. We'll work things out. If your daughter wants to see Cuba, let her see it. Make her happy."

Carlos was caught off guard by this sudden outpouring of counsel. It did not sound like the man who had been sitting next to him a minute ago.

"Okay, Peña. I guess you know something I don't."

"They say that we old Cubans are proud. But the truth is we are realists. We face the truth as we get near the end. And the truth is we are never gonna get back what we had. It's gone. We have to content ourselves with having our freedom. At least we are here. We can talk about the past and reminisce but that is all we can do. It's a secret among us. Only we know it. Our kids who were born in this country or came as children can't understand that because they did not live through it. You can't blame them if they want to get to know their roots. It's their right. So let's leave them alone. If they want to go, let them."

"All right, Peña. You're very philosophical tonight. Let me see you get inside the building so I can leave."

"Don't worry about me. Who's gonna touch me?"

"Get in. I'm watching you."

"Goodnight."

Carlos waited until Peña got inside the lit hallway and disappeared toward the elevator. Then he sped out of the parking lot and drove back to the expressway. The ride home would take about twenty minutes, but he could make it in less time if he pushed his fast Mercedes in the outer lane. He was in his late fifties but had never lost his love for fast cars, just as he had never lost his hair. He switched lanes as he got near his exit and made a right at the end of the ramp. His home sat at the middle of the block in an exclusive development of South Miami. He pulled into the horseshoe driveway and parked his car by the front door behind his wife's BMW. The island in the middle was cultivated with tall banana plants that swayed under the night breeze.

Carlos walked past the porch and opened the two oak front doors. Inside was bright. The foyer chandelier was on, which told him his wife, Lucia, was nearby. As soon as he entered he heard her voice.

"Carlos, why don't you answer your cell? I've been calling you."

"I've had it on vibrate, Lucia. I didn't hear it."

He walked toward the living room sofa where she was sitting and kissed her on the lips. She was an attractive brunette with lively black eyes and an oval face. She sat in the middle of the sofa with her left leg under her right one, across from a wide, flat-screen TV, leaning her elbow on various sofa pillows by her side.

"Did you go take Peña home?"

"I did. I feel a little bit like his protector now. I'm afraid to let him go alone."

"You ought to bring him home more often, Carlos. That poor man needs company."

"He has a family, Lucia. It's not that bad for him."

"Well, your daughter is very excited. She has her mind set on going. She's making all kinds of plans."

"Like what?"

"Like calling the Department of the Treasury in Washington, finding all about the requirements to go to Cuba. She got all kinds of literature printed from the Internet. I actually learned something. Did you know that she is exempted from the ban to go to Cuba even though she was born here because of her background?"

"I'm not sure that that's correct," he said and finally sat down next to her. "She is an American. If she goes, it will be on her record, and it will affect her someday."

"Carlos, but I read it myself. She can go. The problem is that she is organizing this group of friends who want to come along, and I'm not gonna let that happen. If she goes, I'm going. I'm not letting her going by herself."

"I know, Lucia. I know. I don't want her to go alone either."

"Then why don't we all go as a family?"

"You know the reason. We've been through this a thousand times."

"What's the big deal? No one is going to bother you. We're tourists. It'll be just like being in any other country."

"He's there. That's the difference."

"Carlos, he'll always be there. Ignore it and stop living in the past. You know, it's true what they say about us. We Cubans live in the past. We have to stop. It's silly."

"The past is all we have, Lucia."

"Please stop making an emotional issue about this. What matters more to you, your family or your pride?"

"Stop, Lucia, please. I just got here."

"No, but really, answer my question. You're putting your pride ahead of your family. You'd let your daughter go alone before you think of going yourself."

"I said stop. That's not it at all. You don't understand."

"Then what is it? Explain to me. You left when you were thirteen. What possible involvement could you have had in anything? And what possible grudge could you hold against anyone? You were just a kid, Carlos. Don't you want to see the place you came from? I mean after all, it's forty-three years. What do you think is going to happen? Lighting will strike you if you go back or something?"

"It's got nothing to do with fear. It's not pride either. I just don't want to set foot on that island until that man is gone. If I die before him and never see it, then so be it. But while he's alive, I don't want to go there."

"That's fine. That's how you feel and I respect that, but you have a daughter, Carlos. She's our baby, our only one. We owe her, and if she wants to go see the place her parents came from, you should put your idiosyncrasies aside and please her. Don't deny her. Besides, it's silly. It's been so many years. Time erases things. What possible harm is going to come in your going there? All the people you knew are probably now

19

gone. The same ones who you feel may have snubbed you are probably here now. So what does that tell you? That it was all funny. The system created that attitude in them because they felt they had to survive. And you're going to get caught up in that riddle? Carlos, you're wrong. You have to forget what happened. This is our daughter we're talking about here."

There were tears in her eyes, and Carlos looked down at the floor. He remembered a line from a Beatle song: "I look at the floor and I see it needs sweeping. Still my guitar gently weeps." The conversation with Cardona this evening had gotten him thinking about music. It had been mostly '60s and '70s stuff he had listened to, but it all stayed in his head despite the years passed. He felt connected and thought that he was probably living the issue the composer had written about. Human tribulations were at play while something as simplistic as the dust on the floor got his attention. The floor needed sweeping. The dilemma he was living needed to be dealt with. It needed to be faced, not avoided. It needed to be solved.

He turned to his wife once again and saw the tears on her cheeks. He reached out and wrapped his arm around her and brought her close to him.

She whispered the words as she sought refuge in his chest. "Carlos, I love you, honey. You're my everything. We need to do this together. Please don't fail me. I don't want to go without you."

"Why can't we control Alicia? After all, she's only seventeen."

"She wants to know her roots. She wants to go."

"She's not the only one. Think of how many young men and women were born right here in Miami of Cuban parents who have never seen Cuba. They're going on with their lives. I'm sure if there was a change there they'd go, but they're not jumping through hoops right now just to get there. That's because their parents don't want them to go while the current regime is in place. They want to see a free Cuba before they send their kids there."

"Some do, Carlos. Some do go."

"So we're gonna let a seventeen-year-old control our lives. We're not going to put our foot down and keep her from venturing there?"

"A seventeen-year-old who will soon be eighteen. Alicia is so hung up on this, I'm afraid it's too late. If we keep fighting her, we're gonna lose her. You gotta face it. She's obsessed with this. We can't stop it."

Carlos shook his head in frustration. He had never been much of a disciplinarian. To the contrary, he had pampered his only child with attention and given in to all of her whims. Lucia had been stricter as a parent, setting the rules and making their daughter be responsible for certain chores. But now it seemed like the ultimate test of parenthood had arrived and neither he nor his wife were faring very well. He remembered how hard it had been for Lucia during the early years of their marriage. He was ten years her senior, and they had met when she was in her early twenties but immediately they bonded. They married soon after and did not have a child for more than ten years. Lucia had had a miscarriage and their doctor said she would probably not be able to conceive after that. They kept trying and nothing ever happened. They saw specialists and had considered adopting. Then one day, out of the blue, when Lucia was in her mid-thirties, she suddenly discovered she was pregnant. They were thrilled. But the news was to be taken with caution. The doctor told Lucia that she would probably have to endure a very difficult pregnancy, considering her history, and the fact that she was older would not help. There was also the likelihood that the fetus would not develop well. It was a very difficult time for both of them. Lucia underwent a miserable nine months and was forced to lie down for most of the time, experiencing intense effects from the pregnancy, such as constant vomiting and slight bleeding. Carlos stayed by her side, and when he wasn't he stayed in touch by phone. He kept her spirits up.

Then a beautiful, healthy, eight-pound baby girl was born and they named her Alicia after Carlos's mother, who had recently passed away. She became their fascination, and their entire life circled around her from then on. Now she was seventeen, a lively teenager who seemed focused on her goals. She was about to graduate from a private Catholic high school next June, half a year from her eighteenth birthday. The trip to her parents' homeland had been a much-wanted adventure she had craved for a long time.

"There are certain things that just won't go away. I will never forget the way those people treated me. How they despised me and repudiated me when they found out I was leaving. It's an image I have in my brain that won't go away. How could I go back there now after they practically kicked me out? And the conditions, Lucia. The conditions have not changed. They have gotten worse, which is the reason we left to begin with. There's still no freedom of speech, misery is everywhere, the houses are torn, porches are being supported by studs on the ground to keep them from caving in. The whole country is decayed like rotten flesh. What are we gonna do there, pay homage to the very system that tore us apart? No, I can't go there. I can't go back just for a few moments of brief satisfaction in seeing where I came from."

"Carlos, honey, you try to rationalize it but you really don't have to. Remember, I came from there too. My parents had to go work in the fields under Castro's agricultural programs 'for the traitors,' as he called them. I did not have to go because I was too young, but my parents did, and I remember the isolation we lived through, the rejection I experienced at school and from neighbors. Sure I remember, but that was a long time ago. You've got to let that go. Besides, between you and me, let's be real. That's not the reason you won't go back. I think it's your Cuban pride of not admitting defeat. And I'm not criticizing you, but it's true. It comes from our parents and that struggle we all experienced to leave. Our culture is living in the past, not wanting to give in to reality. It's not 1958 any more, and yes, Castro is there and will be there so we might as well deal with it. If we want to see our homeland, we have to accept that he's still there. And that's what your problem is, Carlos. That's why you won't go."

"So it doesn't bother you? It doesn't bother you that you're gonna have to pay him twenty dollars out of a hundred that you spend knowing that the general population will never see it and that you're supporting him?"

"It does bother me, but my family comes first." She said it because she was way too frank not to say what she felt. But she immediately knew that she shouldn't have and that she had hurt him. She placed her arm around him and kissed his cheek. "I'm sorry. I know how much you care about us, but perhaps you should give in a little, honey."

Carlos looked ahead at the images on the giant TV. The news was on. An anchorwoman was talking about Sarah Palin.

"I'm sick of seeing this woman everywhere," Carlos said. "Don't they have more important things to talk about?"

"Alicia likes her."

"She's done nothing. She's only a celebrity, someone who happened to be in the right place at the right time. That's so."

"Oh, I'm with you. She's got no substance, but some people in the media are in love with her."

"The conservative media."

"She gets into everything. Even if they don't talk about her as much in the other stations, she still gets in. I think that's her goal for now, to remain visible."

"So where is Alicia right now? It's almost ten o'clock."

"She's in her room. There are two other girls here."

"So late?"

"They'll be leaving any minute now. They have their cars here."

His cell vibrated and he answered it. It was close-up time at his supermarkets, and he usually got several calls from his managers at this time if he was not around. Tonight he could not be there. The situation at home was developing into a crisis, and he needed to face it. That's why he had quit work so early.

"I don't want to go without you, honey. Can't you understand that?"

He looked at her wistful eyes and saw the predicament that was tearing her heart apart. She couldn't allow herself the luxury of traveling without him. She felt she was betraying him, except in this instance the issue was also about their daughter. She could not let their daughter go even if it meant going with her alone. She clung to his neck as he made an attempt to stand.

"I may have a solution to the whole problem, Lucia," Carlos said, and took the call. "For that will have to wait till tomorrow," he said almost casually as if he were still speaking to his wife. "No, I can't go there now. This is why I left you there tonight, Nick. Come on!"

"Carlos, what is it?" she asked.

Just then a young girl with long black hair came into the hallway from one of the rooms. The house had no stairs and was a one-level ranch, spacious and large, but without a second floor, something Alicia complained about at times.

"A house without a stairway has no life," she had gloomily diagnosed one day, irking her mother to snap.

"As if suddenly you knew," Lucia had retorted. "You haven't been around long enough to know what life is all about. Rule number one is be practical. And don't dream about things you can't control."

In all respects, Lucia Montenegro had been a no-nonsense mother to her only daughter, setting her goals in the right direction and trying her best to keep her grounded. But she had discovered that since an early age, Alicia was not your typical child and when she said something, it was usually based on some observation of her own, never without substance.

"Hi, Daddy," she said as she came toward him and kissed him on the cheek.

Carlos was still struggling with the caller. "Get a plumber there now. That's so. I have to go. I'll call you back," he said and ended the call. "Hi, Alicia. How was your day, honey?"

"Oh, great, Daddy. I made lots of progress in my research. I now have the names of two agencies that can handle the trip. Not that I need them. You know you can get it all almost done online without seeing a travel agent, but I now definitely have three other girls who are in with me to make the trip. Don't you think that's great?"

"Are these girls your age?"

"Yep. They're friends from school. You know them. They come here. They're all excited to go."

"What about their parents? Do they agree with the trip?"

"We're talking about that. You know, it would be really selfish for any parent to oppose. Kids want to know their roots. What's wrong with that?"

"Nothing, except when you're going into a forbidden land."

"Forbidden by whom? Who has the right?"

"Let's not get into that, Alicia. The point is that you need adult supervision. Three or four young girls going in a clandestine trip to an island where our government prohibits people to travel? Of course it's dangerous, and it can't happen."

"Daddy, you're not seeing it. Why can't you understand? Just because the government tells you that you can't go there doesn't mean it's right. They can't decide for you. You have to decide for yourself."

"You want to tell that to Castro, Alicia?"

"Daddy, I'd tell that to anybody. It's my right to know my roots."

"Now it's you who's missing the point. Do you think for a minute that in Cuba you can make decisions such as the one you're making now? You talk about our government deciding for you? Ha! That's a laugh. That is precisely what they do down in Cuba, exactly that. That is why people like me and your mother came to this country, because we did not want the government controlling us, telling us what to do. And you want to go back there looking for the right of free choice? You're doing the reverse of what we did."

Carlos's tone of voice had risen, and unconsciously he had moved to the edge of the sofa, with his legs lodged firmly on the floor and his right hand with an extended index, sweeping the air up and down in gestures.

Lucia came close to him and held his shoulder. "Carlos, easy honey. Alicia, please, let's stop the discussion about the trip to Cuba for tonight. It's enough. Carlos, you said you had a solution to the whole problem, so let's discuss that tomorrow. If you have found a way to work this out, then we'll go with your idea."

"Why can't we talk about it tonight, Mom?"

"Because we've all had enough. Your father just got home,

we're talking, and you go on with this trip again and you get him all upset and frustrated. Stop it. Enough."

"Mom, it's just a trip like any other one. How many times have you discussed the Bahamas or Spain or Puerto Rico for hours and hours with Dad? What's wrong with the trip to Cuba?"

"Alicia, I said stop!"

Lucia sat up on the sofa as a sign that she really meant business.

"Fine, Mom, fine. But I just want you to know whether Dad's solution may just be another hot issue. Don't be surprised if it's only a compromise."

"Alicia, this is the last time I'm telling you. Stop!"

"Fine, fine."

She turned from them and disappeared into the kitchen. Carlos shook his head and closed his eyes for a moment. He kept thinking that he wanted to do right by his family so much. He would do anything, anything to keep them happy, to provide for them and see that they were comfortable. This seemed like a ridiculous situation, that they would argue about such a trivial point. But maybe it was not trivial. It certainly did not seem trivial to his teenage daughter, and it was obvious it had opened old wounds. He could not say for sure whether it did the same to his wife, but however she felt, she was right there behind him, supporting him in his position while at the same time guarding their daughter. Carlos realized how skillful Lucia was in her treatment of the situation, so typical of her when confronted with sensitive issues that disturbed the family peace. He was convinced that Lucia was the glue that held his family together. Without her there would be no home. He let her rub his head and sat next to her without saying anything, perhaps wishing the whole thing would just blow away overnight. His cell rang again.

"I can't believe these people," he said in frustration as he picked up the call.

"But Carlos, why do you have to answer?"

He shook his head. He saw it as part of the downside of being self employed, a temporary inconvenience to be dealt with. This was the price you paid for being a free enterpriser, answering to no one. He had spent more than twenty-five years running food establishments and had given it his all. His managers knew him and how he operated. That's why he got phone calls late at night when something was wrong, because they knew Carlos was a hands-on owner, preferring to make the decisions himself.

"A cowboy's work is never done," he whispered to Lucia as he braced himself for the voice on the other end.

"That's not right, Carlos. This is our time," Lucia complained.

Carlos put out his hand as a sign for her to sit still. "Nick," he said after listening for a few seconds to the voice on the other end. "You've gotta let the plumber decide that one. Whatever it takes, he'll have to do. The thing is, we cannot end up with the freezers down in the meat area in the morning. So tell him to do what he has to. Put temporary PVC lines behind the freezers if that's what it takes. I don't know. Just get it done."

Carlos listened to his manager as he watched his wife staring him down, and for a split second, the thought crossed his mind that she might actually be jealous and doubtful of who he was talking to.

"Nick, I apologize. I really have to let you go. Tonight, I really can't. I'm with my wife, and we are into something really important. I gotta go."

"Thanks, Carlos," Lucia said, reaching out for his hand as soon as he closed the phone.

Carlos laid his head back on the sofa while holding her

hand. The two had spent many years together and were an intimate couple, which made it all the more of a debacle for them to be dealing with the present situation. There had never been an issue in the history of their marriage that had ever divided them. But here it was, and unpredictably and unreasonably involving their only daughter, making it torturous for them to decide how to proceed. They faced a dilemma in that neither one of them wanted to betray their convictions, forged long ago out of the displacement they had endured as immigrants to a new land, and their devotion to their only daughter. The entire problem could have been swept away as simply a teenage whim if it was any other youngster. But this was their daughter, who had inherited her parents' obstinacy and resoluteness, and she thought like an adult. Once she set her sights on a prize, there was no letting go.

"I ask myself once again," Carlos muttered, "why can't we just control this kid? If we say she's not going, that ought to be the end of it. She's only seventeen. My gosh, why can't we just do that?"

"Because she is too much like us," Lucia said.

They cuddled together on the sofa, and Carlos rested his head on her shoulder and slowly dozed off, with the faraway sound of the TV in the background.

Chapter Two

Once four o'clock came, the women who ran the coffee shop at the restaurant *La Carreta* in Southwest Miami knew they were in for a mad rush. The wide avenue off which the restaurant sat became congested with the early evening traffic of people who were leaving work, and cars began packing into the parking lot. Everyone was looking for a coffee break, even in the smothering heat of summer, or a cold drink of *guarapo*, but more than anything else, a chance to chitchat with anybody who came along, and an opportunity to laugh and hear some gossip.

José Cardona was a man who understood that environment. He had lived in Miami for most of his life, and since his early youth he had learned how to peddle for money in the busy cafeterias where he could strike a bargain with a customer in the blink of an eye. At first he sold anything from drugs to fake jewelry, but then he discovered his true abilities as the years went by, and he concentrated on exploiting the emotions of those in need. He understood his culture's eccentricities and appreciated the close family bond so prevalent among Cuban families. It was a feature that he had learned to exploit with great success. In the late seventies, after Castro made his unpredictable move of suddenly allowing Cuban immigrants to return to their homeland

Eralides E. Cabrera

and visit their families, Cardona saw his opportunity. It was what he had been waiting for.

He was skilled in connecting people, providing what they needed. So he began taking so-called "charity trips" to Cuba and carrying everything he could to relatives of those who sent him—for a fee of course. On his way back he would be just as loaded with goods, smuggling cigars, gold, and even birds that he would sell as a high priced item among the old Cubans longing to see their homeland or any items associated with it. It took considerable skill on his part to be able to bring anything out of Cuba. The government was known for its inflexibility and hard stand against corruption, but everything had a price, Cardona thought, and he soon figured out ways to bribe the customs people to get his way.

Then came the Mariel boat liftoff. Cardona was one of the skippers who had made several trips to Cuba during the standoff and brought several loads of people in for a high price. He had to bribe the guards at the port so they could let him leave with a boatful of strangers and come back the next day for more. Yes, it was expensive and dangerous, but at the conclusion of the crisis, Cardona had made a fortune. Not only that, he had established invaluable contacts within the rigid lines in the Cuban government to continue his trade. From then on, it was free season for him. He could bring any amount of people any time, from anywhere, for a fee. Years would pass and he would become even more skilled in his trade. The rule of thumb was, pay everyone off, and learn the routes traveled by the US Coast Guard by paying the people in control. The warning he always got was, once you're in the high seas, you're on your own. That's how it came to more than one occasion when Cardona had to outrun the American patrols in his high-speed boat when he was spotted. After all that, he was still here, a legend in his own time. The one thing he had learned was that everyone had a price.

Cardona leaned against the counter and drank his espresso. It was only spring, but the Miami sun had seen to it that the thermometer would reach ninety degrees this afternoon. It was the first official hot day this year. He paid for the order of the man standing next to him. It was an old habit of his. Pay someone's order, and you're sure to strike a conversation.

"Ah, many thanks," said the chubby-faced balding man, surprised by the gesture. "You did not have to do that."

"It was a pleasure. At your service. What's your name?"

"I'm Francisco Mochoa," the man said, still in somewhat of a shock. "And yours?"

"José Cardona, at your service," he said, extending his hand to him. "Can I ask you something? I saw you taking your time picking your cigars. What's the science behind that? How do you do it?"

"Ah, well, everyone has his own method. Me, I take after my father, who was not only a smoker but an actual grower at a plantation in Cuba. I am from *Pinar del Rio* where, as you probably know, the big cigar plantations were grown. My father used to say that the darker the cigar leaf, the smoother, so I adopted that method. I've smoked since I was a teen and I always look for the darkness in the leaf. The darker the better."

"Yes, but isn't there such a thing as a white cigar, I mean, not literally white but what they call blonde tobacco?"

"Sure there is. And it is very good tobacco, but as I said, it's a matter of preference. For me there's nothing like the dark-leafed tobacco. You try a light cigar and then a dark one and you'll feel the difference. It goes easier on your throat."

Cardona leaned forward as he spotted a familiar face on the other side of the counter. He had a tremendous memory for faces and here was one he had just seen yesterday but that he had engraved in the foundations of his memory with care, perhaps knowing that the moment would come when he would need to retrieve it and associate it with a name. He waved his hand courteously to the other man and smiled.

"That's really interesting," Cardona said to the gentleman next to him. "You know, I have never smoked a cigar. I don't know why. It's the one thing I never craved, not cigars or cigarettes. Coffee, yes, and plenty of it. I drink more than eight cups a day."

"That is a lot," the man said, nodding in amusement. "I can't drink half that."

"It keeps you on your toes," Cardona said. "Excuse me. Let me just slide over to the corner for a moment to say hello to that gentleman."

"Of course. I have to leave anyway. I was on my way home and stopped only for a cup of coffee and a cigar. But I'm much obliged to you, sir. Thank you." He put out his hand, and Cardona gave him a handshake.

"It's been a pleasure," he said. "I hope to see you around here. I'm around almost everyday."

"Well, we'll meet again then. This is a nice place. I come once in a while."

"All right."

Cardona moved over toward the end of the counter and shook hands with Carlos, who had been quietly sipping his coffee.

"Mr. Cardona, it's a pleasure to see you again. How are you?"

"I'm all right, and you?"

"Fine. Just making my daily stop here."

"Would you like something to eat? A pastry or a sandwich? They make them great here."

"No, I'm fine. Actually, Mr. Cardona, I wanted to talk

to you for a few minutes. You think we could grab a table inside?"

Cardona seemed perfectly casual about the request, but inside a thrill had overcome him. It was that great satisfaction he felt every time he scored a job. Now he knew Carlos Garcia was his. He must thank the old man, Peña, who surely must be the reason why such a high-caliber businessman and entrepreneur as Carlos Garcia wanted to talk to him. He did not show the slightest trace of any emotion as he responded.

"Well of course," he said pleasantly. "Let's get a table. Come on. Waitress," he said turning to one of the girls working the coffee machines, "we're going to get a table. Could you pass our bill to one of the other waitresses inside, please?"

Cardona led the way. He opened the glass door behind the counter and moved steadfastly to one of the small tables inside the main room of the restaurant without waiting for the hostess. He waved for Carlos to sit first and then he grabbed the chair across from him.

"What will you have?" he asked again as he signaled one of the waitresses.

"Nothing. I never have anything to eat here. Just the coffee."

"How about a sandwich? Take it home if you don't want to eat it here."

"No, thanks. Listen, I think I could use your services."

"In what respect? I do a lot of different things," Cardona said, smiling.

He was savoring the moment as if it were a grand prize. So he had been right after all. Peña had put in a good word for him. He must remember that.

"I'll get right to the point, Mr. Cardona, and you tell me whether or not you can help me. I have a seventeen-year-old daughter who's got it in her head that she's going to see Cuba one way or the other, as I mentioned yesterday. I don't want her to have a blemish on her record for the future, so I want to get her and her mother to the island for a short visit through some other country where there will be no trace of their going there. And of course it must be something that's 100 percent safe for them. My wife is going because we obviously can't let our daughter go alone, but it must be a safe way. I know a lot of people do these things on their own, but I want them to have a guide, someone who will handle the whole affair for them and get them there safely and back. I'm told you're the man for the job, so I want to discuss how this can be done."

Cardona had listened to him attentively, not missing a gesture or word, and then he put out his hand as if he were leading an orchestra.

"Carlos—may I call you Carlos?"

"Go ahead. That's my name."

"All right. I don't want to take any liberties to which I'm not entitled. But listen, right to the point. First and foremost is safety. I don't deal with anything reckless. Safety for my clients is my first concern. I can assure you that whatever route I take will be entirely secure for your family. Secondly, I try to make my trips enjoyable. I want to make sure that my clients come back happy, relaxed, and at the same time exuberant about what they have seen. What part of Cuba does your daughter want to visit?"

"She wants to go to her mother's town and mine. She wants to see where we came from."

"Well, that's all right. Nothing wrong with that. In fact, it's admirable that children take an interest in their parents' country. How old is your daughter did you say?"

"Seventeen."

"Hey, that's even more interesting. A teenager wanting

36

to see where her parents came from. That's definitely unique. You know teenagers nowadays. They just wanna party, have a good time. I think it's great."

"Well, anyway," Carlos said. "How can I get my wife and daughter in Cuba without a trace? You have them go through Jamaica or one of the other islands I guess, right?"

"No," Cardona responded. "I have them go through Mexico."

"Mexico?"

"Yeah. It's a very safe route."

"The way things are right now in Mexico?"

"Well, the problem with Mexico is at the border. It's a smuggling problem, and a drug problem that brews at the frontier. I have nothing to do with the border or with any of what goes on there. I use Mexico merely as a diving board to get my people to Cuba. That's my goal, to get them there and get them there safely."

Carlos was listening attentively and was quick to pick the point.

"Your operation, it seems to me, deals with a very similar issue as what goes on at the border right now, and that is smuggling. That's what you do. You smuggle people out of this country into Cuba and then smuggle them back in."

Carlos had decided to be blunt. He could take no chances in being soft with a man who was about to become responsible for his wife and daughter. He had to let him know that he wasn't fooling him with his sales pitch talk.

"No, no, wait, Carlos," Cardona said, gliding his open hand in front of him for emphasis. "I don't smuggle people. I provide a needed service to thousands of families who want to see their loved ones or simply want to visit their roots, as in your daughter's case."

"I'm sorry, I don't see it that way. But anyway, why Mexico? Why do you use Mexico when there are so many other places that are far safer now? I mean look at the islands. You can just about use anyone of them. Jamaica, Dominican Republic, Nassau. There's a ton of them. I've heard of so many people flying into those places just so they can catch a plane to Cuba. Why not use one of them?"

"The difference, Carlos, is in the service I provide. In Mexico you're dealing with a major metropolis, a developed country where people can actually vacation and have a good time on their way to Cuba. I offer it as part of the package. You can't do that with the islands. What they offer is limited to a swim at the beach or if you're lucky a trip to a second-class casino. There's more formality in Mexico, more opportunity to be classic, go to a museum, visit the pyramids, or just walk through the city. Ever been to Mexico City?"

"No."

"Well, you're missing a great spot. And like any other big city, you have the amenities, the availability of certain services that are just not there in other places."

"I don't know," Carlos said, unconvinced. "I don't see the connecting country, which is what Mexico would be in this case, as being that important. In the case of travelers to Cuba, what people want is to get where they're going as fast as possible. They're not interested in stopping anywhere if they don't have to. They're focused on bringing all their luggage and loads of goodies to their families. I've seen some leave from the airport here in Miami. They're no ordinary travelers. They're carrying loads of clothes, sometime wearing two pairs of jeans, one over the other, just so they can get one more piece of clothing to their families. So they're uncomfortable and anxious to get there. What do they care about where the plane stops?"

"I agree with you, Carlos. That is in the majority of cases, but when you deal with real tourists like you, and not just people who are going to see their families, it's not so at all,"

Cardona said, shaking his index finger as he spoke. "The country where your family is going to stop on their way to Cuba is a crucial part of the trip. We don't want to ruin the experience of a once-in-a-lifetime trip to their roots by shoveling them through some rinky-dink island. We want them to have a nice memory, so let's land them in a major metropolis with all of the modern amenities that we have in America. Make them comfortable. It's sort of a way to get them ready for the peak of their excursion."

Through the glass door at the right side of the room Cardona saw a familiar face. Francisco Peña was standing by the counter of the coffee shop, holding his espresso cup high in the air, as if to make a toast, a big grin on his face.

Cardona waved at him and the old man gulped down his coffee before making himself ready to walk over to their table. "Mr. Peña is here," Cardona said. "Like clockwork."

"That he is," Carlos said in agreement, turning toward the back room. "It doesn't fail."

"You know something, Carlos? You take that old man, for instance, and it teaches you a whole lot about life and how we end up. I know he's got a family, and I'm sure he enjoys them, but this is the high point of his day. If you took this moment away from him, he'd vanish in a second. And that is because this place was his daily escape from reality all his life. My problem with life is that it is too real, and that's why I crave these little moments. That is why people like you and me seek this temporary escape. We need it."

Carlos pondered over this sudden outpouring of philosophy and quickly dismissed it as another sale's pitch.

"Hello, gents," Mr. Peña said, arriving at the table. "Can you make some room for me?"

"Sure, sit down, Francisco," Cardona replied, looking around for a chair. "Take a chair from another table and bring it over."

Peña walked toward one of the rear tables to fetch a chair, and Cardona took the opportunity to speak while he was not present.

"I assume, Carlos, that it is all right to discuss the trip in front of Mr. Peña, right?"

"Sure. It was Mr. Peña who brought me to you."

"I know, but I wouldn't want to violate any confidentiality. I wanna make sure I can discuss your affairs in front of him."

Carlos did not answer. He took a final sip of his coffee and thought about Cardona's embellished language. It seemed that Cardona really believed what he said and that somehow he envisioned himself as being a professional, giving counsel to a client. *This guy's a little eccentric*, Carlos concluded. He wasn't sure if he was just wacky or was an egocentric. Either way, he was not yet ready to trust him, and certainly not with his daughter and wife on a trip that was against the law and shrouded in secrecy from the government. When Cardona mentioned Mexico as the intermediate country where his wife and daughter would change planes and go through customs without a trace, which was the main purpose why he sought Cardona's involvement, he was taken aback. Mexico? Why Mexico?

Cardona had presented a half-way decent case regarding the issue of the busy metropolis and the comforts that it could offer. Yes, he could imagine his wife shopping in Mexico City, looking for bargains in gold and clothes and comparing the exotic menus of various notable restaurants— but he couldn't see it at that moment. His wife and daughter were focused on only one thing—the trip to Cuba. Their stay in Mexico would probably only help increase their anxiety and wish for a speedy continuation of their flight. Cardona was a businessman and understood that. The idea of a stop in Mexico City did not sit well with Carlos.

"Well, Carlos," Mr. Peña said as he sat. "Is Cardona able to help you?"

"I think so. If I have to agree to this trip, I might as well agree to use someone who knows and who will get my wife and daughter there safely. Which brings me to a point, Mr. Cardona," Carlos said, turning and staring deeply at him. "What about the Cuban government?"

"What about it?" Cardona responded.

"I've heard all sorts of rumors that you have to be authorized by them in advance before you can step on Cuban soil. How are my wife and daughter going to accomplish that? My daughter, of course, has never been to Cuba, and my wife left when she was a child of seven. She doesn't even have a certificate of birth anymore—my wife, I mean. I heard these people will ask you for all sorts of documents and make exorbitant demands. And of course they'll ask for a lot of money. How am I going to be able to comply with all that?"

"Never worry," Cardona said, again sweeping the air with a slice of his open hand. "It's all part of the package. Your wife and daughter will have to do nothing. All you need to tell me is the date they want to leave and I'll get them there."

"I see. You will take care of all the paperwork?"

"All of it. Like I said, you talk to your wife about a date and get back to me with that. I will make the rest happen."

"What about fees? How much is all this gonna cost?"

"I will create a nice package for you. All expenses will be included, but of course you have to decide certain things, like the length of the trip, what sections of the country you will visit, and so on. I recommend that on a trip like this you don't make it for less than two weeks. It may be the only time they visit there, so let them have the time. Make it a lifetime memory for them."

"So you can't give me a ballpark figure, ah?"

"Well, it's not that I can't give you a figure, it's that I'd rather not commit myself until I know exactly what you want. Why don't you speak to your wife and decide some of the details, like the length of the trip and at the very minimum the places they absolutely want to see, and then I can work with you from there. We can come up with various itineraries that include the places your family wants to see and compare prices. How's that?"

"I guess that's right. I was hoping to get an idea."

"Well, it's gonna be reasonable, believe me. For the quality of the services it will include, it will be very reasonable."

"Well, Carlos," Mr. Peña added, "wherever they go, don't let them leave without seeing Valle de Viñales, and of course, Varadero is a must. You can't go to Cuba and not see that beach."

"You know something, Mr. Peña? I never saw Varadero. I've never been there."

"Well, Carlos, you're a country boy, a *guajiro*, what do you expect?"

He hung his arm around Carlos's shoulder and laughed to himself, as if the joke had been meant for him, and Carlos eventually joined him. It was Cardona who remained silent.

"Country people had no time for the beaches or for the revolution," Carlos responded. "It was people among the city masses who gave Castro the fuel he needed to take command. The *guajiros* had no time to think about a change of government. Yeah, it was those beachgoers at the exclusive resorts like Varadero who invented Castro. Batista was not good enough for them."

"Man, are we sensitive," Mr. Peña said. "See that, Cardona? Everybody has a soft spot. All I did was mention the word '*guajiro*' and he's taken the whole thing to a national level."

"In a way, he's right," Cardona finally commented. "People of means were the ones who helped Castro win."

"Oh, come on," Mr. Peña grunted. "From the beginning the so-called revolution was supported by country folks. The war, what little of it was real, was born in the mountains and on the plains. That's where it came from. That's where it was sustained."

"You couldn't be more wrong," Cardona insisted.

"Wait, hold it," Carlos added. "Let's leave that aside before we spark a whole debate among the crowd here. Let's discuss that some other time."

He was cautious, knowing well they had reached too sensitive of a topic for the area they were in. Already Carlos felt the stares of several people at the brink of wanting to yell out their opinions. You did not talk about fault for the rise of Castro in the middle of a popular Miami restaurant. It could be suicidal. A dozen other people would have different opinions and would jump into a war of words in the blink of an eye.

"How about this, Mr. Cardona?" Carlos asked while getting up from his chair. "I'm taking Mr. Peña with me. It's early but we're going to make a stop at one supermarket and then I'll take him home. I already have your number, so at some point tomorrow or the next day, I'll give you a call and we'll meet again to discuss the trip, all right?"

"Sure, Carlos. Anytime. I'm at your service." He stretched out his hand to meet Carlos's and made a slight effort to get up, but Carlos stopped him.

"It was nice talking to you. We'll talk some more soon. Peña, let's go."

The old man did not make a sound. It was a given that he would always leave with Carlos even if he had just gotten here. The fact that Cardona had met with him inside the restaurant to discuss business changed nothing. Peña was Carlos's companion before he was Cardona's acquaintance, and that's how it would stay. Perhaps Cardona would have liked him to remain and smooth some rough edges, ask him to work on Carlos and his insecurities over the trip. But before he could say a word, Peña was waving at him as he walked out the door, following Carlos, and the two disappeared into the restaurant's parking lot.

"Did you talk it over with him?" Mr. Peña asked. "Can he put it together for you?"

"It sounds like he knows his business, Peña. I just don't know about this type of thing. I don't trust it. I think anyone involved in this type of business is a crook."

"You're right to an extent. The problem is that all of us at some point have to deal with people like this. I mean, you tell me, what Cuban family has not ever in their life had the need to get their relatives out of Cuba? Who hasn't needed a visa? We all have done it at some point. We have to."

"Yeah, but this is a little different. This is shipping your family from the United States to visit Cuba."

"It's the trend today, Carlos. Things have changed. Castro cannot survive without the money the visits make for him. He's not only a guerilla fighter. He's also a businessman."

"I know what he is. It's a darn shame we have to deal with shady characters like this guy Cardona to do something illicit. In my case it's because a teenager won't take no for an answer. If it was up to me, she'd be going nowhere."

"Ah, Carlos, leave it alone. Don't torture yourself anymore with this. Let her go and see Cuba. That's what she wants. Honestly, what you should be doing is joining them and going on the trip too."

"Nahhh. I'll never make that trip, Mr. Peña. Nor for as long as the regime lasts. The way I look at it is that if I did not go when my parents were still there and they needed to see me, why would I go now to give my hard-earned money to that bastard? No way. In any case, this guy Cardona, he tells me he wants to send my family on a stop at Mexico

City. Why the heck Mexico? I thought they'd be flying into Jamaica or some other island."

"I don't know why he's giving you Mexico. It may be part of his luxury package now. This guy is like an ambulant travel agent, you know. He's getting more and more sophisticated, and I guess he just wants to provide good quality service. I don't think there's anything wrong with it. It's his ego too. This guy is very egocentric."

"And money hungry too."

The black Mercedes flew down the busy highway 826, through the heart of South Miami, passing fast-moving vehicles on the other lanes. By now Mr. Peña was used to it, but he never stopped whining about it to his friend.

"Any particular hurry that we ought to know about? You're driving like a teenager."

"I just want to get there. Last night the store manager called me at my house a bunch of times over a busted pipe line. That's why I'm going there now, to make sure there are no complaints. I would like to get a good night's sleep for a change. The manager I have at this new place is a prima donna. He draws a salary like you wouldn't believe, yet he couldn't make a decision if his life depended on it. The smallest problem and he's calling me. And it's usually things that can be resolved with a phone call, something like a busted pipe. What do you do? Call the plumber. A switch panel goes down, call the electrician. I mean, common sense."

"Maybe he's trying to save you money, Carlos. That's part of his job."

"Save me money, ah?"

"Yes. You ought to be grateful for that. He's your manager but he's trying to be careful with the spending."

Carlos didn't answer him. He switched over to the middle lane and then to the right one. He got off on Southwest 125th Street and made a right at the end of the ramp. Sections of the street were under repair and new construction was ongoing on both sides. They pulled into a sand-colored brick building sitting at the center of a strip of newly built stores that seemed still unoccupied and under construction.

"Let's go," Carlos said, unlocking the Mercedes' doors.

"This is your new baby, ah," Mr. Peña said, referring to the tall brick building near which they had parked. "It looks like more stores have opened up since the last time I was here."

Carlos came around the front of the car, his cell phone pinned to his ear. He had picked up a call as he got out of the car. "Hello," he said. "What's up, Lucia?" He paused a moment. "No, I'm at the new supermarket with Peña. I wanna make sure we don't get any calls in the middle of the night. I couldn't make my way here today at all so I had to come in before going home. I should be there in forty-five minutes, after I drop Peña."

After a moment he added, "I think I may have the trip situation resolved. Don't worry," he said, and cut the call.

They entered the market, a state-of-the-arts building with a tiled entrance and cash registers equipped with flat screens. It was busy despite the hour, and lines of customers waited with filled carts. Carlos stopped to take a look, and a woman wearing a white blouse and green slacks immediately came toward him.

"Carlos, Nick is waiting for you. They still haven't been able to get those pipes running, and we got two freezers down."

"Estrellita, have you met Mr. Peña?" he asked, ignoring her comments.

"I have, yes. Nice to see you, Mr. Peña. Would you like a *cortaito*?" It was the term used to describe an espresso with a tiny portion of milk. The market had a small cafeteria that catered to the customers.

"No, thanks. I would have taken you up on that if I had not had a cup just half an hour ago."

"All right, Mr. Peña, let's go see what the big emergency is back there."

Everything about the market seemed new. Even the aisles with their racks on both sides sparkled from the polish and shine. Carlos had spent a fortune setting up his new store, and as was his custom, he had put a lot of detail into his new venture.

Carlos's cell rang again as they neared the back of the store. "Yes, Lucia. I'm here."

They walked past the meat displays through a door into the rear of the building. Three men were working on a pipe line, one holding a pressure drill to break through the concrete floor. A fourth one, standing behind them, put out his hand as soon as he saw Carlos entering the room to quiet them.

"Carlos, we still have a backup," he said. "We gotta break further back into the concrete."

"Hold up for a second, Lucia," Carlos said into the phone. "Who was the genius who poured concrete over these lines?" Carlos asked.

"That's how it's done, Carlos," the man replied. "The men do their job. They install the lines and then cover them up."

He was clearly in charge of the crew. Carlos stopped in front of him, holding the phone by his ear but addressing him. "That's what you have safety windows for. You see them in every street corner, and I am no plumber. I don't even know how the City of Miami approved this job. I ought to sue them. Anyway, Nick, when is this gonna get done? That's all I wanna know."

"We might run well into the night tonight. I think the main line is cracked all the way back. It has to be replaced."

"Cracked, Nick? Cracked you say? So then we should

have the contractor back here with his whole crew. Have you called him yet?" He didn't wait for an answer. He switched to a soft tone of voice and told Lucia he'd call her back. Immediately after he was dialing another number. He was getting other help.

Mr. Peña walked towards Nick and shook his hand. Nick Salazar was a big man, about six feet tall with a heavy frame and a large stomach.

"A pleasure to see you," Peña said. "How are things going?"

"Right now, lousy. We got so many plumbing problems in this building that I wish we would have never opened it. It's terrible."

He kept looking in Carlos's direction as he spoke. He had an exhausted look about him, the look of a confused man who did not know what to do to get out of the predicament he was in. He was in charge, true. But he had not been able to handle the problem, and that worried him more than anything else. What if Carlos decided he was not fit for the job? Then he would be out, joining the thousands of unemployed in the City of Miami. Suddenly he saw Carlos put away his phone and walk in his direction.

"A man will be here in ten to fifteen minutes. I'm gonna make my rounds around the place with Peña. When the guy gets here, I'll bring him over and then you take charge of the operation. Tell these guys we no longer need them."

"Carlos, how can I let these guys go? They've been here for more than a day trying to solve the problem. That wouldn't be fair."

"Let them go. They're obviously unfit. Pay them for what they've done and get them out of here."

The two men behind them had heard him. They were standing only a few feet away. They leaned on their tools, looking as if they were ready to lunge at Carlos and Nick at any moment.

"It's not—" Nick didn't get to finish his sentence.

Carlos was on his way to the main floor, followed by Peña.

"Carlos, I think you're being too rash. Why don't you wait till at least the other service gets here?"

"Nah," Carlos replied. "Those guys don't know what they're doing. They're liable to do more damage in the next ten minutes than if I did the job myself. The job will get done. Just watch."

Carlos went on a trip throughout every department of the market, greeting all the personnel, who seemed eager to speak to him at every turn he made.

One man dressed in the green and white uniform of the store insisted on following him. "Mr. Garcia, I was wondering if you could help me."

"What is it?" Carlos said, turning.

"My wife is so sick, Mr. Garcia, and my insurance has only partially covered some of the treatment. I just wanted to ask you, and I'm deeply embarrassed, believe me, if I could take an advance on my pay. There is no income in the house except for mine, and I have two teenagers."

"And we know how teenagers are, don't we?" Carlos said. "I think I got some experience in that. Tell me, what did you have in mind?"

"Well, if I could only bring my utilities up-to-date, the electric and the water, I think I could manage the rest. Imagine if they cut my services with my wife on hospice, what would I do?"

"That's not going to happen. Don't worry. So how much do you need, you figure?"

"About a thousand dollars."

"All right. Go get Estrellita and tell her to come to see me at the manager's office. She'll make you a check."

"Really, Mr. Garcia? God bless you, sir. You don't know how much I appreciate it."

"Don't worry about it, Ralph. Give my best to your wife. I'm stopping at the vegetable section just for a second. Get Estrellita over to the office."

It took Carlos's contractor more than thirty minutes to arrive, but when the two men walked into the store, they were all business. Estrellita received them. They were dressed in gray overall uniforms and seemed to recognize Carlos as soon as they were allowed a peak at him.

"Carlos, how are you?" They greeted him.

"Hey, you guys. How's business these days, ah?"

"Can't say it's excellent," one of them said. "But we're paying the bills."

"These days if you do that, you're doing excellent. Let me walk you guys to the back. I want you to see the project."

He walked in front of them, zigzagging through the aisles and picking up fruit, which he later handed to them.

"Carlos, this place looks beautiful. You built it?"

"Yes. I had it built, but I'm afraid the contractor's plumber blundered the job. Look at this."

They were in the rear section looking at the canal drilled deeply into the floor, exposing the water lines. The men who had been on the job before were gone, and even Nick was nowhere to be seen.

"What the heck happened?" one of the men said.

"We got a cracked line, I'm told. Not sure. But we have a backed-up sewer causing trouble, and now we got concrete over the lines. All I wanna know is this: When can you guys have these lines running and the electric back on those freezers?"

They looked around at the mention of the freezers, looking puzzled.

"So there's electric involved?" one said.

"It seems that the lines feeding them are shut down. Whether it's related to the plumbing I don't know. I need everything working tonight."

There was silence for a moment, but then one took command. He sounded confident. "Get out of here, Carlos," he said, as Carlos's cell rang again. "Give us till tonight."

Carlos picked up the call and headed out back to the market section with Mr. Peña behind him. He waved at them on his way out.

"Yes, Lucia?" he said into the phone. "I'm on my way out. Just wait a couple of minutes. I have Mr. Peña with me. Can you make him some coffee?"

The two walked out of the market and met up with Nick. The poor man seemed disconcerted. His authority had been crossed, as if he were an incompetent.

But Carlos elevated him as he spoke. "Nick, I have to go. It's my wife. I'll be around tomorrow first thing in the morning. Those people I left you back there know what they're doing. Take over and oversee the job. I'll bet you any amount of money they will have this place running in a couple of hours."

Carlos and Peña were already in the car. Carlos opened the driver's window and gave him even more of a lift. He understood Nick. "Don't worry about it, Nick. You did good."

The black Mercedes shot out of the parking lot and made a quick left at the exit. Inside, Mr. Peña complained that it was too late to drink coffee again.

"Then drink whatever you want at the house, Mr. Peña. You can have a beer, a shot of whisky, juice."

Carlos was still on the phone with his wife and talked to her while holding his flat BlackBerry to his ear.

"Tell Lucia we're on our way, and get off the phone while driving."

Carlos nodded as he kept on listening to her voice on the other side of the line. Mr. Peña had been through the scenario many times before and knew just what to do. He fit well in his role of doctoring Carlos, treating him as a son despite the younger man's obvious skills that surpassed his more subtle ways.

"Lucia, we'll be there in a couple of minutes," Carlos said. "Hang on." He put away the phone and focused on the driving. "Lucia is worried, Mr. Peña. That's why I want you to come home with me and back me up on this Cardona guy."

"So you're gonna use him after all?"

"Yes."

"When did you decide that? Back there at the restaurant I got the feeling you were not his fan."

"I thought about it as we were at the supermarket."

"In the middle of all that commotion?" Mr. Peña seemed startled by this revelation but not totally surprised. He had known Carlos for quite some time and knew about his abilities. One of them was a tremendous ease in handling stress. It seemed that he could actually thrive in the middle of the most heated battle of nerves. Always resolute in his thinking and decisive. To Peña that was the secret to his success. A man who could be multi-task as he had shown tonight and actually think as he did was a winner.

"Yes. I think Cardona is right, Mr. Peña. I mean about having them stop at a nice metropolis like Mexico City. It makes it more like a normal vacation. I almost get the feeling that I could go and see after them at least while they're in Mexico City. It would be a nice getaway."

"Why don't you? You should."

"Nah. I can't do that. If I am gonna go, I'll go all the way. But dropping them off in Mexico City and then leaving them alone to go on the rest of the trip doesn't sound too rational. Besides, there are so many modes of communications today. We can stay in touch through the cell phones. I mean, I don't know what will happen when they get to Cuba. I guess the cell phones don't work from down there, right?"

"I don't think so. But I could be wrong about that, actually. You figure Castro's gotta make it convenient for the tourists. That's pretty much his only source of income now, so I wouldn't be surprised if you could even do that. I just don't know."

"A question for Cardona."

"That's right."

They pulled into Carlos's driveway and parked behind Lucia's blue BMW.

"One thing I must say, Carlos," Mr. Peña observed as he got out of the car. "You buy nice cars. That thing must be very fast, no? Does Lucia drive like a teenager too?"

"We all drive the same way in this family, you know that. And we shoot the same way at the range too, me and Lucia, I mean. We're all charged up. Come on in."

The front door was unlocked and they went in. Lucia was lying on the sofa, watching the big-screen TV. She got up as soon as she saw Mr. Peña coming in behind Carlos.

"Mr. Peña, so nice of you to come. I haven't seen you in a long time."

They hugged and kissed each other on the cheek.

"I'm making coffee, real strong as you like it."

"Lucia, you didn't have to. I had coffee not too long ago with Carlos."

"Everybody has coffee not too long ago in Miami, Mr. Peña. That's because it's all over the place. Not a good excuse."

She leaned toward her husband and kissed him and then urged Mr. Peña to relax in the living room.

"Sit down while I go get you a cup." She came back with a small espresso cup on a saucer that she handed to Mr. Peña, who had sat in a loveseat. Carlos had slumped on the sofa next to the bundle of pillows that his wife had mounted one on top of another and against which she usually rested as she watched TV, at times calling him incessantly on his phone.

She squeezed between her husband and the pillows and leaned over. She kissed him again. "What happened? What did you decide?"

"There's this man Peña knows," Carlos began. "His name is Cardona and he makes a living out of arranging trips to Cuba. He sounds very professional and I think he's our best shot for this trip. He can arrange the whole thing, from flights to hotels. There is only one caveat and that is that he would want you to relax in Mexico for a couple of days before you go on to Cuba. It's part of the package he sells."

"Why is that a caveat? It sounds fine to me. My only regret is that you're not coming. Why can't you come with us?"

"We've been over that already. I can't go. I'm sorry. You know why. My question to you is, are you sure you don't have a problem making that stop in Mexico City?"

"No. Why would I? I'm going to visit the Church of our Lady of Guadalupe while I'm there, you know. Neither Alicia or I have ever seen it."

"What worries me is that this is not a good time to be in Mexico, with everything going on down there right now."

"Not the city, Carlos," Mr. Peña said. "The problem is at the border, with the United States."

"I don't know about that, Peña. I think it's spreading everywhere. Even Acapulco has had problems."

"Carlos, don't worry," Lucia said. "We'll be just fine. Or

you could come with us. That way we'd be protected." She broke into a broad smile and caressed his hair, pulling herself close to him. "Come on. Why don't you?"

He shook his head. "Anyway, I think our best bet is to go through this guy, Lucia. We don't have to do anything. He takes care of it all, and you need that when you're going on a trip like this. It's like going into the unknown."

Mr. Peña shook his head and stared at Lucia. "What an exaggeration," he commented. "You would think you're going to the end of the world. Carlos, it's only Cuba. They're going to go and see the island and enjoy it. That's so. Would you lighten up?"

"That's Carlos," Lucia said. "Carlos," she said to him. "Please try to get some rest, honey. Come on, you're tired. Go sit down. I'll take Peña home."

She held his hand as if they were teenage lovers, and he held hers tight for a second and then sat back in the sofa, facing Mr. Peña. The TV was playing the news.

"When are you thinking of making the trip?" Mr. Peña asked.

"My daughter wants to leave right away. She's out of school as of next week. Let me bring her so you can see her."

Carlos reached for his cell and dialed Alicia's number. Even inside the house they dialed each other. Everyone in the family was totally dependent on their cell phones and would not think of being anywhere without one.

"Hi, Alicia. Come to the living room. Peña is here. Come and say hello."

Alicia entered the room dressed in jeans and a tee-shirt, wearing no shoes. "Mr. Peña, hi," she said.

"Alicia, how are you?"

Out of respect toward Carlos Mr. Peña did not mention the trip, but he would have loved to hear her stories about the many sources the young girl had tapped into to get information about the controversial travels to his home island. He had known Alicia for most of her life and knew how intense she could be, unusual for a girl her age but very telling and in many ways something to be admired. Alicia probably had already figured out more ways to visit the island than Cardona himself. But he also knew how Carlos felt about the trip and did not want to hurt his friend's sensitivity. He let her tell him.

"Mr. Peña, did you know that you could even fly into one of the provinces without going to Havana?"

"No, I did not know that," Peña said. "I'm from Cárdenas, which is near Havana, so I would not have any reason to fly anywhere else when I left. But that's good to know."

"Alicia," Lucia interrupted, "your father has it all solved. You don't have to search anymore."

"Oh, how's that?"

"It was actually Peña who solved the problem," Carlos said. "He introduced me to the source. Right, Peña?"

"I did, yes."

"Okay, Dad, so you finally accepted it? You don't object?"

"I did not say that. I object, yes. But your mother and I are trying to make you happy. I have this man who is kind of a broker, you might say, in regards to traveling to Cuba. Right now I don't want to think about his connections with the Castro government because I think that's disgusting, but it's the best way to protect you and your mother. He will take care of everything. We don't have to do anything. He'll set up the flight, the stay, everything. You and your mom get on a plane here and fly to Mexico City, have a little vacation there, and then fly to Cuba for one week. You come back the same way."

"Where do we fly to in Cuba?" she asked, smiling. Her

wish had finally come true. Despite what she considered her father's archaic ideas, she had prevailed. She was going to see the island.

"That's to be decided yet. Your mother and I have to talk."

"Carlos, I think that if we're going to go our home towns we should fly as close to them as possible."

"So where do they fly to?" Carlos asked, turning to Peña.

"Well, you're from Camagüey. Lucia is from Holguín. If you're going to see only those two cities, I guess the best place to start from would be your city, Camagüey. They have direct flights there."

"And then how do they get to Holguín?"

"They'll have transportation."

"Transportation in Cuba is a nightmare, Peña. That's what I always hear."

"Not for tourists. How do you think people get to those northern beaches of the province? They rent cars, tour buses go there, anything. When it comes to tourism, the government bends over backward to please. Of course it is not like that for the general population. We all know that."

"So that's it then," Alicia cut in anxiously. "We fly to Camagüey, Dad."

"Alicia, wait up honey," Lucia said. "Let's wait till we all discuss this. You're getting your wish, right? So then wait."

"Mom, all I'm saying is that if we're gonna go to see Dad's native city, we should fly there directly and then go to your home town, which is not that far away from there. That's the right thing to do, no?"

Lucia and Carlos exchanged glances, both shaking their heads.

"It's gonna be fun," Carlos said to his wife. "Lucia, you're gonna have your hands full down there, trying to control your daughter."

"Dad, stop it."

"Listen, you have to listen to your mother. Whatever she says goes, you hear? That's the condition of the trip. You're not making decisions on your own down there. You do what your mother tells you."

"What is this, Dad? A tyranny?"

"No, it's called raising a kid, which you still are. Tyranny is what you're going to see down there."

"Oh, stop that, Dad. I'm going to see the island where you and Mom come from. It has nothing to do with politics."

"Anyway, Lucia," Carlos said. "I thought you might want to see Havana and then work your way down to our home towns. Aren't you going to go to Varadero Beach?"

"It doesn't matter to me. You know why I'm going. If Alicia is happy with just seeing Camagüey and Holguín, then let's just fly there. I'm only doing it to please her."

"Mom, I would like to see Varadero. Why can't we work our way up to the western side of the island on our way back?"

"Well, that's an idea, I guess."

"So you'd land in Camagüey but leave from Havana. Is that possible, Mr. Peña?"

"I don't see why not."

Lucia handed Carlos the espresso cup she had been holding for a few minutes now.

"All right then. I will settle it with Mr. Cardona that way. And for how long should I reserve, Lucia? One week? Two weeks?"

"No. One week, Carlos. No more than one week."

"Mom, why not? Why can't we stay for two weeks?"

"One week is more than enough, Alicia. Believe me, you're gonna want to come back before the week is up."

"That's not true, Mom. How do you know?"

"I know," Lucia said, staring at Carlos.

"One week," Carlos said. "I'll make the reservations for one week."

Alicia lifted one arm as if declaring victory and then ran off into her bedroom. "I've got to make some calls," she yelled on her way.

"Carlos," Mr. Peña said. "You're all very hospitable, but I gotta get home."

"Oh, sure, Peña. Let's go. Lucia, come on, let's go for a ride and take him home."

She went to the kitchen to put the tray away and then followed them to the driveway. She suddenly felt a deep tribulation. The realization that she was going to go back to the island she had left so many years ago suddenly hit her. Carlos was right. She was in for the trip of her life.

Chapter Three

Lucia felt confident as she exited the gate from the Continental jet that had flown her and her daughter to Mexico City. Alicia took the lead and responded courteously to the two stewardesses and captain who had gathered at the cockpit to bid farewell to the passengers. Lucia had been to Mexico City various other times when traveling to South America or on her way to Acapulco, one of her favorite vacation resorts. But she had always done so with her husband. Nevertheless, they had all agreed as a family that they would please Alicia and at the same time respect Carlos's convictions of not traveling into a pro-Castro Cuba. So she had merrily gone in tow of her excited teen daughter on what was to be a sentimental vacation.

Lucia had not yet fully come face-to-face with the predicament of seeing her homeland after so many years of absence. Perhaps she did not want to, and as she walked down the corridor, she thought that that was probably her husband's biggest reason for refusing to go, the fear of facing the past. A past that, for all practical purposes, most Cubans of their generation had decided to cling to. Perhaps Carlos did not know it, but his insistence that he would not return while Castro was still in power was only a cover-up for the real macabre reason, which was his fear, a fear of unburying the bones of a story that had been told and retold too many times yet was never quite finished. Yes, that had to be it. She felt it too.

She caught up to her daughter as they exited the tarmac. When they entered the terminal, a man approached Lucia and extended his hand to greet her.

"How was the trip? All right?" he asked in perfect English.

Lucia knew Carlos had arranged for someone to meet them at the airport. It was part of the Cardona deal. But she felt surprised that someone would come right up to the gate. Usually the drivers waited for their passengers in the luggage area and identified themselves with signs. Yet the familiar way in which the man addressed her gave her a warm feeling.

"Fine," she replied, slowing her pace.

"That's good. Are you and your daughter ready to see Mexico City?"

"We know Mexico City," she said. "We've been here many times."

Now she stopped and looked at the stranger. He was of medium height and was dressed casually. He seemed totally at ease, as if he had known her a long time.

"All right, what do you want?" she asked, testing him.

She figured if he was not a thief, he would have an answer; otherwise he would stumble.

"I'm supposed to take you and your daughter to your hotel."

"And how did you know who we were?"

"They described you and your daughter to a t. My taxi is outside waiting. Madam, I'm at your service. Shall we go get your luggage?"

"I'll tell you what," she said. "Let me call my husband."

She took her cell phone from her pocketbook and turned it on. She had turned off the power at the beginning of the flight. She was testing him again. She figured if the man was up to no good, he would run off, seeing that he would be discovered. Otherwise he would stay. She waited until the screen came on and then pressed Carlos's name on the contact list and put the phone up to her ear.

"Mom," Alicia said. "You did not call Verizon to get your phone programmed for international service. I did on mine. Here, use my phone."

She handed her mother her phone, a touch-screen BlackBerry, after activating her father's number. Lucia grabbed the phone and noticed that the man was still there.

"Hello," came the voice on the other end.

"Carlos, we're at the airport."

"You made it all right, honey?"

"Yes. We're still at the terminal. There's this guy here who says he came to pick us up. Do you know anything about that?"

"Yes. Cardona is having someone pick you up at the airport. Ask for his name."

"Sir," she said, addressing the man. "What is your name?"

"I'm Alberto. I was sent by Corporal to get you to the hotel."

She noticed the slight drag on his accent, typical in the Mexican manner of speaking.

"Carlos, do you know who Corporal is? He says he was sent by Corporal."

"That's the name of Cardona's company, Lucia. I guess it's all right."

"Oh, all right. Well, I didn't know that. You never told me."

"I heard him say that. He just uses his own name all the time. That's why I never mentioned it. Be careful though. Keep your eyes open."

"All right. We'll do. Listen, I don't think you can reach me on my phone. I forgot to have it set up. Do you think you can have that done for me now?"

"All right. I'll do that right away for you. I'll have one of my secretaries call Verizon. Be careful, Lucia. Call me once you get into the hotel."

She could tell Carlos was in the middle of a crisis, as usual. One of the stores must have been shaken by a hurricane during the night or it could just be simply a matter of a manager not showing up for work. Her husband faced these challenges on a daily basis, and although it did not seem to rattle him, she could, after all these years of being with him, tell when he was on guard even if only a little bit. But she had learned to admire his composure and his wisdom more than anything. Right now there was no one in the world she trusted more than her husband, and even here, in this big city of this Latin American country, she would defer to him on the smallest of details. Hearing him tell her to be careful had a special meaning between them. The casualness with which he said it meant that things were okay and that she could use her own caution, probably the opposite of what it would mean to an average person.

She sized the man up by looking him up and down. "And where is Corporal taking us?"

"They told me to bring you to the *Galería* Hotel, near the *Zona Rosa*."

"Where's your taxi?"

"Outside, waiting."

Lucia did not think about it any more. She followed the slim man who walked at a hasty pace, making it difficult for her and her daughter to keep up. Lucia thought that was rude but motioned for Alicia to hurry. They took an escalator down to the baggage area, where the man set himself immediately next to the conveyor among other passengers.

"How many valises did you bring?" he asked, turning around.

"We have three," Lucia replied. "It's all right. We will grab them."

"No," he said. "That's what I'm here for."

She smiled at him but he had already turned, facing the conveyor belt that was running but so far carrying no baggage. Lucia stayed close to him until she was able to point out her luggage. He grabbed each piece one at a time and then called an attendant, who placed them in a carriage. He asked him to follow.

"You'll enjoy Mexico City," he said from afar as they all walked out of the airport. "The city has grown even more and has gotten a bit more sophisticated."

He turned for a moment as he spoke. "I'm at your service."

She wanted to ask him about the violence that the country was undergoing since recently and whether some of it had spilled over into the city but thought it was not the appropriate time. They went into the airport's parking lot, with Alberto leading the group to a red Chevrolet sedan that was parked deep into the lot. He opened the trunk, and the young man carrying the luggage put them inside. Alberto tipped him, and the porter quickly went away, pushing his empty cart.

"All right, hop in," Alberto said.

Lucia and Alicia sat in the back. Alberto got behind the wheel and drove to the toll booth to pay the fare.

"Are the problems at the border affecting the city?" Lucia asked without thinking, and then regretted she had asked the question.

"No, not really," he said. "The government keeps the city safe. There's too much tourism here. Besides, the head of government is here. It's more or less like Acapulco or Cancún.

They're not gonna let those places be affected by whatever goes on at the border. The border is the border."

"Well, to get to the border they have to cross the country. It all comes from down south, right?"

"Yes, but not the federal district. Everyone knows this is untouchable. It's where the government sits."

They had not been on the highway for longer than ten minutes and the car veered off an exit. Lucia had no idea where the *Galería* Hotel was located, and when the car worked its way onto a local street, she thought nothing of it until it pulled into an empty lot. It seemed to speed through a long stretch of pavement and then suddenly stop next to a black Mercedes.

"Wait a minute," she said. "Where are we?"

Alberto did not respond. He quickly put the car in park and got out through the driver's door. Lucia grabbed her daughter's hand and made for the handle to try to open her door, but she held herself back when it was yanked open by a man standing outside whose face she did not even get to see. It happened so quickly, like a knee-jerk reaction in a maneuver that had probably been practiced many times. He quickly threw a hood over her face, and it seemed like the lights had gone out. She could not see.

"Alicia! Alicia!" She yelled her daughter's name, but her voice was drowned by the dark piece of cloth and a hand that pressed tight against her mouth.

She could not understand what was happening, but she shook in terror as she was carried into what felt like another vehicle. She tried to scream, but no sound would come out. Then she felt a man's hand press her head down and push her inside.

"*Señora*," she heard a voice say in Spanish. "Stay still and be quiet. Nothing will happen to you if you cooperate. Stay down. Your daughter is here with you in the front seat."

She tried to speak, but her words were muffled by the hood covering her head.

"*Señora*, when I say be quiet, I mean be quiet. I'm not playing. One more word out of you and I'll put you to sleep."

For the first time, she was able to filter the meaning of the words. Her anxiety had prevented her from coming into a full realization of what was happening except for her concern for her daughter. She felt the raw rub of steel on her neck and surmised it could only be the barrel of a gun. These people were capable of anything, she thought. But she had to know.

"I need to know that my daughter is here," she managed to say, sucking the cloth as she spoke.

"All right," the same voice said. "She's here. Come on, young lady, say something."

"Mom!" Alicia's voice came from the front seat but was quickly muffled.

"All right. Happy now? Be quiet and you'll be all right."

She felt the gun barrel pressing harder against her neck, and she anxiously asked herself why. A deep fear began to overwhelm her. Up to then she had only thought about Alicia, having a typical mother reaction to a flammable situation the consequences of which had not fully dawned upon her yet. Now for the first time she had actually realized that her life was really in danger. There was a gun being held against her neck and these people, whoever they were, were taking her and her daughter somewhere. What did they want? She felt herself shaking and her heart racing. She wanted to speak again but thought better of it. Then she heard the car engine come to a halt, and for the first time she heard sobbing coming from the front seat.

"Stop," another voice said softly in the front seat area,

clearly to her daughter. "Stop crying right now or I'll knock you out."

"Only four," Lucia heard another man's voice say from the front seat.

She could discern a heavy Mexican accent, more pronounced than the other two who had spoken, and then she heard another voice respond to him from outside the car. This was some kind of checkpoint, she thought. They were getting off the highway and the big city, and that was not a good sign. Where were they taking them?

In the front seat, Alicia was lying in the same weird position as her mother, the mid-lower section of her body sitting but her torso forced to turn to the side. Her upper body was lying down flat, with someone pushing her face tight against the leather. She too had been hooded, and the taut cloth that covered her nostrils made it hard for her to breathe, which caused her to be even more exasperated, trying to break free from her tormentor.

Everything had happened so fast that she had had no time to react, and in the rush of getting her inside the vehicle, her captors had not realized that she was still holding her cell phone in her left hand right after her mother had handed it back to her at the airport after calling her father. The device became trapped under her head, still in her hand that had gotten sandwiched underneath her head and the seat.

As her tormentor pressed her head tight to keep her still, her face made contact with the green dial key of her BlackBerry, which redialed the last number called—her father's. She heard the voice like a faraway echo, never realizing what it meant. She was too upset to focus.

"Hello," the voice said several times and getting no answer back, the recipient of the call ended it.

The car seemed to move slower now, clattering as it negotiated what felt like a bumpy road. Lucia started to think rationally now. She was beginning to sort things out in her mind. It became obvious to her now that if they wanted to kill them, they would have done so already. But what would be the motive? These people were not street thieves. There was some type of organization involved in their operation; that was evident. So the purpose of the whole thing must be a kidnapping. Yes, a kidnapping, she thought, her daughter and she were being kidnapped. They must have realized they were tourists, and she and Alicia just got unlucky and got picked from the crowd. Yes, that's what it was. They were unlucky.

But then she remembered that she and her daughter were on their way to Cuba. They had stopped in Mexico City only for two days of relaxation and sightseeing before boarding another plane to the island. The man Carlos had hired and who had arranged their trip had suggested they do it this way, and she herself had welcomed the idea of breaking up the trip to her homeland into fragments. It would give her some space to breathe, to relax, and in a way prepare for the shock she was sure she would experience upon seeing Cuba again.

But something peculiar struck her as she kept retracing the steps of the trip. The man at the airport had said he'd been sent by Corporal, and Carlos had confirmed that was Cardona's company. It seemed odd now that the man had used the company's name and not Cardona's name directly. That sounded suspicious and she should have picked up on that.

She slid her head slightly on the seat to try to ease the discomfort of lying in such an odd position. Her torso was beginning to hurt. She felt what she could only guess was the barrel of a gun pressing hard against her neck.

"*Señora*, don't move," the man said in Spanish. "I know you're uncomfortable, but we don't have long to go."

Despite the ominous announcement, it did not frighten her. So they were transporting them someplace. That lent more credence to the notion that it was a kidnapping. These people were taking them to some isolated location as hostages. That was the answer. Then she went back to thinking of the scene at the airport and how it had all unraveled. The man who had lured them into the car had known the name of their hotel, the *Galería*. How had he known that? And never mind that he had not mentioned Cardona's name, that after all could have been to make it sound more professional. She began making a conclusion. It had to be, yes. Cardona was in on it. Cardona was part of the conspiracy. He must have realized that her husband was a rich entrepreneur in Miami and he had gone for the chance like a bear after honey. She became so resolute that she went as far as thinking of Mr. Peña as a suspect. Could he too be involved? But she instinctively dismissed that. Mr. Peña was one of those old Cubans who lived life as if it had ended. All he wanted out of a day was his espresso and his daily meetings with Carlos every evening. He was a man who saturated his time and did not have any ambition. No, she was wrong for thinking ill of him. Besides, how could he face Carlos after what happened? And thinking of that, the question popped into her head: How could Cardona face Carlos now? What would he have to say about what had happened?

Lucia could not tell how long they traveled, but she heard voices coming from outside as the car came to a stop. One of the men inside the car responded in Spanish, telling the others that they were ready, apparently an indication that all was well. She had not heard them speak on the phone to anyone, probably because they were being careful not to be traced. There was silence in the car for a few seconds, and she heard Alicia's light sobbing coming from the front of the vehicle. She wanted so much to comfort her but knew that if she spoke, whoever was next to her would lunge at her.

She felt a hand grab her arm and pull her up. "Let's go, *señora*, get up!" He slowly had her step out of the car. She was still hooded and could not see, and she seemed in pain after having spent so much time in a coiled position. The man seemed to acknowledge that and he was handling her carefully. Then she felt someone else pull her hands behind her back and cuff them.

"Where is my daughter?" she asked in despair.

"Quiet. Your daughter is right here."

She heard movement in front of her, and one of the men yelled out to the others.

"I found the girl's cell phone on the seat. It was under her. It's still on."

"Well turn it the fuck off! How did it get there anyway?" another man said.

"I don't know. It must have slipped under her as we carried her inside."

"You idiot! Let's go. Come on."

Someone was holding Lucia by her right arm. She felt they were walking uphill on rocky ground, and she felt the warmth of the sun on her head, making it hard to breathe under the hood. She felt so out of breath that she spit out the words, "Can you take these things off our heads? I can't breathe."

"In time we will, *señora*. Not yet."

"What's the difference? We can't tell where we are anyway."

She felt so suffocated that she stopped walking. She felt the grip on her arm get tighter.

"Let's go!" the man commanded. "Don't make me drag you."

"You might just have to," she said. "I can't breathe."

She felt another hand hold her other arm, this one more aggressively than the other one, yanking her forearm. Because she could not keep up with the pace, her feet dragged on the ground, and she was being carried uphill like a piece of furniture. She wondered how her daughter was faring up front but felt some relief in knowing that she was actually giving them a hard time. She was not so out of breath anymore and was learning about the limits of their tolerance, how far they were willing to go in their efforts to keep her captive, or whatever else they were planning.

Suddenly they stopped. She could not tell where they were standing and heard no sounds, but they next moved her inside some structure where it felt unbearably hot. Next she heard a door slam, and they made her sit down, her hands still cuffed behind her back.

"Where is my daughter?" she asked, determined to keep her pose.

"*Señora*, don't worry about your daughter," another voice answered. "She's fine."

"Where is she?"

"Don't be asking so many questions. Keep quiet. From now on, you speak when we tell you to speak, you understand?"

"I wanna know where my daughter is."

"You wanna see your daughter?"

Lucia's heart seemed to skip a beat. Alicia meant everything to her. She would have traded anything in exchange for her safety right now, injury to herself, torture, even death. She was desperate to know that she was all right. "Yes."

"Then be quiet. Not one more word out of you."

Lucia broke down crying. She had been incredibly strong and held her composure like she never imagined she could in such a desperate situation, but it was obvious she was helpless.

She had no control over anything. She had to do as told or else some harm could come to her daughter. Then, slowly, she recovered. She could not show weakness. Somewhere she had sensed that the men holding her captive had some limits in what they could do. She would try to find the boundaries of those limits and start working on her plan. There had to be a plan. She had to save her daughter from a prolonged captivity that could wreck her life. That had to be her goal.

"I want to see her. Where is she?"

"Never mind that. Be quiet."

"I'm not gonna be quiet. I want to see my daughter."

She felt the cold barrel of a gun again slightly rubbing the bottom of her neck. It felt more like a tease than a threat, but Lucia went tense.

"*Señora*, you don't seem to understand, do you? There are gonna be some rules, and the first one is that we don't repeat ourselves, you hear me? You are gonna be quiet. No talking. Now, we're going to take the cuffs off, but you're going to stay on the chair for now. We're going to cut two openings on your hood, one for breathing and the other for talking when we tell you to. You can't leave the room. This is where you live now until we decide otherwise."

She felt someone grab the black cloth from her face and pull it. Then she heard the tear of the cloth as they sliced it with a knife, making an opening around her mouth. They did the same by her nostrils. It felt good to breathe, but the air felt so heavy she still had a hard time.

"Why can't you take off this hood? I can't breathe."

"Shut up!" one of the men said.

She could not see them but was beginning to identify their voices. The one talking was the same who had been next to her in the car. But there was another voice behind her she had never heard, and he sounded more threatening than the others.

"Be ready to talk on the phone when I tell you to," the voice said from behind her. "You can only say what I tell you to say, you understand?"

His accent was clearly Mexican, she thought. He had that drawl that made the words sound as if they were being dragged. She had always found it an interesting accent in the Spanish language and for some reason associated it with innocence, as if whoever spoke it could not hurt anyone. When she heard it now from these men, it gave her hope. These people could not really do her and her daughter any harm. They must be mediocre kidnappers, if that was in fact what they were, probably poor souls, victims of the misery and poverty that the country was undergoing. The rough tone of the voice from behind her made her come back to reality. This person was serious, whatever his accent.

"Understand?" he repeated.

"Yes," she responded in Spanish. "Why don't you take this hood off? What kind of cowards are you that you are afraid of two women looking you in the eye?"

"Shut up!" the voice before her said. "Shut up!"

She felt the barrel of the gun again rubbing her neck, but then she felt the arm of the man behind her going over her shoulder. He was reaching for the barrel and removed it from her neck. She began to get a feeling that whoever he was he must be in charge.

"*Señora*," he said, "you sound like a tough lady. Perhaps it's nerves that are making you talk like that. Let me tell you something. You don't fully understand your situation. You are a hostage. You belong to us now, and so does your daughter. Things can be worked out, yes. But right now, at this moment, you are our property and you will obey our commands if you want to stay alive. You understand?"

"Cowards," she replied. She wanted to control herself

each time she spoke and yet the words rolled out like thunder, not fully knowing why.

"I guess they gave you a mouth to talk. That's good. We like talkers here, actually. It gives us something to do because we fix them. We fix them real fast. You know what we do with them? We sever their tongues. Ever see a person getting his tongue cut out? It's pretty bloody. Man, is it bloody! And then if the person doesn't die from the loss of blood they are a mess for a long time. The mouth gets swollen, real swollen, as big as a sweet potato, and in the meantime, you know, they can't eat. They can only drink, and that is very carefully because anything can bring the bleeding back. And then you run into the problem of infection. That's the real danger because it is such a sensitive area of the body, and here of course we have no medical facility or nothing, so if you catch an infection, that's pretty much it. You're done. Only it doesn't happen fast. It goes slowly with a lot of pain. Some of them die in the middle of a scream, killed in agony by the pain. Is that how you wanna die, *señora?*"

"You're still a bunch of cowards. You're afraid of having a woman get a look at your ugly faces. You're afraid." She was in shock at the way she was talking to them. She was sure she was not facing the man. His voice was coming from the rear.

"Now, *señora*, if you haven't seen our faces, how do you know they're ugly, ah?"

For the first time, she thought, he was acknowledging her. She had found a way. He was admitting they were more than one. He was reacting to her comments. He wasn't slapping her or trying to choke her as your run-of-the-mill kidnapper might do but had been offended by her comment and had reacted, not in a bad way, almost childlike, but reacting nevertheless. That gave her a hint about his plan, or his orders, as it might be. He had some limits as to what he could do and even when insulted he would not lose his head. Lucia began suspecting that she and her daughter were a grand prize to these people. What they wanted in exchange remained to be seen.

"They're probably white as a ghost from fear. You poor cowards."

"Behave yourself, *señora*. There's no need for violence. I'm gonna have the cuffs removed from you. Now you stay put. You hear me?"

She heard the footsteps of one of the other men and then felt him behind her, removing her handcuffs.

"How about my daughter? Are you removing hers too?"

"Your daughter is fine. She's in the next room," the same voice said. "She's not a talker like you but a crier. I'm gonna give her a sedative to keep her calm. Now, you, I want you to be ready. I will need you on the phone in a few minutes."

"What for?"

"Never mind that. You just do as I tell you."

"You wanna confirm my existence, is that it? You coward! What do you want anyway? What can I or my daughter give you when we're headed for Cuba? We don't have anything."

"You were headed for Cuba. No more you're not. As far as what you can do for us, there's plenty. You will see."

That sounded like an ominous warning, and what immediately worried her was her daughter. Alicia was a beautiful seventeen-year-old, an awfully tempting target to indiscriminate men in a foreign, lawless environment. The exposure to possible sexual abuse was a clear and present danger. Even if these people were looking for a hefty ransom for their exchange, which right now seemed the primary reason for their captivity, it still did not dispel the threat of harm to them. Rape was very much a fear in Lucia's mind at the moment. It seemed that was what the man had just alluded to.

Lucia heard a faraway voice speak, and slowly she realized the man was talking into a phone. She thought if it was a cell phone it showed poor planning on their part and in fact plain stupidity. Cell phone signals would be easy to trace from anywhere in the world. Then she realized the man was not talking into a wireless phone but a secure line.

"The packages are safe and sound. We're ready for you. No, it all went well. Get us through."

"All right, *señora*, you're gonna have to come with me. Get up."

As the voice behind her spoke, someone grabbed her by her forearm and made her get up. She felt someone else hold her from the other side.

"Walk. Let's go."

She could not see where she was going because of the hood, but they were leading her, at times almost dragging her. She did not walk far and could tell they had entered another room. She heard the same voice she had heard before speaking into the phone, except now it was close.

"You will hear her, yes," the man said. "All right, it's your father," Lucia heard the man say. "I only want you to say one word," the man emphasized.

Lucia concluded that her daughter was close by. The man was talking to Alicia. She heard her sob.

"Alicia, is that you?"

"*Señora*, shut up!" the man at her side yelled. He suddenly put his hand over her mouth with his other arm around her neck, holding her against his chest. "Be quiet now. I told you to be quiet. You speak when we tell you to."

"Go ahead," the man on the phone said. "Say 'Daddy, I'm here.' That's so. Come on, let's go."

"Dad?" came Alicia's trembling voice.

Lucia could tell she was only a few feet away. She wanted

to touch her and made an attempt but the men holding her would not let her move.

"All right," the man by Alicia said.

The next thing she felt was the hard round plate of a telephone's speaker pressing against her ear over the cloth of the hood.

"Now, *señora*, it's your turn. Say only 'Carlos.' Nothing else."

She wanted to say much more. She wanted to tell him how much she appreciated him, how much she loved his insight, and how regretful she was in not having listened to him. He had had misgivings about the stop in Mexico and fiercely opposed to their trip to Cuba. He had been right. The whole idea had been a disaster, something they were not supposed to have undertaken, as if it would violate some ethics code that had been secretly engraved in the souls of all their compatriots. And she had been wrong for giving in to the impulses of their teenage daughter, who could never have related to their feelings and the terrible hold that the tyrannical system of their home country imposed on them forever, even from afar. They could never break free of it, regardless of where they lived throughout the entire globe. Its magnetism held against them forever. It did not occur to her at the moment that her present situation did not seem to have anything to do with their trip to their home island. But she saw it as a great mass, interwoven in itself by the evil ego of one dictator who had created havoc for her and her family. The thoughts flashed through her mind like lightening as she heard Carlos's familiar voice on the line.

"Alicia, Alicia! Where are you?"

"*Señora*, speak up!" she heard the man next to her yell.

"Carlos, it's Lucia …"

She felt the phone being snatched from her.

"I told you *señora*, only one word!"

She felt them pull her up and drag her out of the room. They weren't waiting for her to gain her balance and walk. They did not give her a chance to fully stand. They threw her on a chair, probably the same one she had been sitting on when they first came in. Then they firmly pressed her down, as if to make sure she was secure.

She heard them walk away, and one spoke as they were leaving. "I guess you'll try to take your hood off now that you're going to be alone. You can but there's nothing to see."

She heard the door slam and a total silence afterward. She did not hesitate. The man had been right. As soon as he left the room she pulled the black hood off. She felt apprehensive as she did. They had gone through the trouble of cutting openings in it so she could breathe and now they were prodding her to take it off. Were they playing games?

She could see the room. It was totally bare. The walls weren't sheet-rocked as she was used to but bare plaster, thrown against the walls in chunks that seemed in total disarray. It would be impossible to hang a picture anywhere in the room. The ceiling was no better, with frozen tears of plaster that had remained from the splattering manner in which it had been laid. She figured the whole thing had probably been built in one day. But if that was the case, then the structure was not very secure. It was the first time she thought about an escape in the short time in which she had been kidnapped. Then she turned to the floor. It was dirt, nothing but dirt.

"Alicia, are you there?" she yelled at the top of her lungs.

Her words seemed to bounce off the wall, and she did not hear a sound.

She was in a rectangular room, no larger than ten feet by six. There was no furniture, nowhere to sit or lie down. The only door and means of egress or entrance was the shabby door across from her. Although in poor shape, the bolt on it was firmly secured to the frame. There was a slight crack between the door and the frame, which she tried to use right away to look outside but could not make any objects beyond the dirt floor. Then she paced back to the end of the room like a caged animal looking for a way out. She scratched the walls to feel the texture, not knowing why. Then she paced back to the front around the chair and finally sat down.

What did these people plan to do? It was obvious they wanted money. But how had it happened? How did they know about her and her daughter? She went back and forth with these thoughts until she decided she did not know. Whatever had happened, she was now here. She had to endure and see it through.

Several hours passed, and she heard nothing. She paced the room several times. She had no clue as to time or place. How would she know when to sleep? What about food? Would they bring her something to eat? As she asked herself these questions, she could not take her mind off Alicia. She imagined her daughter was on the other side of the room, and she kept touching the wall with her open hand, not knowing on which side she would be so she alternated between one and the other. She began to develop a pattern of pounding sounds that she made with her closed fist against the sharp edges of clay on the wall, but she got no feedback. Even if she did, how could she be sure it was her daughter? These men could be holding more hostages here.

She began getting more and more intense with the tapping, to the point that she did not do anything else but walk back and forth between each wall and pound several times until the side of her hand began to bleed. Then suddenly, as she was about to switch sides one more time, she felt the wall shake from pounding on the other side. Someone was there. She began tapping again, not with her closed fist, but with the knuckles of her right hand, as if she were knocking on a door. Again she got an answer back. Someone was knocking on the other side.

"Alicia, is that you? Are you there?"

"Mom!"

She heard her trembling voice, vague and weak but unmistakably hers.

"How're you doing, honey? How're you feeling?"

"Mom, I'm scared. I'm so scared."

"Don't be, honey. Your father will get us out of here. We'll be out soon."

"Mom, they haven't been back. What are we gonna do here? There's no place to sleep, nothing. What do we do?"

"We just have to wait, Alicia. Wait. They have to come back. Do you have any idea about the time?"

"No."

"I don't either. They took everything from me. Why didn't you answer me before? I've been knocking on these walls for hours."

"I was scared, Mom; I didn't know where I was. It's been like a blackout. I'm scared. What's gonna happen to us here?"

Alicia sobbed. Lucia could hear her pull away. She feared losing control of her.

"No, Alicia, honey. Don't shut down. Stay by me. Let's not stop talking. Everything is gonna be all right, honey. Your father will get us out of here in no time. He'll do anything for us. Alicia?"

She could barely make out her distant sobs and felt a terror that clouded her mind. In the process she would totally forget about herself. It was that motherly instinct so alive in her. Alicia was her only child, and after her husband and her, everything else was secondary.

She began to pound the wall frantically again, trying to get her attention.

She jumped to her feet as the door suddenly burst open. She did not even hear the latch unlock.

"*Señora*! Let's go! Put your hood on! Come on!"

For the first time she saw a face. The man who entered the room was chubby, with large cheeks and a thick, lumpy nose. He had what appeared to be a submachine gun slung across his shoulder and made swift movements with his hands, seeming full of energy. He grabbed her forearm and moved her away from the wall. A second man who had followed him into the room came behind her, and before she knew it all was dark again. He had thrown the hood over her head and tied it firmly around her neck with a string.

Someone grabbed her by her left forearm and forced her to walk. She guessed it was the same man who had first come inside the room because he was now speaking to her.

"*Señora*, come on. Let's go."

"Where's my daughter?" she said.

"She's right behind us. She's coming."

That was a good sign, she thought. At least they were talking to her. Perhaps they would tell her more.

"Where are you taking us?"

"Why do you care? You don't need to know."

"Then at least tell me what time it is. Is it dark out?"

She could already tell it was. Despite the hood covering her eyes, she sensed darkness. She felt the humid air, and her feet dragged over what felt like grass. They were clearly outside. But where were they going?

"It's late," the man said.

She felt another hand grab her other arm, and then they put pressure on the top of her head to make her bend down. They were shoving her inside a car. She tried to slide in as smoothly as possible. She realized that if she did not cooperate, the men might handle her roughly. But it was hard to move without seeing where she was going.

"Alicia?" she said when she felt she was sitting by the end of the seat.

"Mom?" came the answer from the front seat.

They must not want us to sit together, she thought.

As soon as Alicia spoke, she heard the door being shut and the car took off suddenly and fast, and she began bouncing from the impact of the bumps. She felt a hand push her back into the seat.

"Stay down, *señora*."

They pushed her head down until her knees were raised high and her back lay ahead of the seat cover. It was a very uncomfortable position. They were trying to keep her from being seen as they traveled, so she gathered that they were not in as remote an area as she had thought.

They traveled for more than two hours. The further they drove, the more rugged the terrain seemed to get. The car was barely moving at times, negotiating what felt like horrendous bumps one after another. Wherever they were it certainly was not urban. Then came what felt like a steep climb, the engine rumbling from the thrust as it needed more and more force to turn the wheels. Lucia suddenly felt awfully tired and realized she had not urinated during the whole time she had been captive.

"Can we stop somewhere please? I need to go."

"What do you mean you need to go, *señora*?"

"In America that means to go to the bathroom, you idiot."

"Hold your tongue—or have you forgotten the story they told you earlier? We could cut yours out and no one would ever know. You know that?"

"All I know is that I need to urinate, and if you don't stop, I'll do it here, right now. My daughter too."

There was silence for a moment, and she could tell she had had an effect on them. She did not know how many there were in the car but she had a sense they were communicating with each other. Suddenly the car stopped.

"All right, *señora*. Let's go! Get out of the car."

She was struck by the way they let her walk out. They only grabbed her arm after she stepped on the ground, and then someone guided her a few paces away and made her crouch.

"You're behind some trees, *señora*. Your daughter is next to you. I don't wanna see you undress, but remember, there's a machine gun in front of the bush pointed at you. If I see that you move one step away, I'll start firing. Your daughter goes first, then you. You got it?"

"I got it, dumb ass, if you can understand what that means. How're you doing, honey?" she said, turning slightly, thinking Alicia would be there.

"Oh, Mom. I'm so scared."

Her voice actually came from behind her. They had placed Alicia in back of her.

"It's all right, honey. Go ahead and urinate. You have to empty your bladder. We have to survive this. Come on, go."

Clumsily she pulled her pants down and urinated. She would have never dreamed of doing this in front of her daughter if they had their eyes uncovered but took comfort knowing they both were hooded and that neither one could see the other.

"Soon this will be over, honey. You have to hang on. Come on, pull your pants down and go."

"I can't, Mom. I can't."

"Yes, you can. Come on."

She figured she had to make Alicia act as normal as possible, keep her body going and her hopes up although she herself had doubts about their future.

"Are you going, honey?"

She heard the hissing sound of her urine and felt relieved.

"You have to let your kidneys run, honey. Do you need to move your bowels too?"

"I can't do that here, Mom. I just can't."

"If you have to, you go, honey. Don't hold it."

Lucia got up and spoke in the direction where the man had stood.

"When can we have a decent bathroom to go to? My daughter needs to use it."

"Soon," he said calmly.

"What's the use in keeping these hoods on us? We can't see anyway."

"You keep them on till we say so. Come on, *señora*, it's time to move on." He grabbed her by the arm and someone else grabbed Alicia. They were soon in the car, traveling slowly over bumps and mounds. Lucia could not track the time although she tried to. She realized she needed to keep track of her surroundings as best as she could. It could come in handy at some point. She guessed an hour had gone by when they stopped again and were ushered out of the car. She was forced to sit down somewhere inside a structure that she guessed was a house.

"All right, *señora*," she heard the same man's voice say. "I'm gonna remove your hood now. I'm gonna give you and your daughter something to eat."

Lucia wasn't quite prepared for the shock that she was about to receive. As soon as the black cloth was removed from her head, the first face she saw was that of Alicia, and she instinctively made an attempt to get up to embrace her but the man held her back.

"Easy, *señora*," the man said. "Easy. Wait till I leave the room."

She looked up at him as she struggled to push his hand away. It was the same fat face she had seen before for a brief moment. She felt a wave of anger rise up to her head and felt an insatiable desire to spit in his face. But she held back and marveled at her reactions to the very precarious situation she found herself in. She never dreamed for a million years that she could respond so aggressively to captivity. She came from a small family where she had been pampered and raised under the watchful eyes of her parents and two older brothers, without any sisters to compete for attention. She had been brought up to feel that the female sex was delicate and sensitive. She had known no adversity, and after quiet teenage years and college she had met Carlos Garcia, a self-made man who was ten years her senior. But despite it all, it had been a smooth transition from being a single twenty-two-year-old who had never known need to adorning a brand new home for two. Her husband had quickly become her new protector, replacing her parents. But he had also showed her how to be self-sufficient and taught her things that she had thought useless at first, especially in learning how to use firearms. But her love for him had made her follow, and eventually she had blended into his ways, as if besides being her husband he had assumed some fatherly role over her. He had made her stronger and more adept in life, but even after being married to him for all these years, a kidnapping had never been a scenario she thought she could handle without his help.

"Then leave! Get out!"

"*Señora*," the man said, retreating, holding the black hood he had just pulled off her head in his hand and holding on to the strap of his submachine gun with the other. "There's a latrine right in back of this room. When you and your daughter need to use it, knock on the door and someone will take you to it."

Then he and the other man who had un-hooded Alicia turned to leave. They shut the only door in the room and secured it with a bolt that Lucia could hear snap from the outside.

"Alicia!" she said and rushed over to hold her in her arms.

Alicia's cheeks were red from sobbing and her eyes were swollen. The ordeal had taken a toll on her. She cried on her mother's shoulder, unable to speak.

"Alicia, you have to be strong, honey. This will pass. You'll see."

"How … Mom? How … is it going to … pass?" she said, choking on the words.

She held her close and rubbed her back, giving her time to release her emotions. "It will, honey. These people are only looking for money. They are not going to harm us. If they were, they would have done it already. That's why they had us on the phone before. They wanted your father to hear our voices so he would know they have us. They want a ransom. That's what they want."

"So why did they bring us here?"

Lucia hesitated. She thought she heard footsteps right outside their door and placed her index finger on her lips as a sign for her daughter to be silent. Alicia threw her arms around her and sobbed again on her shoulder.

"Be quiet," Lucia whispered. "I think they're listening."

She patted her back and then took her by the hand as if they were going to go for a walk. They in fact did. Lucia walked up front with Alicia following slowly behind her. They walked back and forth through the middle of the room until Lucia felt dizzy and pointed toward the chairs.

"Let's sit down. Come on."

There were two mattresses in the room, one at each side, furnished with two pillows each and a sheet. There was a kerosene light that shined high above them. There was no trace of any electric outlet. Lucia began to consider how tough it would be to survive any long-term captivity with Alicia by her side. She could do it alone, she thought. She could shut down and endure the hardships. She was sure she could make it. However, keeping Alicia going would be tough, and it would make the whole thing twice as hard. She braced herself for the worst.

She moved the chairs close, in front of each other, and she took her by the hand and made her sit down.

"There's nothing to be afraid of, honey. Look, this will pass. You have to try to be strong and not scared. We now need to rest and go to sleep. It's been a long day. Do you need to use the bathroom?"

Alicia shook her head.

"I do. I think you should too. Let me get these guys' attention."

She turned toward the door, but Alicia held her arm. "Mom, don't, please. I'm scared."

"Don't be scared, honey. We'll go together, Come on."

Lucia knocked on the door and almost immediately after heard the latch being pulled back. The flimsy door swung open by itself. A young man, probably in his early twenties, stood blocking the entrance. He had a submachine gun hanging from his shoulder like the other one Lucia had seen before. He did not say anything but looked at her as if he had been waiting for a long time.

"We need to use the bathroom."

He shook his head as in refusal but then spoke to her in Spanish.

"You need to speak in Spanish," he said in an unmistakable Mexican accent. "In America they always say that people need to speak English, so here you're in Mexico. We speak Spanish down here so you need to speak Spanish."

"Except that we are here against our will," she answered him in Spanish. "We speak what we feel like speaking. Take us to the bathroom."

"One at a time," he said. "You come first. Your daughter will have to go after you."

"What is it? You're afraid that two women may prove too dangerous for you?"

"No, there's room for only one at a time. You'll have to live with it."

Just then they heard the sound of rapid gunfire coming from far away. She looked at him alarmed. He chuckled.

"What's that?" she asked.

"You get used to it," he said. "It happens every night. Didn't you hear about what's going on in Mexico?"

"Are we close to the border?"

The man chuckled and then grabbed her arm and pulled her in front of him. Lucia felt infuriated that he would do that.

"That's not for you to know. Come on! You want to use the bathroom, right? Get going!"

"You animal!" she yelled at him without turning her head and began walking.

He did not respond to her insult. She began to realize that she had some cushion with her captors. She had a sense that there was some organization in their operation after all. She and her daughter represented an asset to them that had to be handled with care, at least for now. She had some leeway that she could get away with. Still, she was running an awfully big chance. She was playing with fire and she knew it. But the words just came out. She was reacting naturally to a bad situation.

She was so deep in thought as the man led her outside that she did not get a good view of her surroundings. By the time she became aware that this was her first opportunity to survey her prison, she was outside. It was pitch dark and she had no idea where to go. The man grabbed her arm again and made her turn slightly to her left. It was almost as if she were hooded again. She could not see anything. But her captor pushed the door of what looked like a shanty latrine almost touching her nose. It was even darker inside.

"Go in!" he said.

"In there? That's the bathroom?"

"That's the bathroom. That's where you will wash and relieve yourself."

"I can't. I haven't seen one of these things since I lived in Cuba."

"So you were going to Cuba, no? Make believe you're there. Go in."

"Asshole. Don't you have any idea how to speak to a woman?"

"Shut up."

"It's better that you don't answer. You're too dumb to even know what I'm talking about. How about a light to see what I'm doing?"

"No lights allowed. Go inside and do what you have to do."

She went in hesitantly, feeling her way through. She felt the wood seat, its texture worn from extensive use, and reached the hole in the middle. Her mind went back to the days when her parents took her to their family's archaic farms in the Cuban countryside. No running water, sewer, or modern sanitary facilities. She remembered how shocked she was to find herself in a wooden latrine and swore she would not relieve herself again until her parents went back to the city. But that didn't last, and as soon as nature called and made the pain unbearable, she sat on the worn-out seat again and moved her bowels, jumping away as soon as she was done, wiping with disgust and tossing the paper into the hole and then rushing out of the smelly outhouse. She would have to do the same here. Rush and walk out. But even that would take a tremendous effort against the repulsion she felt. She pushed the thin door closed, yelling again to her tormentor.

"I'm not gonna go with you watching me, idiot!"

She got out quickly, and the man grabbed her arm again. This time, she shook herself free.

"Don't you have your gun at the ready? You can always shoot me if I try to run."

She walked ahead of him, stumbling on the rugged ground until she reached the back door to the house. She noticed the opaque light guiding the way in the hallway. It was a kerosene lamp. There was clearly no electricity in the premises. She walked back to her room and found Alicia sitting on her chair.

"It's your turn, honey. Go with him and make sure you relieve yourself. There's no running water. It's not like home. But we'll have to do. Go."

She sat in her chair and waited. She prepared for the night's sleep. She would have to do her best to get Alicia to rest. She was not sure she could get any rest herself, but she would have to try.

Chapter Four

Carlos got the call while on the highway in the early evening, traveling from one of his supermarkets to another. He was alone in the car and was actually thinking about where to eat supper tonight. He did not want to eat at home. He had his mind set on getting a table for himself in one of the seafood restaurants by Miami Beach. He was going to make a stop at his new store, now officially carrying the name of his supermarket chain, *Prado's*. He picked his cell that was ringing on the seat, thinking it would be his manager again. He had called twice in the past one hour. But when the voice came on in Spanish, he figured it must be a client. The heavy Mexican accent left no doubt he would hear some complaints. Somehow someone had gotten hold of his cell number.

"Listen, Carlos. Listen carefully. Don't get excited."

He reacted quickly. He always did. "Excited about what?"

"We have your daughter and your wife. They're fine. But you're gonna have to do something for us. It's gonna be that simple. We trade your daughter and wife back to you in exchange for one million dollars in cash. No questions asked. We tell you where to leave the money and the whole affair is over. You pick them up yourself at a convenient place or you have someone do it for you if you're afraid. I wouldn't think you are, being that you're such a character. Maybe you like to play rough, but I'm warning you, in this case, don't try. We're talking about your daughter and your wife here, you understand me?"

Carlos could sense the shock he was going to experience and did the prudent thing. He pulled over to the shoulder of the road and remained quiet, thinking.

"Hello, are you there?"

"I'm here," he said. "Who are you?"

"That won't be part of the deal. You don't need to know that."

"Where are my wife and daughter?"

"They're here. They're here with me."

"Where's here? Where are you calling me from?"

"You think I'm gonna tell you that? Now you take a guess where they might be, although that's not going to make a bit of a difference. It's up to you to get them out."

"Get them out from where?"

"From captivity. Don't get me wrong. They're fine. They're well taken care of. But we don't want to keep them. We want to give them back to you, for the right price of course."

"What's it gonna be?"

"I told you. One million dollars deposited in a bank account of my choice. You can pick them up the same day, as soon as the funds are available."

"How do I know this is true? Where are they?'

"They're right here, next to me. You can say hello, but I mean hello only."

One second later, before Carlos had time to even ask, his daughter's voice was on the other end. "Dad?"

Her voice was unmistakable.

"Alicia, Alicia! Where are you?"

He was surprised later at his reaction, but the words just rushed out of him like a sudden outbreak. The idea that his daughter was in some sort of danger had triggered an anxiety in him he had not felt for years. Then, without warning, he heard his wife's voice.

"Carlos, it's Lucia."

She did not get to finish her sentence. Next thing he heard was the same man's voice. "As you can see, they're well. They will continue to be well if you do what I say. What I will do is this: I will call you later with some instructions, after I am satisfied that you are not going to do something foolish like calling the police. It would do you no good, by the way. The police can't help you. Your wife and daughter are in the middle of a fire, and in a way I am their protection. Something happens to me and away goes the shield and who knows then how they'll end up. Do you get my message?"

Carlos sensed he was going to disconnect and tried to stop him. "Wait! What bank?"

But he was gone. Carlos kept the phone to his ear, hoping he would hear another sound. This was his lifeline to his wife and daughter. What would he do now?

Something caught his peripheral vision in his rearview mirror and he looked. He saw the blinking red and blue overhead lights of a highway patrol car that had pulled right behind him. He never got pulled over despite his fast driving, and he despised any involvement with the police. But at the moment his mind was somewhere else, and he could not hear the patrolman's voice coming from the police vehicle's loudspeaker. His mind was far away, trying in vain to get the caller back on line.

"Hello! Hello!"

There was now tapping at his window, and he finally realized that he had to let go. There was an officer standing by the driver's door and another one by the passenger's side. He put down the phone and pulled the lever on the indoor panel to lower his window.

"Yes?" he asked the officer.

"Anything the matter with your hearing, sir? We've been calling you."

"I was on the phone, sorry."

"Well, you're not supposed to be on the shoulder of the road making a phone call. You're not supposed to be on the phone at all, as a matter of fact. Can you step out of the car, please?"

Carlos could have engaged him easily. Of course he could be on the shoulder. Of course he could be on the phone. That's why he was on the shoulder to begin with. But his mind was debating something more important at the moment, and he stepped out of the car absentmindedly, holding the phone on his right hand steadfastly, debating whether he should mention the phone call he had just gotten.

"All right," said the officer, "you can leave the phone inside. No need for that. Now stand over here by the passenger window. Spread both arms. Any emergency that we ought to know about?"

Carlos was still debating with himself what he should do. He got a glimpse of the young officer holding cautiously onto the butt of his gun, but it was a fleeting glance. It had been a strange coincidence that the patrolmen had shown up at this very moment when he had received a call from kidnappers who had taken his wife and daughter. They were God sent. But maybe not. Should he ignore them altogether and not disclose anything to them? Should he not handle things on his own and pay the ransom? He was so deep in thought that he missed the officer's instructions.

"I'm gonna say it just one more time, sir. Bring your arms down."

Carlos did as asked. The officer had patted him down and inspected his wallet and money that he retrieved from his front pants' pocket. Then he pulled Carlos away from the car to look into his shirt's pocket. The other officer was looking inside the car.

"Can I ask you something?" he said, looking at him curiously. "What seems to be the matter? You're a businessman, I can tell that. Why is it that you're so aloof? You haven't been drinking, have you?"

Carlos shook his head. He was disconnected. His mind was wherever the call had come from, which he guessed was thousands of miles away, or maybe not. He suddenly remembered the trip. How many times had he warned them not to go? Yes, Cuba. They were in Cuba, not thousands of miles away but actually ninety miles from Florida, a stone's throw from Key West, one hour and a half by boat ride. Yes, that's where they were. He figured it out then. They were captives of those sons-of-bitches on the island. Had he not said it to Lucia and his daughter a million times? You could not trust the Castro regime. Never, no matter how many years may have passed. Despite all the rhetoric you heard about what an altruistic system he had established where supposedly there was no class, free education, free health treatment, in the end, it was nothing but a tyranny, imposed by a most heinous assault against the human spirit. In such a system anything was possible. Any free human visiting the island could be subjected to any atrocity at any moment without any possibility of defense. Holding you captive was not off limits, and demanding money for your release, knowing that your family had the means to deliver was also a possible scenario, at least in Carlos's mind. He felt a tremendous hatred for the Castro name again, like he had felt throughout his life but now more personal, more internal.

"Sir?" The young police officer tilted his head forward, trying to get an answer from Carlos. "Are you feeling all right?"

Carlos came back. He realized he was in a bind. He had to decide what to do. "Actually, I'm quiet disturbed about my family. I just got some very bad news, and that's why I pulled over, so I could take the call. And no, I have not been drinking. I do not drink, officer, only coffee."

"All right. Well, I'm sorry to hear that. But this is the shoulder and it's quite dangerous to use it on this highway. We gave you a couple of instructions through the loudspeaker before. We were telling you to move forward, and you did not respond, no reaction whatsoever from you. Do you mind if we look at your car?"

"No. Go ahead. I've got to get going real fast. Something's come up."

"Well, you're gonna have to wait for a few minutes till we look inside, and if everything's all right, then you can go."

Carlos saw the officer's wide grin and thought it was rather unusual. How old could he be? Maybe twenty-two or -three at the most. That was the trouble with power, he thought. This was how freedom was lost on a small scale. It began like this, with a young man who was given a gun and the power to impose on people, and then he became cocky and things got out of hand. This is why you needed libertarians in any democracy, people who would take the police to task to keep it within its boundaries. You needed it in any free society. Here he was, worried to death about his wife and daughter, who seemed to be in mortal danger, and this young punk was playing games with him. Did he not see the obvious? That he was a working man, busy, worried about his family? He watched as the other patrolman came around and opened the driver's door, swinging it wide and dangerously close to the vehicles cruising by on the inner lane. And here they were lecturing him about the dangers of the shoulder when they seemed to show little concern for its implications. He shook his head in disbelief as the other officer sat inside and went through the contents of the glove compartment. Carlos kept his car in neat condition. Not a paper out of place. There were no CDs strewn inside, no old notes, cigarettes, or maps, just the registration and insurance card and the car manual. There was a log on the passenger seat with the names of all of his stores where he stopped on a daily basis. There were notes next to each name that he made as his rounds. After looking over the contents of the glove compartment, he saw the officer pick up the log and spend what seemed like an eternity reading it. What on earth?

Then, oddly enough, he thought he heard the vibrations of his phone that he had left lying inside his cup holder. He intuitively made a jerky movement with his hand and immediately realized how foolish he had been.

"Sir, do not move," the other officer said from behind him.

He had remained standing in back of him as his partner went through the contents of the car.

"My phone," Carlos said. "My phone is ringing. I'm waiting for a very important call. I have to pick it up."

"Why?" the officer asked from behind.

"Look, it's an emergency. It's my family. I've got to pick it up."

"Stay still," the patrolman said. "Greg, give me that phone."

The other officer passed him the phone from inside the car, and the young patrolman looked at it for a second, trying to figure out its operation.

"A Verizon BlackBerry," he said. "Very expensive phone. What business are you in?"

"Officer, it's not the time for games. My phone is ringing."

The patrolman put the phone to his ear and Carlos yelled out. "No! Don't answer that! Don't!"

"Why not? What are you afraid of? Hello?" the officer said.

Carlos felt a sudden urge to knock his teeth out. He was so close to him, he could have just snapped him, but he held back.

"No, it's not Carlos," the officer said. "Who are you?"

"Give me the phone," Carlos said.

"Sir, stay still!" the other officer yelled.

He had suddenly jumped out of the car and stood between his partner and Carlos. He shoved Carlos toward the rear of the vehicle.

"He can't come to the phone right now. You're going to have to deal with me," the patrolman was saying into the phone. "I'm his partner. What's up?"

Carlos was watching him carefully over the other officer's shoulder. These idiots were imagining that he was some kind of dealer, Carlos thought. The young patrolman was taking a call that could ruin whatever chance he stood of saving his wife and daughter. Carlos grew desperate.

"Look, you guys don't know what you're doing," he said to the other patrolman, who was standing so close to him that the two could almost rub chins. "You don't understand. That call is meant for me only."

"Oh, really? And why is that, sir? Is it a business call, maybe? Is that why you don't want us to handle it? We may just find out what business you're in, ah?"

"Shut up, you idiot. You don't know what you're saying."

The officer shoved him again and Carlos almost lost it. "It's my family, stupid. It's my family. Give me that call!"

"Hold it, sir, or I'll throw the handcuffs on you."

"Greg!" the other officer called. "Get him over here, fast!"

The officer grabbed Carlos's arm and pulled him toward

his partner. Carlos saw the look of fear in the other officer's face. Gone was the cockiness he had sensed earlier in the young man. Maybe he had come to realize what a grave mistake he had made and how unprofessional he had been. But none of that mattered right now. It was all about Lucia and Alicia.

"Here. Talk to them," the young officer said, handing him the phone.

"Yeah," Carlos said on the line.

"Who's the asshole that took the phone? Didn't I tell you I'd be calling back? Don't you care about your wife and daughter or what?"

"Oh, never mind him. He's just a friend who happened to pick up my phone."

"Instruction number one," the voice said from the other end, "you carry your phone with you at all times for as long as we're talking, you hear? It is kind of absurd that you would let someone else pick up the phone knowing the situation your family is in, isn't it? It's crazy and stupid. I mean, how do I know that you did not call the police? Not that it would help you. Still, this has gotta be on a one-on-one basis, you hear me?"

Carlos was trying to decipher his accent. The man spoke perfect English, which led him to believe that this person knew a lot about him and his family. But all through the conversation, he was trying to pick up traces of any nationality. There was a slight drawl, but it was definitely not the Miami-Cuba slang. Whoever it was had learned the language somewhere else. That only reinforced his previous suspicion, or conviction, you might say.

Somehow the Cuban government was responsible. But then again, Carlos always thought that the evil regime was behind every aspect of his life. Although he would never admit it, he was fixated by the idea. It was as if he had never left the island or that the island had never left him.

"I hear you. Can I talk to my family now?"

"No, no, no. You already talked to your family. Instruction number two is Bank of America. That's where the money goes to. Five deposits of two hundred thousand each at different branches. You got until eight in the evening of tomorrow. You'll get more details later."

"Wait, wait. I need more time."

He looked at the BlackBerry, but the caller was gone. Then he looked back at the young officer who seemed to have a look of deep concern about him.

"What's going on?" the officer asked.

"I can't say. I told you not to meddle. This has to do with my family."

"It's too late for that now. We're already involved."

"No, you're not. This is way over your head. Stay out of it."

"It doesn't work that way, sir. Greg, wait out here with him."

The other officer got inside the patrol car and picked up his band radio. "Car fifty-nine to station, over."

"Station, over," came from the speaker.

"We have a possible security discussion," the officer said into the mike. "Instructions? Over."

"Call on a secure line," came the response.

The officer sat still for a few seconds, thinking of how to proceed. He felt a little edgy. He had come to realize that he had stumbled onto a very delicate situation and knew he must be cautious as to what steps he would take next. His career could be on the line. Already, he feared, he may have mishandled the situation by overlooking the obvious. The man out there was someone of economic influence and apparently clean. This was no ordinary hoodlum, maybe not even a drug dealer, as he had first jumped to conclude. And he happened to be the victim of some kind of extortion involving his family. Was there a kidnapping? The question was how he should face the problem. He needed to act as a professional. He could not walk away from a crime scene, but at the same time he must do all he could to protect the innocent and not endanger the victims. He was a simple patrolman, not knowledgeable in how to respond to high-profile crimes. Yet the man out there was not willing to cooperate and would not come to the station willingly, and he understood why. He thought for one more moment and an idea came to him. He called the station and requested a backup. When asked to classify the event, he told dispatch it was that of a witness to be interviewed. He got out of his car and went to speak to Carlos.

"Now, here's what we're gonna do, sir. We're gonna let you get in your car. Another patrol vehicle is coming, and it will be right behind you. We're gonna lead the way, and you're gonna follow us. We're bringing you to the station. There will be a Federal agent there to talk to you. You hold on to your phone and answer it if you have to until we get there. Try to keep your cool."

Carlos looked surprised. What had brought this round about change?

"Am I under arrest?"

"No. But we can't let you leave now that we know what's transpiring. We're trying to help you."

The young officer exchanged glances with his partner, who was still clueless about what was happening.

"Go ahead, sir. Get inside your car."

"What the heck is going on, Walt?" the other officer asked, as Carlos made his way into his car.

"I think this guy is being extorted, Greg. His family may have been kidnapped, and we may have broken in as he got the ransom call. We're gonna bring him to the station and get the FBI to handle it. This is way over our heads."

"He doesn't seem to want our help," Greg said.

"Naturally not," Walter said. "He doesn't want to involve the police for fear of hurting his family. He's probably looking to get the ransom that the kidnappers are demanding. I talked to them. But we can't just walk away knowing what's happening, and at the same time, we gotta be careful not to meddle too deep. Let's go. Here comes our backup."

The police vehicle that came down the highway and pulled onto the shoulder had its overhead blinkers on, and Walt did not wait for him to stop behind Carlos's Mercedes but began pulling out of the shoulder at the same time with his own overhead lights own.

"Come on, man," he said to himself, as if he were talking to Carlos.

"This is a little risky, Walt," his partner said. "What if our man decides to get away?"

"He won't," Walt replied.

"I'm not worried about what you think. I'm worried about what our captain may think. Leaving our detainee behind us in his own car does not sound very smart."

"Greg, if the man gets another call and we're around him, we might just blow it for him. And he's not our detainee, by the way."

"What is he then?"

"Someone we're trying to help."

"I just hope this doesn't turn into an ugly chase. I mean, we would have to chase him if he goes on the run, no?"

"I'm on the phone with the station," Walt replied. "Wait up."

It was only a short ten minutes to the patrolmen's station, and the first police vehicle in the lineup of three cars pulled into an empty slot in the parking lot, followed by the black

Mercedes that parked right next to it, and then the police car that had traveled behind it.

"Let's go inside, Mr. Garcia," Walt said to Carlos.

By now he knew quite a bit about Carlos's life. The station had filled him in on the way here. A Federal agent had been summoned and was on his way. The secret, one of Walt's superiors had said, was to be able to convince Carlos to stay and wait. They could under no circumstances force him, as that could jeopardize his family's lives. But at the same time, they had to try. A crime was being committed, and the department knew about it. Something had to be done.

As soon as they walked into the station, a captain came in to receive them. They did not have to check at the desk. He ushered them in, immediately going to work on Carlos.

"Mr. Garcia, it's so good of you to come, sir. You're doing the right thing."

"I didn't have much of a choice, did I?"

The captain ignored the remark and opened the door to a large office, right at the beginning of a hallway.

"Mr. Garcia," he said inside. "Believe me, I know what you're going through, and I've taken great care to see that we don't put your family in any danger by our presence. We're just trying to help you out."

"Captain, is it?" Carlos asked, still unsure of his rank.

"Yes. Sorry. I'm Captain Solowsky." He stretched out his hand and shook Carlos's.

"Well, captain, your men brought me here, and I followed, but now that I'm here I'd like to leave. Unless, of course, you're placing me under arrest."

"No, of course not. But I'd like to persuade you to wait for a few minutes until you speak with an agent. You can make your decision then. Give it a chance, please. You owe that to your family."

"Captain, you realize that by forcing me here, you could

be doing great harm. I do not want your help. I made that very clear to your men. Why do you have to get involved in things that do not concern you?"

Even at this point, Carlos was still not admitting to the term "kidnapping." He could not afford to. But he understood clearly that these men knew.

"Carlos," the captain said, addressing him by his first name for the first time. "The reason we are involved is because there is a crime being committed. We have to be; that's what we're here for. We fight crime. I praise my officers for having handled the situation as professionally as they did. They did the right thing by bringing you here."

Carlos exchanged a glance with Walt, the young officer he had at first loathed. He had the opportunity to spit out a few derogatory comments in front of his superior officer, teach him a lesson, but he did not do it. He was, deep inside, a bleeding heart and outside a hard shell. What good would come out of it? Maybe the young man would learn his lesson—and after all, he had meant well. He was trying to help in the only way he knew.

"Captain, you brought me here, and I listened to your officers but now I'm done. Thanks for your concern."

"Wait Carlos, I ask only that you wait. A Federal agent is on his way here. These guys know what they're doing. They're experts and they deal with these situations every day. Please wait."

"No, captain. Time is gold for me right now. I've already lost enough."

Carlos turned and opened the door. The captain pleaded after him, but Carlos did not turn back. He walked at a fast pace, right past the receiving desk where an officer sat with an inquisitive look that seemed to be waiting for an order from the officers in the rear to stop him and hold him. Carlos was not so sure he would make it out the front door of the building, but that was secondary in his mind at the moment. He was holding his BlackBerry in his right hand and picked it up immediately as it rang. He was already out of the building when the call came in.

"Where's your friend?" the voice asked, now in Spanish.

Carlos was surprised by the change in language, not that he did not expect them to speak Spanish; he knew they could. But he was not quite ready for the shift. And why now, anyway? The answer came quickly.

"I don't want our conversation to be picked up by anyone else. You understand me?"

"Yes."

"Good. So where is he?"

"He is not here," Carlos said, and turned away from the main door of the police station.

He did not want the officers to hear him. Right now, he thought of them as much of a threat to his family as the kidnappers themselves. If the caller realized that he was at a police station, they could take it out on his wife and daughter. This was no game.

"I'm going to give you a number," the man said. "There will be no games played, you hear? You will only use that number to make the deposit of the funds and that is it. If someone goes into the account for any reason whatsoever other than to make the deposit, the deal is off, you hear me?"

"I hear you, but I don't have the money right now."

"You got until eight o'clock tomorrow, I said. Surely you can manage that."

"I'm not sure I can," Carlos said hesitatingly, not sure how far he could push him. But he had to try. "And what guarantees do I have that my family will be released? Where are they going to be?"

"You'll be told once the funds are in."

"That's no guarantee. How do I know this is not just a bad joke?"

"They're not where they're supposed to be, are they?"

It was a revealing statement, and Carlos recognized it immediately as such. This people knew where his family was headed, and they knew they were not there. Lucia and Alicia had been booked for a hotel in Mexico City. Things had been moving so fast that Carlos had not even had a chance to check with the hotel. That would have been the first thing to do. But what did the man mean then? That they weren't at the hotel or that they weren't in Mexico? For a fleeting second he thought about the police captain. As much as he hated to admit it, there was some truth in what he had said. This needed to be handled by a professional, someone who knew about these situations. He was bogged down by his abhorrence toward a system that probably had nothing to do with what was happening. This clouded his thinking. He would always be suspicious of anything having to do with the Castro regime, and although his family's ultimate destination had been Cuba, he suddenly remembered that they should have been in Mexico right now.

"I don't know that."

"Stay by the phone," the voice said, and the call was terminated.

Carlos held on to the phone for a few seconds, as if he could somehow make the voice come back. It was the only link to his family.

He held the phone tight and walked to his car. A blue Dodge pulled up behind him, and a man got out. He was dressed in a jacket and tie and looked nothing like a law enforcement officer.

"Sir, can I talk to you for a second?"

"No. I gotta go. Please move your car."

"Sir, let's talk for a minute. I'm with the FBI."

The man produced a badge from his wallet, identifying himself as an FBI agent.

"I don't want to talk. I gotta go."

"Hold on one second, sir. This is way over your head, sir. You wanna protect your family? Then let me help you. Look, this is not a job for you. You're gonna hurt yourself, and in the process you're gonna get your family hurt."

"Let me ask you something, sir," Carlos said. "Let's say I agree to accept your help. What can you possibly do for me?"

"I can monitor the situation. We work in stages. First, we just listen along with you and let you handle the calls. The emphasis is on finding the location: where they're calling from. Once we get that, we move on, we get forces in the area and evaluate it, we see what we're dealing with. Meanwhile, you keep talking to them and play as if we're going to give them what they want. The goal is on getting your family out safe."

"I'm not sure about that—detective, is it?"

"Yes. I'm a detective."

"Well, I think your focus is on catching the bad guys, and that's what I'm afraid of. I have nobody to catch. Yes, there's one guy right now whose neck I'd like to wring and I'm gonna look for him as soon as I have a chance. But right now I'm steady on getting what I need to save my family."

"Don't do it, Carlos," the detective said. "Don't wring his neck. That would be the worst mistake you could make."

"Anyway, I've got to get going. I need to put some things together."

"Carlos, let me come with you. We can set up shop at your home if you prefer and monitor the situation from there."

Carlos reflected one last time before speaking again. If he did, he would finally admit that his family was being kidnapped and there would be no going back. But he eyed the detective with some apprehension and got good vibes. He was gentlemanly looking, with a steady look, black eyes that clamped you down and signaled they would not leave you. What a difference from the patrolmen who had nearly arrested him. Carlos saw them approach out of the corner of his eye.

"You can come with me in my car if you wanna help. I need to do some things. These guys cannot be involved," Carlos said, pointing to the captain and the patrolmen now almost behind them.

"Deal. Let me move my car."

"You're doing the right thing, Mr. Garcia," the captain now said.

Carlos turned and ignored him. He got inside his car. Once behind the wheel, he felt he was being unfairly unjust, so he powered the window down. "Captain, thanks for your advice. You and your men did good."

He knew he didn't mean it, but there was no sense in slighting anyone. Not now. There needn't be any more casualties. He was actually saying a prayer for his family when the detective got in the passenger seat. He backed out of the parking lot and took off like a bat out of hell.

"I need to use your cell, detective. I want to keep my phone open in case they call."

"Call me Steve. I have a feeling we're gonna get to know each other well. Just one call though. I gotta report to the station and let them know what we're doing."

"No problem," Carlos said, grabbing his cell from him and dialing Peña's number.

The old man took time to answer. He carried an old model phone in his pants pocket and usually took a few minutes to retrieve it.

"Hello?"

"Peña, where the heck are you?"

"Carlos?"

"Yes. It's me. Where are you?"

"I'm at the restaurant. Hoping you'd drop by."

"And where is that fuck Cardona?"

Carlos sensed some hesitation, and that put him on guard. Peña had, after all, been the one to put wheels on his family's trip by recommending Cardona.

"I don't see him here yet. Why? You need to see him?"

"Yes. I need to see him."

"Well, stop by then. I'll wait for you. He might show up any minute."

"All right. I'll see you later."

Carlos handed the phone back to the detective.

"Who was that, Carlos?"

"It's a long story. He's an old friend I see almost every day. Actually, Steve, I need to make a couple of phone calls. Can I keep using your phone?"

"I'd rather you wouldn't right now," he replied. "I need to report to my station. Besides, we need to set up the operation, and I don't want you losing focus. Let's drive straight to your house."

"Steve, you forget I gotta come up with a large sum of money here. I got to make a few phone calls."

Steve gave him an eyeful from the passenger seat. Carlos had already taken the Palmetto Highway and was driving down the outer lane of the road, doing well over eighty mph.

"Let's not touch anything until we discuss the situation. We'll talk about the money. Right now we got to get those calls monitored. Slow down, would you? We don't need any more local police stopping you."

"I've got to make this one stop. It's not far from my house."

"What? A stop? No way. Drive straight to your house."

Steve got on his phone and called headquarters. "I'm on 826 with subject. We're in a black Mercedes, moving fast. Can you put out the word to local police? I don't want them stopping us."

Suddenly, Carlos crossed over into the inner lane and took the exit for S.W. Fortieth Street.

"What are you doing?"

"This will be quick. It's not out of the way."

He darted through the heavy traffic at that hour by swerving around the cars lined up at the lights, moving on the opposite lane at times until finally reaching the parking lot of *La Carreta*, where he found an empty slot in the front narrow area across from the restaurant. He darted out of the car and went to stand at the counter, where he saw Peña sipping espresso coffee.

"Is Cardona here?" he asked him.

"I haven't seen him, no," the old man said. "Did your family get to Mexico all right?"

Carlos hesitated. Right now he wasn't sure who to trust, not even Peña. Just then he thought about calling Cardona. But he wasn't sure whether he should. The feds were now involved. Peña turned toward the man following Carlos, someone he identified immediately as an American.

"Yeah," Carlos answered, watching for any reaction in the old man's body language.

"You want coffee?"

"No, I guess not. I have to get going. I have to bring this gentleman to the new store."

"Well, here comes Cardona now," Peña said.

Carlos spotted him as he came through the tiled hallway under the eaves of the restaurant's roof. He seemed calm and composed. Carlos was about to lose it, and his face went red with rage. Seeing his reaction, Steve grabbed his right arm, discreetly but so tightly that it made Carlos turn.

"What is it?" Steve asked.

Upon seeing him, Cardona headed straight toward him and gave him his open hand. "Carlos, how're you doing? You miss your girls yet?"

Something was not right, Carlos thought. He was ready to jump for his jugular and would have done it were it not for the agent's grip on his arm that got tighter each second.

"Yes, a lot," Carlos said.

"Talk to them yet?"

"Yeah."

"And how do they like it? Excited to go to the island?"

"Oh, yeah, very much."

"Listen, Peña, can you come with me?" Carlos said, turning to him.

"Wait it a minute," Cardona interrupted. "What's the hurry? Can we get something to drink? My treat."

"No, I'm afraid not today."

Peña left his half full cup on the counter and followed Carlos and Steve to the car. He sat in the rear, still wondering but not asking about the identity of the man who took his usual place in the front seat.

"Peña, I didn't introduce you but this is Steve, a friend of mine. We're going to the house for a moment, and then we'll go visit two stores. There are some things I need to do."

Steve wasn't keen on bringing someone else into the secrets of a kidnapping investigation. If he allowed the stranger to participate, he would have to keep him from leaving the area to prevent leakage. He figured he would have to put his foot down.

"You wanna tell your friend who I am and what I'm doing here?"

Carlos swiped a quick look at him but did not slow the

car down. They had gone back on 826, and he was working the Mercedes's engine unmercifully.

"Mr. Peña," Carlos said. "This man is with the FBI, and the reason he's with me is because he's helping me with my family. Now, what I'm gonna say is top secret—"

"Carlos, wait a minute," Steve interrupted. "I did not tell you to disclose any details. I just said I wanted you to tell him who I am. You realize that now I'm gonna have to hold this gentleman until the situation clears up."

"Steve, it's okay. Mr. Peña is all right."

Carlos had rather abruptly decided to let Peña into the story. He had concluded in his typical fashion that Peña had nothing to do with his family's kidnapping. It was Cardona that he was not sure about.

"Still."

Steve now turned around on his seat and introduced himself to the bewildered Peña, who seemed more confused by the minute. "I'm Steve Hartzman, and I'm a federal agent. I know you just walked into this, sir, but you're here. This is an investigation, and we cannot have you disclose anything you hear. Do you carry a cell phone, sir?"

"Yes. I have a cell phone."

"All right. Let me have it."

Peña handed him the phone. At that very moment Carlos was getting off the highway and squeezed past the line of cars waiting at the light to get into the surrounding suburbs. Peña was thrown to the side by the thrust of the turn.

"Slow down! You're gonna kill us!" Steve yelled.

Carlos's phone vibrated, and he immediately picked up. "Hello," he said, expecting to hear the same raspy voice.

"Carlos, I'm having problems with the electric in the freezing room. There's no power."

Carlos hesitated. It took him a second to realize that it

was Nick, his rather inept manager, who was calling him again.

"Nick, have you tried the electrician?" Carlos asked sarcastically. "I don't have the time tonight."

"Carlos, I don't want to call—"

"Nick, I don't have the time tonight. This is what you get paid for."

Carlos cut him off and turned to Steve. "That's one of my managers. I cut him off to keep the line free. Imagine calling at a time like this."

The Mercedes made the turn around the horseshoe driveway and stopped abruptly right across from the front door of the home. Carlos had noticed the two Lincolns, each parked on opposite sides of his driveway, and was on guard as he saw the men walking toward him. Steve walked up to meet them.

"What the heck is going on, Carlos?" Peña said as he exited the car.

Carlos did not respond right away, as if he still were hesitant to discuss the whole affair out loud.

"They kidnapped Lucia and Alicia," he said, turning to open the front door and struggling to fight the tears.

"What?"

"Just like I said. They've been kidnapped. I have these guys calling me for a ransom. That's why I wanna keep my phone free. They could be calling me back at any minute."

"But how? How did it happen?"

"I don't know, Peña," Carlos said, frustrated, collapsing on the sofa.

Detective Steve Hartzman walked into the room, followed by two other men wearing suits who were carrying equipment. Steve explained what they were about to do.

"We are going to set up a monitoring station in your house. I know you're getting calls on your cell right now but in the event that a call comes in to the regular line, we wanna be ready to trace it. Our main station has already set up surveillance on your cell line so that every call that comes in is screened. We can trace the calls from wherever they come from. So we should be able to tell where they're calling you from."

Carlos listened attentively and then spoke. "Will the caller be able to tell he's being traced."

"No, he won't. They'll know absolutely nothing. Now, we need to talk about this gentleman. He seems to have been involved with the other fellow that set up the trip, right? You wanna tell us how you know this man, sir?"

He was addressing Peña, who was still in a daze after hearing the news.

Carlos interceded. "Peña speaks only broken English. I don't think he knows much about what's happening."

"It's not a problem," Steve said. "We can have one of these agents ask him in Spanish. John?"

He pointed to one of the other officers, who was busy working with one of the phone lines that fed into a phone on a side table in the room.

"There's no need for that," Peña said. He went and sat down next to Carlos in the sofa. "I recommended Cardona to Carlos," Peña went on with a heavy accent. "Carlos's daughter wanted to go to Cuba to get to know the island where her parents came from. I know Cardona, the man you saw at the restaurant, from many years back. He makes a living out of arranging trips for people who want to go to Cuba and having goods delivered there. I used him myself on one occasion and it turned out okay."

"You went to Cuba?"

"No. I had things delivered there to my older brother."

"And what was the arrangement? What did he do for you?"

"I paid him a sum of money, and he arranged for the deliveries, medicines, clothes, anything I wanted."

"Wait," Steve said, not being able to catch some of the words. "We're gonna have one of my officers translate. John, can you please?"

The other officer put down the small box he had been fidgeting with and came to stand next to Steve.

"Now, I know you speak some English. But we really need to get this cleared up. I don't want any misunderstandings. So you go ahead and speak in Spanish. John here will translate."

Peña went on with his story in Spanish as John translated. It probably would have served Steve better if he had allowed Peña to continue in English, and Carlos caught on right away, but as it happens many times with law enforcement, they rely on a translator even when his skills are questionable and when the speaker can probably do better without him.

Steve was particularly interested in Cardona's operation—how it worked and how he conducted his business. It seemed odd to him that anybody would pay for services that were hard to justify.

"I just don't get it," Steve said. "You seem like a smart man, knowledgeable about your own culture. Why would you pay anybody to set up a delivery to your family when you can do it yourself? What's so difficult about sending the goods there? I mean, I know it's regulated but as long as you stay within the regulations, you're fine."

"But you can't send anything you want. If you use Cardona, you pretty much get everything through," Peña replied. "As far as the trips to the island, I'm not as knowledgeable there but I know that there are a lot of things that you have to do to deal with the Cuban government. You have to get a passport, depending on how long you've been away. You have to get permission to enter the country. It's a process. And then there's the movement inside Cuba. You need to have a place to stay and to travel inside the island."

"No big deal. They can stay with their families. That's why they go there to begin with."

"No. The ones who travel are not going to rely on their families. People don't have anything in Cuba. Everyone is very poor. They have nothing to eat, no clothes. They live on the bare necessities of life, so no one is going to abuse their hospitality and impose on them. That's why they hire Cardona to set them up at a hotel and arrange the whole trip. Besides, he has connections down there that make it easier for you to move around."

"He has connections? What kind of connections?"

"I don't know. He seems to get his way down there. He knows people."

"I see. Have you referred other people to him?"

"Yes, some. Here and there."

"And you've gotten a fee for doing that from him?"

"No. I have gotten no fee from him. I just referred a couple of people to him, that's so, like I did with Carlos. I introduced Carlos to him and that was it."

"Did you get a fee for Carlos's referral?"

"No."

Carlos's phone vibrated in his hand, and he immediately signaled to Steve with his other hand. The room became quiet as Carlos picked up the call. One of the other two officers got on his cell to tip the station.

"How is it going?" a voice, now in English, said.

"All right," Carlos replied, keeping his composure.

"You with anyone?"

"No. I'm home trying to work things out."

"Good. You got pen and paper?"

"Yes."

Carlos got up quickly and took a pen from Steve's pocket. He then found a notebook in the side table's drawer.

"Write this number down. It's one, five, six, eight, zero, zero, five, five. You got that?"

"I got it."

"Now, that's just one account. I will be calling you back with more numbers."

"Wait a minute," Carlos said as Steve tried to get his attention with a wave of the hands. "I need some time here. I can't just come up with this huge amount of money like magic. I need more time."

"You got plenty of time. You got plenty of money. You're lucky it's only one million. You're worth much more than that."

Steve was trying to tell him to keep the call going, but Carlos was not getting it. It did not matter. He kept pleading for more time and by doing so, the call went on for a few more seconds. Then, without a hint, the caller simply got off the line.

"He's gone," Carlos said. "I didn't even get to ask about my wife and daughter. He's gone."

"Carlos," Steve said, walking over and sitting next to him. "The station is working on getting that location. Sit still for a minute. Now, here's one observation for you. The fact that these people are calling you repeatedly like that tells us that they may be amateurs. It's way too early to conclude, but that is a sign. We're probably dealing with people who are not very good at what they do."

"What does that mean, Steve? What does that do for my family? They're still being held somewhere against their will and in danger of losing their lives. What do I care whether these people are professionals or not? They still have my family."

"You should care. And I'll tell you why. This tells us that

119

we're dealing with people who may not be very organized and are unsophisticated in the way they operate. It's important because it gives us an idea of how their operation runs. Am I saying that they're not dangerous? Of course not. Unfortunately, and I must tell you this, they may be even more dangerous than if they were a highly organized operation. You know, you are dealing with people who are more unpredictable and who don't necessarily follow a pattern. That could be troubling. Yet on the positive side, because they're disorganized and maybe inexperienced, they're bound to make mistakes and we can find them faster. As a matter of fact, we may already have a reading on them."

The agent who was standing by the side table had snapped his fingers high, and Steve was looking over his way.

"What you got?"

The agent seemed secretive, and Steve got up and walked over to him. The two began to talk in low voices. Peña sat on the sofa next to Carlos. He put his hand on his friend's shoulder and nearly broke down in tears.

"Carlos, I feel responsible somehow for what's happened. It was me who took you to Cardona."

Carlos hesitated a moment but then spoke flawlessly. "There's no need for you to feel any guilt, Peña. It's not your fault. This guy Cardona may not even have anything to do with what's happened. Like this detective said, it sounds like these people are unprofessional. My mistake was in giving in to Alicia. I should have never allowed them to go to Cuba. I had a bad feeling about this from the very beginning. It never sat right with me. I should have never let them go." Carlos shook his head in frustration.

"But Carlos, traveling to Cuba is not the problem. Something must have happened. It could have happened right here at the airport for all we know."

"No, it couldn't. It's them. It's those fucking communists again."

Peña knitted his eyebrows in disbelief. "You don't mean that Cuba has anything to do with this, do you?"

"I mean exactly that. I bet you any amount of money they're behind this."

"No, Carlos. I don't think so. And if I may say so, I think you maybe taking your hatred of the system, which I share by the way, just too far. They may finagle them for money at the airport or something like that, but kidnapping? No, they wouldn't do that."

"Okay, so what's your explanation for what's happened? Where are they?"

"I think you have to give these guys a chance," Peña said, pointing to Steve and his two aides, who were still gathered in a group near the house phone talking. Steve had actually grabbed the phone and dialed a number and he was listening to someone on the line.

He then handed the phone to John and came over toward Carlos. "That last phone call came from northern Mexico," he informed him. "We tracked it down. We are tracking the area more specifically right now. We should know in a few seconds. See what I mean about these guys? These guys are sloppy, Carlos. And that's in our favor."

"So they are in Mexico. That's where they were kidnapped."

"Yeah. That's where they are."

"Where in Mexico?"

"We don't know just yet. We're working on that."

"They can't be too far from Mexico City. That's where they flew into."

"My bet is that they would have moved away from the big city right away. But then again, we're dealing with amateurs here, so I would not be surprised if they're not too far."

Carlos crossed glances with Mr. Peña. He had intentionally avoided his gaze. He did not want the old man to feel guilty, but right now he had a strong urge to strangle Cardona. It was he who had convinced him to fly his family to Mexico on their way to Cuba. Why such interest in Mexico? Cardona had to know something. He now felt like a fool for having fallen into a trap. But then he came to the obvious question. If Cardona had somehow orchestrated the affair, right now he would be in hiding. He had to know that he would become a suspect once his family's fate was known. Could it be possible Cardona had not known? Carlos thought about the grim news that was constantly coming from Mexico: cartel wars, torture, and kidnapping near the border. He closed his eyes for a moment and blamed himself. There was no one else to blame, he thought. How could he have been so blind? Mexico was the most dangerous place to be at the present time. Innocent people were being killed on a daily basis. How could he have allowed this to happen?

He missed Steve's question, and the detective had to almost shake him to make him come back to life. "Carlos, listen to me. I want you to think back and tell me everything that you discussed with Cardona about your family's trip. Let's start from the beginning. It's important that I hear every detail. Don't let the old man's presence bother you. He too will have his chance to tell his story. In fact, Mr. Peña, I want you to step out of the room for a minute. Let Carlos and me have some privacy."

Peña made a move to get up but Carlos held him back. "Leave Peña alone, Steve. He's got nothing to do with what happened."

"Carlos, that may be so, but this is how we conduct an investigation. Let me do my job."

"In this case, Steve, I'm gonna take my chances. I was wrong once for letting my family go to Mexico. I was wrong a few minutes ago for thinking that the Cuban government had something to do with this. But I'm gonna do this my way. Peña stays. He introduced me to Cardona, that's right. But he did nothing wrong. And by the way, Cardona may not have either. I'll tell you all I know. I don't know that it will help. We are losing time sitting here. I need to get the money ready so I can get my family back."

"Let's have it. Tell me everything."

Chapter Five

Lucia opened her eyes to the rays of light filtering in slowly through the cracks around the boarded window in the room. She had not slept much, lying still for hours on her mattress in order not to disturb Alicia, who had finally succumbed to sleep late during the night. Then Lucia dozed off around the time she heard the unmistakable sound of a rooster crowing, a sign that morning was coming.

When she woke, she instinctively looked at the kerosene lamp mounted high on the opposite wall and noticed that it had gone out. Either it had run out of kerosene or someone had entered the room at dawn and put it out. *What was the use?* she thought. If she had wanted to use it to burn the place down, she could have done it early the previous night.

And then it occurred to her—her captors were really inept. How could they allow her to keep a potential means of destruction in the room? Perhaps they came to realize their mistake early in the morning. Yet on the other hand, they had been obsessed, it seemed, with the hoods. *What's the use of the hoods?* she thought. She could only use the information about their identities if she survived the ordeal. She had no idea where her captors were anyway. Unless these people operated from a fixed location, which she doubted, her whereabouts would be of no use to the authorities in the future.

She sat up and looked toward Alicia. She was still asleep.

Eralides E. Cabrera

Lucia didn't want to disturb her, so she lay back on her pillow and waited.

Her captors must have known about her movements, because immediately after, the door was pushed open and two young men with submachine guns slung across their chests entered the room. She looked at their faces and did not recognize either of them.

"Time to get up," one said, standing close to her mattress.

"Shut up, asshole, my daughter is asleep."

As had been happening with her during her few hours of captivity, the words just rushed out as if she were talking to some imprudent driver along a Miami highway. She only thought about it because these men were different guards she had not seen before. What if they decided not to tolerate her?

The answer came flashing back in a second. One of the men swung the gun backward and yanked it down with vigor. The butt of the gun struck her jaw like a sledgehammer, flipping her back from her sitting position. She felt a bolt of pain travel down her lower body, and she thought she heard the bone in her jaw crack. That would have been bad enough, but the impact must have wrenched the man's fingers far enough to push the trigger, setting off a discharge of rapid gunfire that tore into the ceiling of the poorly ventilated shack. The young man jumped back in shock. His companion took a step back, and not knowing what to do, loosened the shoulder strap that held his gun and pointed it toward Lucia.

Lucia sat up on the mattress and felt her head spin. Her maternal instincts made her look toward the other side of the room, searching for Alicia, who had been awakened by the noise.

"Mom?"

Lucia tried to answer but a sharp, pounding pain traveled down her neck as soon as she tried to speak. She heard the hurried footsteps of someone who came rushing into the room.

"What the hell happened?" a man yelled excitedly as he walked in. He was the same young man who had walked them to the latrine last night.

"My gun," the man who had fired said, trying to explain himself.

"You dumb ass! Don't you realize what you've done? They're gonna know we're here. And what did you do to that woman?"

The armed young man didn't have the chance to answer. She jumped on him like a beast of the jungle, surprising him because she came at him peripherally, as he had turned sideways to talk to the other man. Lucia totally lost control, feeling overpowered by a wave of anger that drove her to do the insane, ignoring her own crippling pain.

"Fernando, move out of the way!" the other young man hollered, trying to get a good shot at Lucia.

But the other man who had entered the room last grabbed the gun's barrel and moved it sideways. The gunman tried to break away from his grip as Lucia fought desperately with the other gunman. She had caught him by surprise and grabbed his neck in an attempt to choke him. Small-sized and of slender built, he could not shake her off and had to let go off his gun to push her back. That was when Lucia made a go for it, grabbing his gun with both hands by the bolt and chamber area and yanking it back with violent tugs that actually dragged the young man toward her from the strap as she scurried backward. It had now turned into a struggle for possession of the weapon, and the man was having a hard time keeping hold of it.

A shot went off as they fought for it, hitting the wall.

Eralides E. Cabrera

Alicia was screaming in the background. Then suddenly Lucia lifted the gun above the young man's head as he tried to snatch it back by grabbing the handle. The strap came over his head, and Lucia lost her balance and fell back from the tug of her own pull. But she had the gun in her hand. She probably would have done nothing if it had not been for the young man's delay in reacting.

As he recovered from his own loss of balance and walked toward her, he found himself staring at his own gun's barrel. He did not stop. He did not think, and neither did she. It happened quickly. It was her crazed and desperate attempt to hold on to the weapon that made her hold its midsection and grab the trigger with her thumb. She did it blindly, not realizing she was firing, but she was.

The bullet struck the advancing youth in his midsection, ripping through his stomach and splattering him with blood. He fell forward, almost on top of her, and at that point she had the sense to move farther back, almost to the corner of the room, walking on top of her mattress. She was now thinking clearly and not merely reacting. She knew Alicia was far behind and in danger of the other two, who were still fighting for the gun. She pressed the trigger with her thumb, this time deliberately.

She hit the younger man with the rifle right in his chest. She immediately fired again. This time two shots came out of the automatic weapon, one striking the other man. One shot went through his neck area and the other one whizzed past him. But both men were mortally wounded and fell in a heap on Lucia's mattress.

"Alicia, let's go!" she yelled, feeling the lightening pain in her jaw as she spoke. "We gotta get out here! Grab that gun! Come on!"

But her daughter was in no state to comprehend what was happening. She kept yelling at the top of her lungs. Lucia was now thinking clearly. She pushed the tittering, dying body of one man away from the one underneath and hauled the gun out. She swung the strap around her shoulder with some difficulty, switched the other gun to her right hand, and grabbed Alicia with her free hand. She ran out of the room with her daughter, past the open door, pointing the gun in every direction as she moved around the empty house, looking for anyone who might still be around.

There were only two other rooms in the shack, and once she realized they were alone, she took her time looking for a phone. There was a pile of clothes in one room but no furniture. She found a chest in the other and looked through every drawer. Nothing. Then she turned around and saw the two cell phones, lying inside an open metal box on the table. They were hers and Alicia's.

"Alicia, take those! Come on!"

Alicia had calmed down somewhat. Sobbing slightly, she clung to her mother's hand as if it were her lifeline. She extended her hand to reach the phones inside the box, as if afraid to get close.

"Let's go!" Lucia said. "Come on!"

"Mom, where are we gonna go? Where are we?"

Lucia looked around. She moved quickly toward the only window, located at the side of the front door inside the small house. She pressed her face against the window bars to get a better view of the surroundings. It seemed desolate. The house was sitting at the crest of a hill on rugged terrain with sporadic vegetation. *It was built here for a reason*, she thought. It could be spotted from miles away and probably was being watched from somewhere in the valley below.

Then her eyes met with a stunning finding, which in the confusion and her anxious state she had initially failed to spot. There, to the side of the house, sat a gray Chevy Blazer with tinted windows and oversized tires. Lucia's mind raced.

She tugged her daughter back into the room where they had been held captive.

"Mom, what are you doing? Shouldn't we be getting out of here?"

"Alicia, put your hands inside that man's pockets and see if he's got any keys."

"Oh, no, Mom. I can't."

"Come on! Do it! We have no time. I'm afraid to let go off these guns. Hurry!"

It was a horrific scene, and Lucia knew it. Even she had a hard time handling it. The man she kept pointing to was lying on top of another and was bleeding profusely. Lucia noticed the slight shaking of one of his legs and instantly pointed the gun at him but knew he posed no danger. The man was clearly dying and his body was probably undergoing involuntary movements. She egged Alicia to search his pockets. Alicia stuck her hand slowly into the man's right pocket, standing at a distance from him, scared to touch him. It took her time to search inside, and after some difficulty she pulled something out. She held it still for a moment, not realizing what it was.

"Those are the keys," her mother said. "Let's go."

"Mom, I got blood on my hands, look!" She held her hand up high. Smudges of blood ran across her fingers.

"Don't worry about it, Alicia. Let's look around for some food and get ready to go. Come on! Hurry up!"

Lucia took a good look around the outer room. There was nothing but a table shoved against the wall. Two medium sized bags were filled with men's clothes. She found a loaf of stale bread on one of the chairs beside the table. The house had no kitchen and no storage room that she could see. She figured the men had used the house strictly for captivity and the food was being brought from somewhere nearby—one more reason to get out of here quickly. But where to go?

Where were they? She had no idea. She had been brought here blindfolded and had no visual recollection of the path they had followed. But still, she had her sense of direction, she thought. They must go, and fast.

She grabbed her daughter by the wrist, still holding the automatic weapon in her hand and the other one slung across her shoulder.

"Open the door," she said to Alicia, getting close to the front door held together by planks that ran diagonally across it like in a movie from the old west.

The two moved outside, and she told Alicia to close the cabin door. Then they ran quickly toward the vehicle. She let go off her daughter's hand momentarily to open the driver's door. She did not have to use the keys. The door was unlocked.

"Get in!" she said. "Go in, fast!"

Alicia climbed into the driver's seat and climbed clumsily over the console to the other side. Lucia jumped inside after her and shut the door. She was careful with the guns, laying one on the backseat and taking the other from her shoulder, squeezing it against the edge of the seat at the console. She set the handle low but in a position where she could pull it out rapidly in case she needed to fire. She was sure that moment would come. Then she got the keys from her daughter and started the car.

"Mom, where are we gonna go?"

"We're going back the way we came," she said as she checked the needle of the gas tank.

It was three quarters full. She turned the ignition key and got the engine going.

The electrifying pain traveling from the left side of her jaw down her neck almost paralyzed her. She could hardly open her mouth and had been able to withstand the pain only because of the adrenalin flowing through her body. But now, in a more normal state, she was beginning to react to the injury.

"Mom, what's wrong?"

Alicia saw her reaching for her jaw.

"I think one of those guys really hurt my jaw."

"It's not broken, is it? Mom, what are we going to do?"

"We're gonna get out of here. That's what we're gonna do."

She put the Blazer in reverse, and holding onto her jaw with her hand, she looked at the rearview mirror as she raced back and then quickly jammed on the brakes when she realized she was at the edge of the mount. She had no idea how precipitous the downfall was. The rear end of the Blazer had reached a vacuum.

"Shit!" she cursed.

"Mom, what happened?"

"Alicia, sit still honey. Keep your head down."

She quickly shifted into drive and stepped on the gas. She spun the Blazer in a semicircle in front of the house and took the rugged path leading down to the bottom of the hill. She almost lost control of the vehicle as it careened through a string of bumps that boosted her and Alicia toward the roof of the car. The path was not graveled and was not travelable at more than ten or fifteen miles per hour. She slammed on the brakes and brought the Blazer to a stop.

"Are you all right?" she asked her daughter.

Alicia was crying, holding her head with both hands. "Mom, you're gonna kill us! You're gonna kill us! You don't even know where we're going!"

"Alicia, try to calm down, honey. We're gonna get out of this. You'll see."

Lucia checked the butt of the automatic weapon to make sure it hadn't shifted position from all the commotion. She checked the other gun in the back. It had fallen off the seat from the impact, and she placed it back on. The last thing she needed was for one of the guns to accidentally go off. Slowly she moved forward, now negotiating each bump or uneven ground she saw. She worried about anyone who might have noticed her but saw no signs of life around. Perhaps not yet.

"Mom, do you know where you're going? How do you know which way to go?"

"Do you remember anything, Alicia? Were you concentrating when they brought us up here?"

"No, Mom. I was too scared. And they had us blindfolded. You know."

"Well, I figure it this way. There's no road from the back of the house, so we couldn't have come from behind it. That means that at least for now we're on the right track. I do remember the bumps as we were coming here, so that fits in with where we are headed. The question is what will happen if we run into more than one road on the way. How will I know which one to take? I'll just have to see."

But her real fear was not even the choice of roads. She just could not tell her daughter. She felt terror thinking that at any moment they would meet someone. Surely their captors in the house were not alone. There had to be some backup nearby. And the shots that had been fired in the house were sure to have been heard from a distance, she thought. But then again, maybe not. There was turmoil in the area. Last night they had heard shots, a sign that the notorious violence that had overtaken the country was not far from them. Her captors had not seemed concerned and even joked about the firings. But something told Lucia they were not part of that terrible slaughter that was happening in the country. In her estimation, these were untrained hoodlums who were trying desperately to make some money by kidnapping two women tourists who happened to be on their way to Cuba. Yes, they were unscrupulous and would not hesitate to kill, but they were poorly trained. The result of what just happened spoke for itself.

She kept maneuvering the Blazer around the bumpy road. *At this rate,* she thought, *I'll never reach civilization.* Then she realized she had reached flat land and began to get concerned. She looked around. As far as she could see the place was desolate. Vegetation was almost nonexistent, and the rocky terrain made it look more like a lunar space station than the region of north Mexico where she could not have known she was. Lucia knew they had traveled far and thought their only chance of survival was to find some populated town before they ran out of gas. In the meantime, it would be a miracle if she could remain undetected. There was nowhere to hide, and her vehicle, traveling at slow speed through the makeshift road, was bound to be spotted at any minute.

"Mom, do you have any idea of where you're going?"

"Alicia, you've asked me several times. No, I don't know. I'm trying to get as far away as possible from the house. Will you sit still, please?"

"Oh, Mom, please." Alicia moved over and leaned against her mother. She began sobbing with such intensity that she was making her mother shake.

At that moment Lucia spotted the van coming toward them in the opposite direction and trembled inside. She instinctively slammed on the brakes to grab the gun but then realized that would be a mistake. She must keep going and try to camouflage herself as a local. But how? If the occupants of the van were part of the gang that had kidnapped them, they would recognize her immediately. She must be ready.

"Alicia, move over, honey. Someone's coming."

Alicia immediately jumped up and cried out in fear.

"Stay down, honey. Stay down." At that moment she would have given anything to have Carlos with her. She felt lost without him. True, she was knowledgeable about guns because he had taught her how to handle them. But she had never before until today fired a weapon without him being at her side. And she had just killed three men.

She kept the Blazer moving at a slow speed and then carefully pulled the gun from the edge of the seat. Because of the length of the barrel she had to let go off the wheel momentarily to grab the middle of the weapon and set it at an angle on the edge of the window. Her right hand held it firmly with her finger on the trigger as she held the wheel with her left.

"Mom, what are you doing?"

"Nothing, Alicia. Just stay down, honey, and don't come up no matter what you hear."

Right now, her thoughts went back to her husband. How would he handle this situation? Carlos was quite a marksman, and through the years he had developed an attachment to target practice with his .45. Since early in their marriage he had persuaded Lucia to join him at the range, and he had taught her how to shoot handguns and rifles. She became knowledgeable in the use of every weapon, even semiautomatic ones. She should know as much as he did, he had insisted. But she could never keep his pace.

She certainly was no expert in the use of an automatic weapon and had almost fumbled her firing back in the house. What she did not realize was the magnitude of the success she had achieved so far. She had killed three men. For a fraction of a second she looked down at her weapon and suddenly realized what she was holding: An M-16, the standard US Army and Marine Corps primary infantry rifle. She had shot from one many times at the Miami range under Carlos's watchful eye. Thoughts went through her head and she began to regain her confidence. Why, she had just used the weapon back there. But it had all happened in the spur of the moment, trying to survive. This was deliberate, calculated warfare. She looked down again and viewed the fire mode selector on the left side of the weapon. She moved her hand up and placed it on semi automatic, 3 round burst fire. Now, she thought, she was out of her daze and knew what she was doing. She needed to. Her daughter's life depended on it.

She could see the face of the man behind the van's wheel. He was wearing a baseball cap. A passenger sat beside him. The driver had his eye on her, as did the passenger, as the van approached closer and closer. She was trying to decipher their movements as they became more visible, realizing she could not afford to slip for a second. If the men were in fact connected to her kidnappers, they were sure to take some action, and more than likely they would start shooting. She could not take the chance. At the same time she did not want to indiscriminately shoot someone. But clearly the men in the van had the advantage on her. They were in familiar surroundings and probably apt in armed assaults. What could she do?

She saw the van slow down and the driver lean forward, as if to take a better look at her. She pressed the window's automatic button and put the window down. She pushed the barrel of the rifle forward, jutting it slightly outside. Then she saw the driver make a move as if to reach down for some object. She did not wait. She pressed the M-16's trigger and the gun wobbled as it spit out three bursts of fire. Then came the shattering sound of the van's windshield as it smashed into pieces from the bullets, hitting the driver. As if she was on some kind of automatic pilot, she slid the gun slightly to the left and fired again. Three more bursts of fire and she saw the passenger's head explode from the impact of the projectiles.

She stopped the Blazer and waited as the van moved slightly off course, away from the dirt road. It came to a stop almost parallel to her position. She noticed the driver had slumped forward, his head resting grotesquely on the wheel. It was then that she became aware of her daughter's frantic screams.

"Alicia, be quiet, honey. You need to stop."

"Mom, please! I can't take it! I can't take it!"

"Alicia, be quiet! Listen up. I'm gonna get out of the car for a moment. I need to check that van. I'm going to collect those men's weapons and maybe some money and food, whatever I can find. We need to survive. Who knows how long we're gonna be here?"

"No, Mom, please don't leave me alone! Please don't!"

"Stay down, honey. I'll only be a minute."

She got out of the Blazer with the weapon's strap slung across her chest, looking much like one of her former captors. She was not hesitant anymore. She knew what she needed to do and had a plan to survive. She reached the van and opened the door.

The scene inside was pretty grisly. The driver was still alive, shaking and gasping for air. Strangely, the scene did not faze her. She moved him back gently and moved the shift to the park position. The engine was still running so she turned it off and took the keys. She leaned over and collected the submachine gun that lay on the other side of the driver, the one he had tried to grab. Then she searched his shirt pockets, taking a bundle of papers and a phone. She searched his pants pockets with great difficulty because his body was heavy and she had to move it from side to side as she got her hand inside one. She found a bundle of Mexican bills, his wallet from the back pocket, and a knife belted to his waist. Then she went around the other side and searched the passenger side, an even more gruesome task as half the man's head had been blown off. She found additional bills and a handgun. She looked throughout the cabin, avoiding the blood and skull fragments that lay scattered everywhere. She could not find any food but found two half full bottles of water. After she was satisfied there was nothing else, she closed the door and tossed the keys toward the sloping rocks on the side of the road.

"All right, Alicia," she said, back inside the Blazer. "Pick up my phone and see if you can make contact with your father."

She put the Blazer in motion and continued along the makeshift road. Despite the throbbing pain to her jaw, she was now in full command of her situation, deeply concentrated in what she had to do. Her deepest concerns were not knowing where she was going, and even more frightening, what would happen when she ran out of gas. It was bound to happen. She looked at the gas gauge and watched the needle. It had not moved from three quarters full. At least now she had some local currency, she thought. She could gas up once she reached civilization. But where was that?

"Mom, my phone is dead. It has no juice. It needs to be charged. Do we have a charger?"

"No, we don't have a charger, Alicia. Where do you think you are? Those creeps must have let our phones die. Who knows what they did with the rest of our stuff? Try my phone. Come on! This is crucial."

Alicia grabbed her mother's phone, a far cry from her touch-screen Blackberry. She opened the cover in her mother's Motorola Backflip and pressed the connect button. At first it did not seem like the screen would come on, but she noticed the small white circle turning in the middle of the screen. It could very well be that it would never reach full activation, but at least there was some power.

"Mom! Mom! We got power!"

"Good, honey. Dial your dad's number as soon as it powers up."

"I don't know if we'll get service, Mom."

"I had Carlos call the company before we left so we could make calls from outside the country. It should work."

"I mean that there may not be enough power. Wait—it's coming on very slow. Oh, God!" Alicia watched impetuously as the small ring of light kept twisting in the middle of the dark screen. Suddenly the screen lit up, and she saw her own face come on. Her mother kept it as a home screen image. "Mom, it's on! It's on!"

"Good. Press contacts, Alicia, and look for Carlos."

Lucia stopped the Blazer and opened her window. She waited for her daughter to make contact with her husband. If anyone could operate a cell phone with eyes closed, it was her seventeen-year-old daughter. But this was a special situation. There was no room for error. Alicia had clicked on her father's name and put the phone against her ear.

"It's going, Mom. It's going."

She heard the crackling sound of a distant ring.

"Come on, Dad, pick up, pick up!"

In her anxiety, she had not realized that she had pressed the speaker option. When Carlos's voice came on, Lucia and her daughter both screamed.

"Dad! Dad! It's me!"

There was some hesitation but then the unmistakable lively voice they both knew.

"Alicia, is that you?"

"Dad! We're here! Me and Mom! We're here!"

"Where are you? Where—"

Then they heard the sound of static on the phone.

"Dad! Dad! Are you there?"

"Give me the phone, Alicia!"

Lucia grabbed it from her. But the screen darkened, and she knew they had lost power. She pressed the on button and waited. Nothing.

"We have no power. We need to charge the phone. Look around, Alicia, look around. We may get lucky and find a charger. I've got to get going."

She placed the Blazer in drive and kept going. At some points the road was barely visible. It was lost among the rocks and dry terrain. Lucia could only pick up traces here and there, like tire tracks that became visible on the dustier areas. There was no sign of life.

"Oh, Mom, we're gonna die! We're gonna die!"

"Alicia, we're not gonna die. We're gonna be just fine. When we find our way out of this area, we'll pick up a major road and get some help. You'll see."

"Mom, you don't know where we're going. I'm hungry and I'm thirsty. What are we gonna do about food?"

Lucia handed her one of the water bottles she had found in the van. "Drink up. But drink slowly. Don't drink it all in one shot. I'll see what we can do about food."

Alicia took a long sip from the bottle and then gazed with teary eyes at her mother. "Mom, there were people inside that van, right? What did you do to them? You killed them, right?"

Lucia was silent. She had tried not to expose her daughter to the slaughter, but that wasn't exactly all of it. She had discovered something strange inside herself, something she had never known she had. She was capable of real violence. She had killed other humans and had done it flawlessly, without hesitation, as if it were second nature. Had she been lucky, or was it the result of a hidden ability? That she did not know. She realized she was unconsciously trying to hide it. She did not want her daughter to know.

"Alicia, don't think about what happened back there. Concentrate on what we're doing, please. Try to help me find a charger."

"Mom, you killed them, right? You did, right?" Her

speech was slurred from her sporadic sobbing. Whether she sobbed for fear of the terrible situation they faced or for the abrupt discovery she had made about her mother, Lucia did not know, but now more than before Lucia felt a peaceful serenity that invaded her whole being and let her think rationally. She held firmly to the butt of her M-16 that she had again slid between the edge of her seat and the car's console, ready to retrieve it at a moment's call.

"Can you look for a charger around the car, please?"

"Okay! Okay!"

Alicia knelt on the seat to look through the back, still sobbing. "Mom, you got a whole bunch of guns back there!"

"Alicia, please, look in the glove compartment, under the seat, anywhere. Forget the back seat." Her daughter did as told, slowly and with trembling hands.

Lucia kept her eyes in the horizon. She thought back about the man she had talked to in the car while still hooded and then at the house. She had seen his face. Had he been one of the two in the van? She almost felt sorry that he might be one she'd killed. She thought about the two bodies she had left in the van, one still breathing. She had barely looked at their faces. Their wounds were far too severe for anyone to survive them, especially out here in this remote area, so she let them be. But now she asked herself whether there were more. There had to be.

She tried thinking about their trip last night. It had taken more than two hours, and at some point they had left a paved highway. If she could only reach that point again, their chances of survival could dramatically improve.

"Mom, there's nothing here. What's the point in even looking? You know we're not gonna find anything."

"All right. Then sit still. Be ready to duck down when I tell you to. If we meet any cars along the way, I don't want them to see you."

"Why, Mom? Are they chasing us?"

"I don't know, honey. I don't know. Just sit tight. Keep your eyes open and let me know if you see anything."

"Mom, you really think we'll get out of this?"

"We will, honey."

It was now around noon, and the sun was hot. They had not eaten anything since the day before, and Lucia had hardly slept last night. Fatigue was beginning to set in. Driving the Blazer through the rough terrain required full concentration, not to mention the constant vigilance to avoid being surprised by any vehicles that might appear on their way. Lucia kept her eyes on the far horizon but also kept checking her rearview and side-view mirrors. They could come at her from anywhere.

Out in the distance two black SUVs were moving toward them. She thought about how she would handle it. The question in her mind was always whether they could be merely locals traveling somewhere and not necessarily linked to their captors. What if they were friendly? But she could not chance it. She had to assume they were out to do her and her daughter harm, not only out of self preservation but even logically. They were in a country ravaged by drug wars and fights to the death among criminal factions who wanted control. It was chaos at its peak, and in such a situation one cannot assume anything but the worst.

The fact they were in a remote area only made it easier for any band of thugs to slaughter whoever they ran across. Who would ever know?

Thoughts flashed through Lucia's mind. How should she handle it? Should she stop? Should she go on? She decided to keep going. There was a chance the vehicles would simply pass her by. This was wishful thinking and she knew it.

"Mom, someone's coming."

"I see them, Alicia. Get down. Get under the dashboard. Come on."

"Oh, Mom. What's going to happen?" Alicia was sobbing and crouched under the dashboard, her torso resting against her knees that she wrapped with both arms.

Lucia had not time to console her. She had slid the M-16 from the edge of the seat and placed the barrel discreetly on top of the dashboard, without showing the rest of the gun. For some reason, she did not feel the need to open the window and point the gun out as she had done when meeting up with the van. The two vehicles grew in size as they got closer. They both had shaded windows, which she interpreted as a bad sign. She could not see inside. But still, she kept on. If they were going to fire at her, she figured she would pick up some movement. But she noticed nothing as the first vehicle came within a few feet of the Blazer and then slowed down. She kept moving at the same speed.

The driver's window rolled down, and a hand moved out as if to wave—but no gun. She put her own window down and waved back. As they passed each other, the driver kept signaling for her to stop but she merely waved at him and kept going. She would not stop. Then the second SUV was passing her. The driver of this one did not open any windows but merely drove by. She did not look at him. She had slyly moved the gun down to avoid having them notice it.

When she had passed them she breathed in relief. They had seen a woman driving alone and did not attack her. Could it be possible? She watched cautiously through the rearview mirror as they slowly kept moving further and further away until they disappeared.

"All right," she said. "You can sit again, Alicia."

"Mom, what happened? Who were they?"

"I don't know. They passed us and did nothing, so I'm not going to complain. It's hard to tell whether they are related to the others, but one thing's for sure—once they run into that van back there, all hell will break loose."

"They're gonna come after us, Mom?"

Lucia realized she had said too much. But she was living in agony, accompanied by her daughter but holding back in her comments so as not to worry her. She realized that her chances of getting away depended on how soon she could find the road. She looked at the gas needle. It was smack in the middle. She had already used one quarter of a tank and had not been driving for more than one and one half hours. She knew she needed to find a major road soon or she and her daughter would be in trouble.

"Drink water, Alicia. It's good to keep the fluids coming."

"Mom, I don't wanna worry you, but water is only part of it. We need food."

"I'm afraid you'll have to take a rain check on that. Soon we'll be on the road, and we'll find food."

"How do you plan to find food? We need money. We have nothing. We've lost our luggage, our wallets, everything."

"I've got my ways," she said, and she discreetly felt the wad of bills she had taken from the dead men in the van.

Alicia stared at her in silence. She had a look of amazement about her, as if she found it hard to believe that this was her mother. "Mom, you've changed. I never thought you could be like this."

"Like how?"

"Like so tough, Mom."

"I'm as far from tough as we are from home," Lucia said, laughing. It was the first time she had laughed since they had started the ordeal. She found it refreshing and tried to appreciate their situation. They had escaped from an abduction in Mexico, the center of the most intense violence around. That in itself was an unbelievable feat. And she had a car, some water, guns, and plenty of ammunition. Yes, she had plenty to be thankful for. The rest must work itself out somehow. She had to concentrate on getting to a town, somewhere she could make contact with her husband again. That brought her thoughts back to Carlos. She knew her husband. If she had to bet money on it, he would be on her track right now like a bloodhound. He was not sitting slothfully in some Miami restaurant waiting for the next call right now. He would be desperately looking for a way to rescue her and Alicia. All she had to do was get to civilization and keep her eyes open.

The late spring's afternoon sun was merciless. There seemed to be no end to the bare landscape with little or no vegetation and no signs of life. When would it end?

Alicia broke into her thoughts. Or maybe she had been talking all the while and Lucia had been in such deep deliberation that she had not heard her. "Mom?"

"Yes, honey."

"Did you hear what I said? I never knew you had it in you. I always thought Dad was the tough one. You always seemed like you just followed him, like you made no decisions on your own, you know."

"Really?"

"But it's not like that at all. You're so strong. Where do you get it from?"

"I don't know, honey. I guess I put on a good act."

"No. Things like that don't get faked. Something's happened to you out here. Something changed you."

"I don't know that either. I don't know."

"It's almost, you know. It's almost scary." Alicia said, staring at her.

Lucia saw the fear in her eyes and blinked. She was disturbed by the thought of her daughter seeing something horrible inside her, something that she herself was afraid to acknowledge.

She turned onto the dirt path ahead and held the wheel. She glanced at the needle in the gas gauge and saw it leaning slightly under the halfway mark and her heart trembled. Then she turned to look ahead again, and it occurred to her that the path she had been following was actually a road now. This could only mean one thing, that they were getting close to a major highway. There was hope.

"Did you hear what I said?" Alicia repeated.

"It's your imagination. I'm no different than I was yesterday. We've been under a great deal of stress. Stress does funny things to you. It makes you see things different. Your mind takes over your body and it makes you see funny things. Nothing's changed, babe. We're both the same as before. We just have to get out of this place."

Alicia shook her head in disagreement and began sobbing again. She turned to gaze outside the passenger window.

Lucia reached out behind her and caressed her hair. It made Alicia cry more. "Oh, Mom, I'm so scared," she said in between sobs. "I think this is all my fault, dragging you here. Dad was right. That man brings out the worst in everything and everybody. That's why Dad hates him so much. That's why he won't go back to Cuba. Look what's happened to us. Look what's happened to you."

"Let me tell you something, honey. That's got nothing to do with our situation. We've just happened to have made a bad judgment call. We should have never stopped in Mexico. We should have flown straight to Cuba, like most people do. It's a bad time here now, but Castro or Cuba has nothing to do with it. Don't let that part of your father influence you. It's not right. We've just gotten caught in a bad situation, but we'll get out of it.

She shook her head as if she could not bring herself to

agree and kept looking away. And she remained detached, leaning her face on the glass of the window for almost an hour until she heard her mother shriek as she slammed the Blazer into a stop.

"I see a highway! We've made it! We've made it!"

"What?"

"Look, Alicia, it's a road. It's a paved road. That means we're close to a town. All we need is a bit of luck now, and we'll be fine."

Lucia put the car in motion again. What she didn't tell her daughter was that she was terribly afraid that the Blazer would run out of gas before she found people who could help her. But it was true. They were coming to a highway. That meant other cars, traffic, and the possibility of finding some help. She kept her eyes on the patch of road that kept getting wider and wider as they came near it. There was no barrier around it, and she could see the tire tracks of other cars left on the rocky ground right off the road.

She brought the Blazer to a full stop and leaned forward to look both ways. Now she faced the decision of her life, the one that could make the difference between life and death for her and her daughter. Which way should she turn? She had no idea about the cardinal points but knew she needed to move north to get close to the border. But which way was north? She looked for signs on any visible portion of the highway but saw nothing. She finally decided that she would take a chance. At some point there had to be a sign pointing to the next town or at least its direction. Then she would have to test her memory and see if she remembered where it led to. She could not remember the last time she had looked at a map of Mexico, and her knowledge of the geography was very limited. She did not think of asking Alicia, and without any further thought, she made a right and got on the highway.

"Mom, do you know where we're going?"

"No. I don't. You're gonna have to help me here, Alicia."

The single-lane highway looked desolate, but it felt good to drive on a paved road again, and she rapidly gained speed. She brought the Blazer to eighty. Then she saw the small sign to her right that read they were twelve and a half kilometers from Rio Grande.

"Where's Rio Grande? Where are we?"

"I don't know. I have no idea."

"That's where we're headed. It's only a few miles ahead. I think we're gonna make it." She was referring to the gas content in the vehicle. She looked at the needle and saw that it contained less than a quarter tank. She was fairly sure it would make another five miles, which she believed was more or less what she needed. She kept thinking that if she made it into town, any town, they would be safe. But then she thought about the situation that the country was undergoing and thought that being in a city, especially as a foreigner, could be just as dangerous as being in the countryside. To make it worse, nightfall was coming.

"Mom, I don't know. I haven't even heard the name."

"What do they teach kids in high school these days? It seems like you learn less and less."

"Why would we learn about Mexico?"

"We learned about everything when I was in grammar school. Do you know where Mexico City is at least?"

"It's the capital, no?"

"Gee, great, you got that right."

They looked at each other and laughed. Lucia felt good inside all of a sudden. Alicia had laughed, the first time she had done that since they arrived in Mexico. She felt pleased. As long as her daughter was okay, she was willing to take whatever punishment came her way. Alicia was the reason she had come on this trip, and then it dawned on her. Imagine if she had let her come alone! Her daughter alone in

Mexico! Thank God she had insisted on escorting her, even at the price of annoying her husband, who thought Lucia was merely contributing to the whims of their teenage daughter in her obstinate desire to travel to Cuba. Alicia would have never survived alone.

Lucia felt a tremendous relief as the first vehicle passed in the opposite direction. It was an older model pickup with several passengers sitting inside the truck bed. This would never happen in the United States, she thought. There would be cop cars surrounding the pickup, the passengers in the back would probably be arrested, the driver too, and the truck would be towed. Now she really knew she was in Mexico.

The road led her right into town. Walking energetically along the side of the road, most in pairs, were flocks of men wearing long straw hats, some carrying tools over their shoulders, who apparently were coming from the fields. It was an agricultural town. Then, out on the side of the road, across from a row of wooden houses, she noticed what appeared to be a gas station. She pulled the Blazer beside the green pump that looked like a throwback version of an Exxon tank from the seventies. She opened her door and looked back to make sure the gas tank was on the driver's side. When she looked up, she saw a short swarthy man standing before her.

"What will it be, *señora?*" he asked in a heavy Mexican accent and staring at her swollen jaw.

She checked her pocket to make sure the bundle of bills was still there. "Can you fill up my tank, please?" she said in the best Spanish she could muster.

Although she spoke Spanish as her first language, she knew she would be spotted immediately as a foreigner among the Mexican population. Her Cuban accent gave her away, and she knew that in her situation, she would have to strive to remain as unnoticeable as possible. She could not trust anyone.

The man glanced at her as soon as she spoke, and Lucia could tell he knew. He paced back toward the rear of the truck and began filling the tank. Then he moved back to the driver's window. "It's going to be one hundred and twenty pesos," he said, and gazed toward the inside of the cabin.

Then she remembered the guns in the back seat. She pushed the door open as if to make him back up. He did. She let the .45 drop discreetly on the seat as she stepped out. She gave him a one-hundred-peso bill. She thought she was being ripped off, but under the circumstances it was better not to make fuss. He took the bill and waited. She went through her roll of bills until she found a twenty and gave it to him. There was no doubt in her mind that he had picked her up as a foreigner. But what worried her the most were the guns. She should have hidden them.

"Do you know of any hotels nearby? I'm coming from the federal district and need some rest." She offered an explanation in the hope of sounding casual.

He kept his eyes on the pump and spoke without facing her. "Are you staying the night?"

"Yeah. Me and my friend inside."

"There is a good place right on this road. It's called the Rio Grande."

"Just keep straight on this road?" she asked.

He nodded and again stared at her swollen face. She waited for him to finish pumping, blocking his way in case he decided to walk back.

"Well, that's it. You got a full tank," he said.

"Thank you." She got in the Blazer and stuck the .45 under her waistline, letting her blouse drape over it.

"Mom, what are you doing?" Alicia asked. "What's happening?"

"Nothing. You know, Alicia," she said, now speaking with difficulty from the swelling in her jaw. "We're gonna look for a place to stay. I think I have enough money to do that. Once we have a room we can have the phone charged and then we can call your dad again. But while we're here, you don't say anything to anyone. We can't trust anybody. I have a feeling this place gets rowdy at night."

She was back on the road, driving through what appeared as a meager version of a residential strip of northwest Miami. The houses were mostly wooden with a few adobes between, and then right at a corner was a multi-floor building with the Rio Grande sign. She stopped at a parking space across from it and sat behind the wheel, looking at it.

"Mom, I think before you go anywhere we ought to go to a hospital. Your face is getting more swollen."

"I don't think my jaw is broken honey. It hurts but I can bear it. Besides, I'll bet you there are no hospitals in this town just like there's no police. They've all fled from the violence."

" Are we going to go in then?" Alicia asked.

"Nah," she said after a moment. "Of all the places there may be in town, this would be the one I wouldn't stay in."

"Why?"

"Because he told us to come here. That guy is probably the connection to everyone who comes into town. If you do not want to be noticed, you don't go where he sends you."

"So where are we gonna go? This looks like such a small town, Mom. There probably isn't anything else. Why don't we just keep going?"

"Because we don't know where we are yet, honey. We need to get our bearings."

She went further down the street. Alicia was probably right. There wasn't a lot to choose from, and everything she saw seemed like small, cheap cantinas that did not feel suitable for two women fleeing from their captors. She had to turn around and go back after it seemed like they had passed the whole town. She settled for a medium-sized motel with several rooms on the side. She checked the rates advertised at the window and counted her money. Until then she had had no idea how much she had. It was more than enough for the lodging and a meal. She left her daughter in the car and went inside to make the arrangements with the host, an older, overweight woman who seemed actually happy to have a guest.

"No, I do not have a charger for your phone," the woman said after Lucia showed her the cell phone. "You would have to ask someone. I don't know."

"Do we have a phone in the room then?"

"Yes, you can use the phone in the room. We don't charge extra for anything local. If you're calling out of the area, you'd have to call here first, and then we will direct your phone call out."

"I'm calling collect," she said.

"It doesn't matter. You still have to call the desk."

"All right," Lucia said, taking the keys. "Can I park the car in front of my room?"

"Yes. It's better that you do, actually."

"And where can we get a good meal?"

"There is a restaurant down the road called La Ronda. They're open till late."

She backed the Blazer into the parking space assigned to their room. It was still light out so she could not take the chance of pulling the guns from the back seat, so she placed them on the floor, hoping they would not be noticed.

The first thing she did when she walked into the squalid room was look for a phone. She needed to call her husband. He was the lifeline to the outside. Alicia had barely walked in and Lucia was already on the line, going through the operator. Lucia gave her Carlos's cell number. She could hear the faraway ring as she waited anxiously for his voice to come on.

"Hello," Carlos said.

"It's me, Carlos, it's me!"

"Lucia, where are you?"

"Carlos, we've made it to this town called Rio Grande. We're at a hotel here, but I don't know how long we can hang around. Carlos, you wouldn't believe what we've been through."

"Is Alicia with you?"

"She's here. She's fine."

"Lucia, stay right where you are. I'll come and get you. Where the heck is Rio Grande? Isn't that a river?"

"Carlos, I have no idea. I don't know where I am."

"Don't worry, Lucia. I'm coming. Put Alicia on."

Chapter Six

When Carlos got the first call from Lucia, he was again on the highway. The previous night had been a bad one, sitting in the house with the detectives as he waited for more calls from the captors, but none came. Then he tried to get some sleep, with Peña keeping him company. The old man had been so concerned and taking the whole thing so personally that he refused to leave Carlos alone. It had been all for the best. Carlos needed a friend. The two had dozed off around 4:00 in the morning, both on the living room sofa, with a detective hanging around just in case a call came in. Carlos's cell lay close to him as it was plugged into a charger. Then around 8:00 in the morning they were up. Still no calls.

Carlos decided he needed to gather the ransom money. He could not wait any more. Detective Hartzman had left the previous night and said he would be in touch, but as of early this morning, he still had not called. Carlos told the detective at the house he was going to work on the money. If a call came in, he would immediately call Carlos, but his phone was being monitored anyway. The detectives had traces on all the calls that were coming in, either on the cell or on the house phone. Maybe that was why no other calls had been received, Carlos thought.

Carlos and Peña were on N. W. Thirty-Sixth Street,

approaching one of Carlos's supermarkets, when the phone rang. A detective had come along with them and was sitting in the back seat, watching their every move. Carlos picked up immediately.

"Dad! Dad! It's me!" he heard.

His heart skipped a beat, and he carefully pulled the car to the side of the road. "Alicia, is that you?"

Peña was on guard upon hearing him utter his daughter's name.

"Dad! We're here! Me and Mom! We're here!"

"Where are you? Where in the world are you?"

He heard nothing but static and felt a tremendous rush of energy. "Please don't go now! Alicia, Alicia! Are you there?"

He called her name at least five times but got no response. The line was dead. "I lost them," he said to Peña.

The detective in the back moved uneasily on his seat.

"We got a trace on your cell too, Carlos. They'll call back."

He was going to ask him how the hell he knew but at that moment the phone rang again, and he picked up in a rush.

"Carlos, we got them," a voice said. "We got the location of that call."

"Where are they? Where did they call from?"

"You need to come back to the house. Steve is coming. Stay off the phone."

No sooner had he said it than Carlos made a U-turn in the middle of the street and headed back to the Palmetto Expressway.

"It was only a darn detective," Carlos said sarcastically.

"Take it easy, Carlos," Peña said.

"They're out, Peña! I can feel it. They're out! They're out somewhere and I don't have a clue where. I've got to do something fast. If they've broken out, their captors are gonna go after them like mad."

"You don't do anything," Carlos, the detective said from the back. "You stay cool."

"They're out? Out of where?" Peña asked.

"From wherever they were being held. They've broken out."

"Is that what they said?"

"No, it was Alicia I spoke to but she didn't have to say anything. She sounded excited, like she was free. I just lost the connection. I couldn't hear them any more. Peña, they're in trouble. My two girls are in trouble."

Peña felt for him, and had they been anywhere else he would have reached out and patted him on the shoulder. But Carlos's frantic driving had him on edge, and the presence of the detective in the back did not help. He did not dare move a muscle.

"What did Alicia say?"

"She just yelled out my name, real emotional. I just didn't have time to speak more to them. But I know they're out, and that's why I'm worried."

"Yeah, I know what you mean. It's dangerous down there right now. Did you get to speak to Lucia?"

"No, we got cut off."

There was a moment of silence as the car raced down the highway, and then Carlos turned to Peña. The detective in the back had picked up his cell and was calling someone.

"You know, Peña, that had to be my wife. Yeah, if I had to bet money on it, I'd put it all on Lucia. She did it."

"What do you mean?"

"Lucia's tough. She got away from them. You noticed how I've not gotten another call from those guys?"

"Right."

"Because they're dead."

"What?"

The detective in the back stopped speaking.

"Lucia must have gotten hold of a gun and wiped everybody out."

"Carlos, I pray everything turns out all right but don't go jumping into conclusions. Wait, these guys are helping us. Heard anything detective?"

He turned around to face him. Carlos went on speaking as if he wasn't there.

"You've seen her with a gun at the range, Peña. Underneath that soft-looking shell is a tough woman. Lucia can outdo any man with a gun. Have you seen how she handles herself with those automatics? I know she did it. Someone probably got careless, gave her an opportunity, and she took it. They're out of there, wherever they were, and now she and my daughter are roaming the country, looking to get out. That's what happened."

Peña remained thoughtful. He wanted to say it but didn't. If that was the scenario, it could be worse. The war-like conditions in Mexico at the moment made it a very dangerous place. He could not tell his friend that, of course, when he himself felt guilty for their present state of affairs. Had he never introduced Carlos to Cardona, this never would have happened to begin with. And then for him not to object when Carlos made the decision to let them stop in Mexico on their way to Cuba was unforgivable. Here he was the older and supposedly wiser of the two and not foreseeing the obvious danger. He felt tremendous guilt.

"I can't let them down, Peña," Carlos said as the car pulled swiftly into the horseshoe driveway."

The three men got out of the car and one of the detectives inside opened the door as they approached. "Steve is here," he said.

"Okay," Carlos replied, squeezing himself in. "Can you guys show me the area where the call came from?"

"We will. Come on, let's go in."

The detective led the way. They went into the living room, where a large map had been set against an easel, standing by the sofa. Steve Hartzman was sitting there talking on his cell. As soon as Carlos and Peña walked in he got up to greet them.

"How are you doing, Carlos?" he said, extending his hand.

He seemed cordial but something about him made Carlos suspicious. Carlos shook his hand and nodded to the other agent who was sitting in front of the coffee table, operating what appeared to be a monitoring device.

"So what have you found out? Where are they?"

"It seems that they are in the Zacatecas area. We're not sure where exactly but we know that's where the call came from. We're trying to find out more."

"Any idea why the call got cut off? Do you know?"

"No. Now, let me ask you something, Carlos, you've been to Mexico a couple of times, haven't you?""

The two exchanged glances. The question suggested that Steve was beginning to suspect that Carlos was involved in the kidnapping of his own wife and daughter. It took Carlos a moment to collect himself and not lose it and he would waste no time in letting Steve have it but first he had to let him know about Lucia. He was so proud of her and here was this moron wasting precious time. He regretted allowing him and his team to be involved in the case. As far as the phone cut off, yes, it could have been anything. The phone battery could have died. Maybe it was human interference. They could have even been caught by their captors while making that call. But Carlos knew it had to do with Lucia. He knew her capabilities better than anyone else.

"Steve, you know what? I'm going to ignore that stupid question. And let me tell you something, if you're gonna waste my time making me a suspect to my family's kidnapping tell me now and I'll just head out to the bank, pay the fucking ransom, get my wife and daughter back and forget about you. You should be ashamed. You can't even figure out what's happening right now. I know it better than you. I'll tell you what's going on: they broke away from their kidnappers. That's right, they broke away," Carlos repeated, staring him down. "They're roaming the countryside right now. That's what's happening! You know how I know? Because I know my wife. You can't keep her in a cage. She'll eat you alive. I bet you she killed those suckers and got away. My fear is that they might get caught up in the middle of some shootout down there, unrelated to the kidnapping. How active are the drug cartels in Zacatecas?"

Steve was slow to answer, and Carlos got tense. You couldn't tell whether the lawman was genuinely offended by Carlos's badgering or he would simply let the matter drop.

"Not as bad as other places, let's say."

"But bad enough that you're worried, ah? Well, tell me something, Steve, what can you do for them right now? Do you have men in the area?"

"No, we don't, but the Mexican authorities have been notified. They're on the go with this. They'll be purging that area soon."

"What Mexican authorities, Steve? The Mexican army is under siege at this moment. They're lucky if they can survive. What my wife and daughter need now is a rescue team. Someone who goes down there and gets them out. Can your department do that?"

"I'm afraid we have to defer to the Mexican government, Carlos. We can't interfere."

Carlos said nothing. He turned to Peña, who knit his eyebrows as a sign of discontent, as the old Cubans tend to do when things don't go their way, and instinctively both men went and sat on the sofa.

"It never occurred to me to ask you, but what do you actually plan to do to get my family back? Do you have a plan? I mean, do you plan on using a SWAT team and actually go to Mexico to get them back or what?"

"Carlos, I can't say yes or no, right now. We're looking into it. First of all we have to determine whether Lucia and your daughter are really out. Then, as a matter of procedure, I have to take this high up. This involves an independent country and the possibility of having to fly into their air space to get people out. This is major leagues."

"So what do you intend to do? How are you going to proceed?"

"We're feeding the information to our higher ups right now. We're working on it. We're in touch with Mexico's Department of Defense. They've been given all the information. They have sections of the military assigned to different trouble areas such as kidnapping, and they have this case. It would be much more desirable that they make the actual rescue than us getting people down there."

"What does all that mean? Is there someone right now actively looking for Lucia and Alicia?"

"We're moving in that direction right now."

"You're moving in that direction," Carlos repeated. "What a solution you're giving me, Steve. The only thing I got are my four years of naval service and my limited skills with weapons and I think I can do better than what you got going for yourself right now. You know that?"

"Carlos, don't even think for a minute—"

"Yes, I'm thinking for a minute. I'm thinking for a lot more than a minute about what I have to do!"

Carlos abruptly got up from the sofa and walked out of the living room. Peña signaled to Steve with a wave of the hand to stay put.

Steve yelled out to Carlos. "Carlos, one thing I do need

is for you to try to make contact with your wife. We need to confirm that they're out. Let's talk this over, come on. We're gonna get your family back."

Steve got on the phone for a few seconds and spoke to someone. He hung up when he saw Carlos enter the room again.

"You know something? This reminds me of the Bay of Pigs. This is what's wrong with America. The liberalism, the stupid ideology that we can't do this because 'what the world is gonna think' and we can't do that because it's immoral and whatnot. Meanwhile the whole frigging society is falling apart. This is why we Cubans are so enraged. You train men, you tell them you're gonna help them, and you even send them to invade the island. Then, when it's time to really deliver and send support, you say, oh no, we can't get involved. Even if it means walking out on those men and abandoning them in the swamps as you did, you do it because all of a sudden you can't get involved. That's why Castro is still there today, because of that mentality with the Kennedys and his clan. This here is no different. My wife and daughter are stuck in the middle of a drug war and suddenly, after you've led me to believe they were safe in your hands and that you would get them back, now you hesitate to get involved. Oh no, it's against the law. It's another country, we gotta be careful. You know what, Mr. Hartzman? It's Mexico, damn it! What has Mexico done for you in past one hundred years? Do they respect our air space when a ton of weed and coke get across our borders every day sent with love from Mexico? You know, Steve, thanks a lot. I don't need you to get my family back. I never even wanted your help. A couple of young police officers don't have enough to do and stop me for being on the shoulder of the road while I'm getting a call from somebody who's just kidnapped my daughter and wife, and these cops blow the whole thing apart. Had they not interfered, I probably would have my family back by now. I gave in, thinking you were actually going to do something. But I see what's going on. You're just wavering, Steve. Now it's the Mexican government that's being cast to solve the problem. You know, Mr. Hartzman, why don't you just go on to your next gig? Leave me alone. I can solve my own problems."

Carlos was upset, but he was quite coherent in his speech. As usual, he saw a parallel to the Cuban debacle over which he seemed so obsessed.

Steve let him finish and then got up and addressed him calmly. "First of all, Carlos, I wasn't even born when the Bay of Pigs took place. It has absolutely nothing to do with what's happening here. The point is we can't impose our own legal process on another country. We have to respect their laws and defer to them. That doesn't mean we're not going to try to free your family, but we have to do it by the rules."

"America does not interfere in other countries' affairs? Is that what you're saying? You could have fooled me, Steve. What the heck are we doing in Iraq, Afghanistan? Come on, Steve, get a clue. I know America better than you do and I wasn't born here. You don't interfere when it's not convenient for you but when you're after something, you find a thousand ways to move in. You've done it a million times through the history of this nation. Don't give me that crap!"

"Look, let's not turn this into a political debate. This has nothing to do with politics. This has to do with a family that was kidnapped in Mexico and we're trying to get them back. Let's work together on this thing, not against each other. We've already got the Mexican military alerted as to your family's location. They will get to them. In the meantime, let's keep doing our share here. Try to contact your wife again. Try to get her on the phone and learn more about what happened. Let's stay on top of the situation. That's our job."

"I don't know," Carlos said. "I'm not sure my family needs

the FBI right now to help them find their way, and even less the Mexican police or army, whatever it is. I think what my family needs is me down there. We work well as a team. Lucia's probably out there right now giving them hell. Lucia can be your worst nightmare."

"The best way for your wife to protect your daughter right now is by staying calm and not ruffling any feathers. The men who have kidnapped your family can be savagely cruel."

"The people who kidnapped my wife and daughter are dead, I bet you," Carlos said with an assurance that led Steve to believe that Carlos knew something he didn't.

"How do you know?"

"Intuition. Listen, you're listening to the same thing I'm hearing. You're good at that. Americans are good at eavesdropping and keeping an eye on other people. You would have made great communists, you know that?"

"Oh, stop that bullshit. What? You're not American now all of a sudden? You've been in this country for longer than I've been alive. You can't disown it now."

"I've never disowned it, Steve. There is no Cuban that you find who does not love America. That's why we came here. But I can't forget how the politicians betrayed us and we've had to endure Castro all these years. Do you realize that this very situation that we're living right now with my family would not be happening if the right decision had been made back when? We'd all be in Cuba—Peña, Lucia, my daughter, even me."

"In the little time I've known you I've come to realize how tortured you are by this 'Castromania,' shall we call it? I mean, you connect everything that happens with it. You know, you're a smart man. You've got to let go of that obsession. He's not important. Let it go. We're talking about your family here."

"Lucia and Alicia would not be in this mess if it wasn't for that son of a bitch. It is a curse that follows us Cubans. I can remember my daughter having this natural curiosity about Cuba since she was a little girl. I fought her every step of the way, tried to persuade her not to ever go there, but she got older, and I lost control of her. That's what happened. Her mother did the best she could, and I know Lucia agrees with me. She never would have thought of going back with Castro in power, but with Alicia so desperate to visit the island, she had to act against her own instincts and do the very thing she hates, and that is go to Cuba. All to protect our daughter. She thought of our daughter first and put her pride aside. She did it only to protect her and make sure Alicia would be safe on the island. Now that is what you call a lady. I on the other hand would not give in. My hatred for the system would not let me." Carlos was as close to tears as he could ever get.

"Quit punishing yourself. I understand how you feel. But none of this is your fault. I agree with you there, you've got a dynamite lady for a wife. But you've done nothing wrong. You know what I think? I think you know your wife better than anybody else, and you've come to depend on her. If Lucia had not been there to keep your daughter company on that trip to Cuba, you would have gone. The reason you were able to resist that fateful return was that you could depend on Lucia to look after Alicia. But were it not for your wife, you would have been along on that trip in a heartbeat."

Carlos was thoughtful for a moment. "I'm real worried about my family, real worried. They're out there in the middle of nowhere, probably in danger of getting caught by one of those wild mobs ravaging the country. I don't know." He turned and went into the kitchen.

Peña got up and followed. "Maybe you should try to get some sleep, Carlos. You hardly slept last night. As you said, Lucia got things under control down there. She'll get Alicia into safety in no time and these guys will get them back. You'll see."

Carlos sat by the kitchen island, holding his cell phone. "I was debating whether I should keep working on getting the money ready for the ransom, Peña. I practically have it ready. But at this point it doesn't seem like there's gonna be any need for it. I don't think I'll get another call from these kidnappers. That's pretty much a given now. The thing that I have to figure out now is how to get down there."

"What do you mean, Carlos? What are you thinking?"

"Lucia did her part. She's got herself and our daughter out of captivity. Now someone has to get them out of Mexico and bring them back here. That's my job."

"You're not thinking straight, Carlos. That's suicide. You'd never make it. Let the FBI take care of it. Give these guys a chance. They're working on it."

"The FBI? The FBI? You were out there and heard Steve talking. You see what he plans to do? Nothing. Absolutely nothing. He was even considering me a suspect. Did you see that? That was totally stupid. It shows how off the beat these guys are. And then this thing about calling the Mexican government. What does he think the Mexican government is gonna do? You think they're gonna go out of their way and risk getting a few of their men killed just because two American women tourists have run astray? They are too busy with these cartel wars."

"I think you should listen to Steve."

Carlos was not hearing him. He was constructing a plan. He had already made a decision, as he always did in the middle of a crisis. "You know, I need you to do me a favor—one last favor, that is. I want you to come with me to the new market. I have two Mexican guys working there who just came back from Oaxaca, they were telling me. I think I'm gonna talk to them, and I want you to come along. You're the person I want at that market while I'm gone. You don't need to do anything. Stay by Nick, just help him, and he'll show you how to stay in touch with the other markets from there. I want you to be the link to the whole enterprise while I'm gone. You make the decisions after you check with me. You stay in touch with me twenty-four-hours. You think you can handle that?"

"I'll do anything for you, Carlos, you know that, but where're you going?"

"Guess."

"Don't do it, Carlos. You're gonna make things worse than they already are, and on top of it, you're gonna put yourself in danger. Besides, Steve will never let you walk out of here. You know that. Just let these guys do their job."

"Nah. These guys won't get anything accomplished, Peña. It was a mistake getting them involved to begin with. One thing I would like to do before leaving is knock that guy Cardona on his ass."

"No, let me handle that part."

"All right, Peña. Let's go." Carlos quickly got up from his chair. He suddenly looked refreshed and hopeful. He seemed like a new man.

"How in the world do you think we're gonna walk out of here with these guys around? What are we gonna tell them?" Peña said, leaning forward to prevent being heard by the others.

"We're going to escape," Carlos said. "Let me go to my bedroom for a second to get some things ready. You might as well get that coffee going."

Carlos darted out of the kitchen and walked by the living room where Steve and another agent were studying the Mexico map.

"Where're you going, Carlos?" Steve asked him.

"To my bedroom for a minute, Steve. I'll be back."

Steve made a gesture as if he wanted to keep on talking but Carlos disappeared into the hallway. He got to work quickly. He went into the master bedroom closet and took a long flat box down from the top shelf and retrieved two pistols. He lifted a heavy box from the floor and examined its contents. It was full of different calibers of ammunition. He took some time sorting through the supplies, loads of single bullets for the pistols that were inside small boxes and that he stacked one over the other. Then he gathered the long racks of pointed missiles for his M-16 and folded them carefully into packs. It was going to be hard to pack all this stuff in the car and even harder to get them out of the house without being noticed. He went to the closet and took two small cardboard boxes from the shelf. Inside were two grenades. He would need them too. He reached inside his breast pocket to make sure he had his passport.

The master bedroom was large. It had its own bathroom and walk-in closet. A double mahogany door led into the stairway, and French doors led onto a balcony. Carlos had been deeply involved in the building plans for the house and had insisted on having more than one exit out of every room. It was having that second option that he always thought of. In his mind, you always needed more than one way to do things, more than one way to get in and out. He grabbed the long box with the M-16 inside first and went to what seemed another window in the room. But behind the curtains was a door. He opened it and walked through a dark hallway, carrying the box in under his arm, until he reached the garage. It was another feature of the house that he had insisted on. When you lived with an arsenal in your closet, you needed to have a secret passage to make a fast getaway. He opened the door at the end and found himself outside, by the driveway. Cautiously, he got to his car and placed the box in the back seat. Then he loaded the ammunition box and put the two pistols in the back, covered by his jacket. He had placed the two grenades underneath the driver's seat where they could not be noticed and would have enough cushioning around them. Then he went back in the house and entered the living room.

Steve was on the phone while his aide was sticking two red pegs in the map as if he were playing a game.

"It's now been two hours and I haven't gotten another call. I think I'm gonna get back to my new market and deal with some of the everyday problems. If a call comes in, Peña and I will be in touch."

"Not a good idea, Carlos," Steve said. "You should stay put. What if you miss a call?"

"How can I when you're right here picking them up? Another thing, Steve, I don't need one of your guys with me in my car. If you're going to send someone to keep an eye on me, let him use his own car."

Steve shook his head in dismay. Controlling Carlos was almost as hard as monitoring the situation with his family.

"Well, don't worry. I won't miss any calls. You want some coffee?"

"I'll take some regular coffee, yes. I think Ralph would too."

"You'll have to do with the espresso. It's all we have here. Peña made it. Peña, is it ready? These men are craving coffee."

"Not in particular," Steve murmured, looking at his partner, Ralph. "That stuff you guys drink is like fire."

"I'll pass," Ralph said. "Maybe we can have someone bring us some Dunkin Donuts coffee."

"I can't believe that you, an American family, do not have regular coffee in this house," Steve said.

"No, we all drink the espresso. Never got used to that dirty water you call coffee."

Steve shook his head again. "What is it with you and this cultural bind? You're in America, my friend. Live like an American."

"And you should begin living like the South Floridian that you are. What person in South Florida does not know what espresso is and drink it?"

Peña walked in the room holding a tray with four small cups, steaming with hot coffee. He gave one to Carlos and then offered the rest to Steve and Ralph, who politely declined. Peña took one and set the tray on top of one of the coffee tables in the room.

"It's gonna be a long night," he pointed out. "You might change your mind later about these."

"Let's go, Peña," Carlos said, taking one last sip from his cup and laying it down on the tray. He waited for a reaction from Steve. Would be object to his going? Would he try to force one of his agents on them? "We gotta do what we gotta do."

Steve remained silent. It was an omen, and Carlos, in his own sly way, knew it. Yes he had much to do. He had already planned how he would carry out what he thought of as a rescue. He left the house convinced the men inside would not be able to help him and that he had actually wasted precious time. Before the day was over, he would be on his way to Mexico and would find Lucia and Alicia, even if it cost him his life.

The black Mercedes shot out of the driveway. It went back on the Palmetto Expressway and later got off onto S. W. Fortieth Street, heading toward Carlos's newest supermarket. The whole time, Carlos kept his phone clipped by his belt. Most of his business connections knew not to call him since he had warned them that he needed to keep his phone line free. But every so often, Carlos looked down at his phone as if to verify that no calls had come through although he had the ringer on.

"Are these guys going to be following us?" Peña asked. "It seems like at least Steve does not trust you completely. And if he suspected what you're about to, he'd hit the ceiling. Carlos, Are you sure that you wanna do this?"

"It's the only way. It's the only way I can get my family back."

"Those men down in Mexico who are fighting the drug cartels, they are real professionals. They know what they're doing. What makes you think you can outdo them? You have no expertise. I mean, you're a businessman from Miami who has some knowledge of guns, granted, but that's not enough. You're not trained for this. You're gonna get yourself killed."

"If I get myself killed at least I'll know I died trying to save my family. I can't just sit here and wait for something to happen. Because nothing will, I guarantee you. These guys are not gonna do a thing for me."

"But that's suicide. You can't think that way. You are of more use to your family here, where you can provide for them. I wouldn't be so quick in judging these guys, Carlos. They're doing what they can to help. Besides, what makes you think that you're just gonna show up somewhere in Mexico and bring Lucia and Alicia back without any trouble? Don't you know that there are deadly gangs hanging around the whole place?"

"I'm well prepared," Carlos said smiling.

They had pulled in to the market's parking lot, and Carlos parked the black Mercedes on the side as close to the building as possible. He jumped out of the car and waved for Peña to follow. He went straight into the market's office located on a high platform.

He went inside and spoke to the young woman sitting at a desk. "Estrellita, can you get Guillermo over here?"

"Guillermo? Guillermo, Carlos?"

"Yes. Guillermo, the Mexican."

"All right."

She paged him on the loudspeaker as Peña took a seat next to her and Carlos sat behind another desk, laying his cell phone in front of him on the table. The man who entered the room was small in height and slightly overweight.

"Yes, boss?"

"Hey, Guillermo," Carlos said. "I need your help. Let's go outside."

There was real concern in the man's eyes as he stared at his boss. He had gotten the job two weeks ago, having just arrived from Oaxaca, Mexico, from where he had traveled in his pickup as he had been doing every spring for the past ten years. He had been lucky in landing the job at the new supermarket. His skills as a connoisseur of vegetables and fruits had certainly helped, but Carlos had been emphatic about his requirements. He needed a full-time, year-round helper. The seasonal trips to Mexico would have to stop if he wanted the job. Guillermo had agreed.

"Let's go to the parking lot, come on."

"Is there anything wrong, Mr. Garcia?"

"No, nothing's wrong. Let's go talk outside. Come on."

It was late afternoon, and the always prevalent Miami heat was beginning to set.

"There's a favor I need from you," Carlos said as they walked outside the store. "How's your pickup running?"

"It's good, Mr. Garcia. My pickup is in great shape."

"Where are the Mexican plates for the pickup?"

"I have them, Mr. Garcia. I have them at home."

"Is the paperwork still good for the pickup in Mexico?"

"Oh, yes. I mean, I was going to let it expire this year since

I am not going back to Mexico in the fall, but everything's still good. I got it registered here in Miami now, but the old paperwork is still good."

"Good. I need to borrow your pickup, Guillermo."

Guillermo seemed to hesitate. He was thinking about his job status more than anything else, but now his boss's request sounded like a real intrigue. Carlos wanted his truck? "Well, sure, Mr. Garcia. I have the keys right here."

He reached for the keys from his pants pocket and pulled a key ring with the green, white, and red stripes of the Mexican flag.

"Wait," Carlos said. "Walk me to your truck."

Guillermo's pickup was a blue 2002 Dodge Ram. Carlos checked it thoroughly outside and then went inside the cabin and started the engine. He liked to get a good feel for any car that he drove and imagined how he would fare during the many hours of traveling inside the truck's cabin. But he came out of it with a good feeling.

"How do you think this truck would do on a trip to Mexico?"

"Mr. Garcia, I've taken it to Mexico about five times. Never had a problem."

"All right. Let's go back inside and talk. I wanna borrow your truck to take it to Mexico on a trip. Can I do that?"

"Sure. Yes, sir."

"Let's go talk to the secretary so she can arrange a rental for you. What kind of car would you like to have while I have your truck?"

"No, Mr. Garcia. You don't have to get me any car. I can get by just fine. My brother can bring me to work."

"Nah. We can't do that in Miami, Guillermo. You need a car."

Somewhat dumbfounded, Guillermo followed him

inside the supermarket. Carlos brought him in the office and made him sit next to him at the desk.

"Estrellita, I need you to schedule a Chevy rental for Guillermo," Carlos said, addressing his secretary. "He's gonna need a car for a few days."

She paused and looked at Peña. Something was going on. "Does Guillermo have a license?"

"Of course he does," Carlos replied, not looking at him.

"Well, he can drive a rental without a license, just so you know. He just can't rent a car without a license."

"I'm renting the car," Carlos said. "Besides, Guillermo does have a Florida license. He has been in the United States for many years and has immigrant status. That's how he's able to get in and out so easy."

"Well, Carlos, you'll have to pay extra to allow him to drive as a second driver."

"Rent a Chevy pickup, four wheel drive. That's what he wants. Let me know when I can pick it up."

Carlos went back outside with Guillermo and discussed a few more details about the truck with him. An hour later he was almost ready with the Mexican plates, the registration placed carefully under the seat and an atlas map of Mexico on the passenger seat. It was early in the evening and was still light out. He would prefer to transfer the weapons from the Mercedes into the pickup after dark but time was running out. He felt satisfied with the arrangements he had made and was anxious to get going. He knew it was going to be a dangerous trip, but the sooner he left, the more of a chance of success.

He began to walk back to the supermarket to talk to Peña some more. Only he knew what Carlos was going to do. That's when he heard the ring on his cell phone and picked it up immediately.

"Hello," he said.

"It's me, Carlos, it's me!"

"Lucia, where are you?"

"Carlos, we've made it to this town called Rio Grande. We're at a hotel here, but I don't know how long we can hang around. Carlos, you wouldn't believe what we've been through."

"Is Alicia with you?"

"She's here. She's fine."

"So, that means you're out. You broke free, right?"

"Yes."

Carlos sensed the confidence in her voice and knew then that his premonitions had been right. He was going to ask her how she had escaped but thought better of it. A funny thing went through his mind. The Feds were listening. No, he should talk to his daughter and assure her that everything would be all right. She was probably hysterical and giving her mother a difficult time. Right now, the best way he could help Lucia was by giving their daughter reassurances that she would be safe soon. He spoke to her for a few moments and then asked that she pass the phone back to Lucia. He needed to get more details, and as he spoke to Lucia he walked back to the truck and made notes on the map of everything she said. Then he gave Lucia instructions to stay indoors and not see anyone. After they hung up, he looked up the town of Rio Grande in the region of Sacatecas. He immediately saw that his family was sitting in a trap. The nearest major city was Torreón, or Gomez Palacio, places that probably were hard for Lucia to reach without being detected by some of the ravaging bands now hot after her trail, he was sure. No, the die was cast. He would have to go through Texas and cross the border. He studied the map, not even thinking about the Feds who were now deeply involved and surely would want a say in the matter. When the phone rang he picked it up absentmindedly, not realizing its significance.

"That was good," Steve Hartzman said. "You had them on the phone long enough for us to pick up their spot on the map. They definitely are where they said they were. Come on over right away. We need to discuss this."

"I can't right now, Steve," he said, as he drew a red circle around the small black dot on Highway 49, around the name of Rio Grande on the map.

He had already decided that he would cross into Mexico many miles east of El Paso no matter how dangerous the roads. It would save him precious hours of traveling.

"Right now this is priority, Carlos. You need to come over so we can talk in person."

"I'll be over as soon as I can."

Carlos didn't care what Steve sensed. He was no longer interested in Steve's plans. He concentrated on what he was about to do. It was the best hope for his family.

He tried to cut the conversation short. "I'll call you as soon as I can get back," Carlos said, cutting the call off.

He got back to the store and called Peña onto the main floor. "I'm leaving right away," he began. "If I wait Steve will be here with his aides and stop me. You're the only one who knows where I'll be. I'm giving you the keys to my car. You drive it and stay on top of things around here. I'm not worried about the other markets. Talk to Estrellita and let her know I'll be away for a couple of days. She's my top manager and knows how to run the operation as if it was me. She's done it before. Just hang by her side and help her out. I'll keep in touch. You're going to need to carry a cell phone. I know you don't like them but you need one now so we can communicate. Estrellita will give you one. Here are the keys. Drive slow."

He smiled sarcastically as he handed him the keys to the Mercedes. Peña looked like he was about to cry. "Carlos, why don't you change your mind? You realize what you're doing?"

"I'm the only chance they got, Peña."

"And what am I gonna tell these Fed guys when they come looking for you?"

"You don't know where I am."

"Easy for you to say."

"Come on, Peña. Don't tell me you can't handle the Feds."

Peña was thoughtful for a moment. "I'll tell you who I'm gonna handle—that sleazy bastard Cardona. I'm gonna get him if it's the last thing I do. This is all his fault."

"Don't do anything till I get back. We don't know enough about what's happened. We don't even know that he's involved. This is what I mean about these guys. This guy Hartzman hasn't even questioned Cardona. I mean, at least try to find out who's behind it all. But no, we hear nothing. That's what frustrates me."

"Carlos, you don't know. They're not gonna tell you what they're doing. They may be after Cardona like a house on fire. We just don't know about it."

"Anyway, go inside. I don't want you mixed up in anything. Tell Estrellita to call me on my cell if she needs me. But I doubt she will. She'll know what to do. She is so close to Lucia that she has begun referring to her as my second wife. When no one else can get hold of me, she can. When I get unreasonable, the managers call her and ask her to intercede. She knows my weak side better than anyone else. I admire her. Part of it begins with her name. She has such a Cuban name, like someone who came from a program from the fifties, when the country folk sat around their radios at night to listen to the never-ending-salt poppers. For certain, one of the characters was bound to be named Estrellita."

"All right, I will hang around her. How long will you be gone?"

"Beats me, Peña. You know the mission. It could last two days, a week, a month."

"How should I handle Lucia if she calls?"

"She knows I won't be here. She won't call."

There was no hesitation, but the slow tone of voice left no doubt about Peña's concern. "Be careful," he said.

"Careful is not the word," he said, giving Peña a wink.

Peña walked with him to the pickup, parked next to the Mercedes at the far end of the parking lot.

"You should go inside," Carlos insisted. "I don't want to get you mixed up in anything that might hurt you."

"I'm already involved, Carlos. Besides, you're my friend. What do you need?"

"All right. Make sure no one gets close. I need to shift some things around. I need those keys one more time."

He opened the Mercedes and discreetly began to move his guns to the cabin of the pickup. He did it quickly, knowing that time was of the essence. He knew Steve would soon figure out that something was amiss and he would come looking for him at the supermarket. Later, before reaching the border, he would hide everything in strategic places where they would not be detected. But now, it was time to go.

"Carlos," Peña said, "I know you made up your mind to go and nothing I say will make you change it, but you have to concentrate on getting Lucia and Alicia back, nothing else. Avoid a firefight rather than looking for one. Your goal should be to find the girls and immediately run back. Don't go looking for trouble, Carlos. You can't beat those guys down there."

Carlos listened attentively. He could not deny that there was a little rebellion inside him, a thirst for revenge for what they had done to his wife and daughter. Peña was trying to put his fire out, and he was right. The strategy should be get in and get out quickly. He wanted to think that a confrontation would not necessarily be unwelcome. But that was his cockiness that he recognized should have no place in this venture. Peña was a smart man. He had touched on his Achilles heel, and Carlos could not help but admire the old man one more time. Not only had he proven to be a true friend but wise. There was something about these old Cubans that was never quite understood. They were smart men who had given up everything they once had to come to a new land, give up their entire past, and start over. Anyone who did that had to have a lot of insight.

He reached out to his friend and embraced him, patting the middle of his back. "You're right. Now's not the time to be a cowboy at the expense of my family. Don't worry. I won't even think about it. You'll see me back here in no time."

"Okay." Tears filled the old man's eyes as Carlos got behind the wheel of the pickup and turned the ignition.

Carlos waved at him without opening his window to prevent any further uncomfortable conversation. There was no time. He had to get going.

The map was on the seat of the pickup, but he didn't have to look at it to know the shortest route that would lead him out of Florida and west into Texas. He could easily have installed a GPS but preferred not to. He knew the routes. Besides, there was no guarantee the unit would work in Mexico, and there was no time. He needed to get going.

He took the Florida Turnpike north from 826. From there he planned to take Route 75 north and then Route 10 west. The question was how long he could drive without sleep. He had had little of that in the past two days, and after all, he could not forget the fact that he was carrying weapons in his vehicle. He could not just pull over to the side of the road and catnap as he was used to doing when he drove long distances with Lucia. That was a sticky point between them. Lucia would suggest they book a room at any roadside motel and get some sleep. Carlos on the other hand insisted on driving and getting to wherever they were going as soon as possible. Then Lucia, always the fast sleeper of the two, fell asleep in the passenger seat, sometimes waking and finding herself at a rest stop with Carlos napping behind the wheel.

"A half hour nap is all I need," he would say.

"You're going to kill yourself and me in the process. Why can't we just go to a motel and sleep like normal people? What's the hurry?"

That would be her answer but it would get her nowhere, and because she was such a light sleeper, she would only succeed in getting her husband back on the road, supposedly looking for some lodging, and then she would doze off again, not realizing that her husband had no intention of stopping anywhere.

Carlos was in the vicinity of Orlando when he got the first call. He had expected they would come. He looked at the screen, hoping it would be either of the familiar numbers for Lucia or Alicia, but to his disappointment he noticed a Florida area code. "Hello," he said.

"Carlos, where are you?"

"Steve Hartzman," Carlos thought.

"Out somewhere," he answered.

"I'm at your supermarket. Mr. Peña is in front of me. He has not told me anything, but I have a pretty good idea of what you're doing. Let me give you a warning—"

"Wait, Steve. You're not gonna give me any warnings. I gave you plenty of time to solve my family's situation, and you've brought me nothing but empty promises. Whatever I have to do for my family I'll do, and there's nothing you can tell me or do to prevent that. So instead of you giving me a warning, let me just say that you can do either of two things: go against me or join me. Tell me on whose side you're on."

"Carlos, you don't understand. This has become a Federal investigation now. You can't interfere with it."

"I can do whatever it takes to save my family. You wanna help me? I'll take it. Take one of those nice CEO-type of planes the Feds have and join me in Tallahassee. The two of us can drive to Mexico."

There was a pause on the other end, which Carlos did not interpret as any serious consideration of his proposal. He had little faith in the Feds.

"Carlos, you know I can't do that. Not in any official capacity."

"Then do it in an unofficial capacity," Carlos shot back.

There was another pause on the other end, and Carlos could feel the hesitation. He was going to tell him it was only a fluke, that of course he was not serious. He would say he understood his position and was only daring him. That he wanted to see how far Steve would go. He wanted to see if he had guts, but Steve spoke first.

"I couldn't do that, Carlos. I have orders to follow. I'm a professional and have to behave like one. What I must do is to urge you to turn around and come back home. You don't belong out there. This is not a job for you. It's in the hands of the law at this point, and that is how it's going to remain.

I gotta tell you that if I have to get some officers out there to stop you, I can easily do it. And Carlos, it's not gonna be pretty when they apprehend you. Let's not make this harder than it already is."

"Steve, why don't you use your time more fruitfully, like trying to figure out where my family is for instance, ah?"

"We know where your family is."

"Then why aren't you doing anything to get them back? What's your plan, Steve? I haven't heard any action from you since this whole thing started on how to get them back except to say that you can't get down there, that Mexico is another country, blah, blah, blah. It's the same old story with you guys, Steve, all talk and no action. If you had not become involved in this thing, maybe I would have my wife and daughter with me by now."

"I'm telling you one last time, Carlos, turn back! This is my case."

"Like hell it is! If you really have any guts, meet me on the way. Otherwise, don't call me again."

Carlos disconnected the call and put the phone next to him on the seat. Lucia could be calling at any moment, he thought. He would drive as far up as he could. Maybe he could get out of Florida before he had to stop. He had just taken the Florida Turnpike and stopped for a toll. He must be careful not to get stopped for speeding. If Steve was serious, the word would be out for the troopers to stop him. But if they were looking for a Mercedes, Carlos thought, they had another thing coming—unless of course Peña had failed him and gave him away. But something told him the old man was too smart for the FBI. An old Cuban dinosaur who had lived under Castro's iron fist and survived was way too much for any gray-suit wearing Federal officer, Carlos thought, as if to reinforce his own beliefs that the Cuban exile experience was one of the giant milestones in human history.

"I'll bet I know what Peña did," he uttered. "He probably hid the black Mercedes in the back of the building as soon as I left, anticipating that Steve and his boys would show up."

At that moment the phone rang, and this time he did not look at the screen. It had to be Lucia. He picked up.

"Carlos, it's me."

"Where are you, Lucia? Where are you exactly?"

"I'm at this little motel in Rio Grande. It's called La Cantina. It's in the middle of the main drag—at least I think it's the main drag. We're about to grab something to eat. Where are you?"

Carlos knew the Feds were listening. He could not tell her he was on the road. But the two had developed ways of communicating with each other in furtive ways when it was needed.

"All I can say is that Castro is still ruling our lives, Lucia. We still have to live as if we were in Cuba," he complained. "I'm still in Miami. But you just stay put, we'll get you out."

Lucia knew better than anyone else her husband's obsession with the dictator's system. He blamed everything on it, even small daily events. If the air conditioner at one of his stores shut down unexpectedly, it was Castro's fault. If business suddenly became sluggish or a hurricane hit, it must somehow be linked to their past in Cuba. But for him to start a sentence with such a prologue meant only one thing: that someone else was listening, like the experiences they had lived in their native island when they were kids. Someone else was always listening. You had to watch what you said. Carlos could not say where he was, but if Lucia was to bet, her husband was flying through the Florida turnpike right now, trying to get to Texas so he could cross the border into Mexico. She knew her husband.

Chapter Seven

Lucia and Alicia walked into the restaurant the hostess at their motel had recommended. It was a stucco building off the main road, with one large room of about ten tables, all covered with red tablecloths. There were no more than three customers inside, all men, scattered at different tables. After what seemed like a long while a young woman came to their table and asked them in Spanish what they wished to order. Lucia tried to think about Mexican dishes and held her hand up as a sign to Alicia to wait.

"I'd like some *tortillas* with *frijoles* and *guacamole*. I think she'll have some *quesadillas* with pork shops if you have them."

Alicia was going to protest but Lucia held her hand up again.

"We have them," the young woman said. "You want something to drink?"

"I'll have a *jarrito, tamarindo* flavor. Bring the same for her," Lucia, said slowly, aware that the waitress was coyly looking at her swollen jaw.

"Mom, since when do you order for me?"

"Believe me, Alicia, I got the mildest things for you. I don't want you making a spectacle out here and vomiting or something."

"Mom, for someone so cunning you can be so cruel. I don't eat any of this stuff."

"Aren't you hungry?"

"Starved."

"Then you'll eat it. I made sure you got no spice. You know that everything is spicy around here. Just eat. You have to eat and gain your strength back. Then we have to get some sleep."

"What are we gonna do? Shouldn't we just keep going?"

"I think we're gonna stay put down here. Your father knows where we are, and he said he's coming to get us."

"But how's he gonna get down here?"

"I don't know. But if I know your father, he's on his way. We'll call him again when we get back to the room. For now, keep your eyes open and don't make a whole lot of conversation. I don't know who's who around here."

The waitress came back with their food and proved Lucia right. No sooner had the plates touched the table than Alicia began devouring the *tortillas* with *frijoles*. She gave no hint that the spice bothered her. Lucia looked discreetly sideways to see how the other customers might interpret it, for she quickly came to the conclusion that everyone around here knew each other and were somehow connected with all the violence. Perhaps she was unfair in making such a harsh assessment, but it was a strategic one. If she judged everyone a suspect, she would always be one step ahead of them and that was the idea: stay ahead and survive. She visualized the older men in their chairs, sipping on their beer as being collaborators with the local gangs or cartels, probably sizing her and her daughter up to try to determine their purpose here. Were they some rich tourists merely passing through? But what about the fact that they spoke Spanish? That sure gave them something to think about.

"Mom, even if Dad could get here, wouldn't it make more

sense for us to simply drive out of here and get to the nearest airport and leave? Or what about the police? Can't we get the police?"''

"Actually, Alicia, I'm debating that myself. I want to call Carlos as soon as we get back to the hotel, but I wanted us to eat first. We also need to get some sleep. I'm just a little afraid. As far as calling the police, no, I'm afraid that first, there's no police around here, and second, they're so corrupt that they're bound to be worse than the kidnappers themselves."

"You're afraid that these guys might find us, Mom?"

"That, yeah." She wasn't telling her about her biggest fear. There was a strong possibility that they would never be able to make it out of the town. Their car was marked and the word would have gotten around by now whose car they were driving. If they went on any highway, they ran the risk of being spotted and massacred. But then it was also not very safe to stay put. What if they were spotted here? She needed to talk to Carlos again. She had to be sure of what to do.

Her thoughts suddenly veered to her cell phone. The hotel receptionist had finally found her a charger, and she had left the phone connected to it. She needed to have it ready in case they decided to leave. The waitress came over their table again. She placed the soft drink bottles on the table.

"She was hungry," the waitress said, smiling. "She didn't wait for her pork chops."

"She likes *frijoles*," Lucia said. "I'll have one of those pork chops myself. Alicia, do you mind if I take one?"

"No, Mom, go right ahead."

"Where are you from?" the waitress asked.

"We're Cubans," Lucia replied, reaching under the table to touch her daughter's lap and get her attention.

She said it loud enough so others in the restaurant could hear her. Lucia knew there would be a follow-up question. It was inevitable for people to ask where Cubans came from since the island's population had been so split by the fifty-year-old exodus.

"Cubans? Cubans from where, Miami or Cuba?"

"Cuba."

Again, Lucia tapped her daughter's lap.

"We're here on a medical mission. We're headed for Chihuahua."

She did not know her Mexican geography very well but had reviewed the map in the room and Chihuahua stuck in her mind. It was north.

"*Señora*, your face looks very swollen. Are you all right?"

"Oh, yes. I hit the bed post with my chin, almost fractured the bone but I'm all right."

"Are you a doctor by any chance? I know that your government sends doctors here."

"I am, and my daughter here will be one soon too, so the government allowed her to come with me."

The girl stood still for a moment, tray in hand. She was short and dark-skinned. She was suddenly staring at Lucia with imploring eyes. "Ay, *doctora*, do you think you could do me a favor? I would be so grateful if you could come to my house. It's about my daughter."

"What about your daughter?"

"She's five months old and has been running a high fever for two days."

"Have you taken her to a hospital?"

The girl shook her head, fighting tears.

Despite her anxiety, which was now running high, Lucia took pity on her. She could see it was a money problem.

"I live all alone with my mother and have no money for a private clinic. The hospital doesn't help much. I've asked my boss to help me, and he said he would but I …"

"I don't carry a lot of medical supplies with me, but of

course I could look at her for you. I'll be glad to. Do you live far from here?"

"No, no. A few meters off the main road. I would really appreciate it." Tears were now rolling down her cheeks, and she pulled her apron to wipe them. Lucia handed her a napkin.

"Where's the nearest pharmacy?"

"Down the road from here there's one."

"I'll need you to show me. We need to go there first and then you can take me to your house so I can treat her. Alicia, we're gonna have to finish supper fast, honey."

"No, no, *doctora*, I don't mean to trouble you. Please finish your meal. Can I bring you anything else?"

"No. Get ready to come with us."

Alicia was dumbfounded. She looked at her mother in dismay, afraid to speak. "Mom, how are you going to treat her daughter? You're not a doctor," she whispered.

"But I've been a mother, Alicia. I know about babies."

Alicia shook her head in disbelief. "I can't believe it."

"Believe it. Listen, we have to face the situation. I can't refuse. Don't you understand? Let's go, come on. Let's get going."

"I haven't finished."

"I never knew that you were fond of *tortillas*. What's come over you?"

"I'm hungry. We haven't eaten. Who knows when we'll eat again?"

"Don't worry about that. I'll stock up on food if we have to drive out of here. But that girl has a sick baby. If she doesn't get attention, the baby could die. We may be her only chance. Maybe God put us here for a reason."

"Mom, you're not a doctor. What can you do?"

"I'm not a doctor but like I said, I raised a baby. It's common sense, Alicia. Someday you'll get to experience

189

it yourself. A mother always knows what to do and if she doesn't she learns. She learns very quickly."

Alicia sipped from her soft drink bottle and smirked. "What is this stuff? It's so sour."

"You've had it before. It's all over Miami. The supermarkets sell it in a can. Goya makes it."

"What's it called again?"

"*Tamarindo*. It is a tropical fruit. It is very sour, you're right about that, but only in its original form which would be in pulp. The one you're having has been processed. It's more like any other soft drink."

"I'm so thirsty, I'll drink anything."

Lucia got up from her chair and waved to the waitress, who kept talking to a man standing by a door at the back of the room. She came racing toward Lucia, her face still wet from tears.

"How much do we owe you, honey? I want to pay you and get going to my hotel so I can return and get you. I'll only be a few minutes."

"My boss is giving me a hard time about leaving. I'm telling him that I would be right back. It's because of the hour. We get busy here in the evening. Maybe if you spoke to him, *doctora*."

"Me? What could I do?"

"He might listen to you. You're a doctor." She pointed to the short man with straight black hair standing by the door. Lucia sized him up and wondered what she could say to persuade him. She still wasn't sure as she crossed the floor guided by the waitress.

"My name is Lucia Garcia," Lucia said, extending her hand to him. "Nice to meet you."

"Did you like the food?" the man asked, ignoring her greeting.

"Oh, yeah, it was great. You know, I was just talking

to this young lady here, and she told me she has a very sick child at home who has not been medically treated. Because I am a doctor, she's asked me to go look at her baby, and I was hoping you would let her go for a few minutes. I will bring her back here myself."

"You're a doctor from Cuba, ah?"

"Yes, that's right. I am from Cuba."

"We don't see many Cubans in these parts. They stay mostly in the federal district. I've heard of some of them being sent to Doahuila and the Sierra Madre to treat the poor people. What is it? Castro has too many doctors in that island?"

Lucia found his irony distasteful, but the worst part was that she would actually have to stick up for Castro's idea of exporting medicine, although she knew it was one of his shrewdest propaganda moves. But she had no choice. This man seemed to be portraying a certain disdain for her nationality and anybody else who wasn't like him. Perhaps he was just a miserable, unhappy fellow who hated everyone around him.

"Oh, it's not like that at all. Doctors go out to help people, young ones, old ones, everybody. That's why we are here. Right now I'm a little concerned about your waitress's baby and I'd like to help."

"Ahhhh," he murmured with a tone of abhorrence.

"And your name is, sir?" Lucia asked him, putting her hand out to shake his again.

He didn't refuse to shake it but did it without looking at her.

"It doesn't matter. Go ahead. Go see her baby. You have a car, no?"

"Yes."

"Well, just drive down the street from here," he said, pointing to his right with his finger. "Take the first dirt road you see on your left and stop at the wooden house that's painted green on the left. It's about one kilometer in. You don't need her," he said, pointing to the waitress with his chin. "Just knock on the door and someone will answer. If you're a doctor you should know how to do those things. Another thing, *doctora*, don't let anybody else beat you up. Your face looks like a coconut."

"No one beat me up," Lucia answered with disdain.

Lucia was in shock at his lack of compassion. She felt rage and felt an urge to slap him, but of course she had to hold back. She walked toward the young waitress, who was standing a few feet away.

"I'll do my best to find your house and treat your baby. Where do I find the pharmacy?"

"Down the street from here. It's on the left hand side too."

"All right. Well, I'll check with you later. Let's go, Alicia."

They went to the register, and Lucia paid for their meal. She went back to their table for a moment and left what she thought would be a sizeable tip for the waitress. She felt the boss's gaze on her and turned to look at him as she began walking out. He had a deadpan face, looking serious yet aloof. But what she noticed most was that look of loathing on him. Whatever he had heard, whatever he knew about her, he did not like. Perhaps he was a grouch; perhaps simply a hateful person or maybe even he was somehow connected to the kidnappers. This last thought got her nervous and she held her daughter's hand. All throughout the evening she had not felt nervous and acted almost normal, but now a new twist had been thrown into her lap. She had been asked to help a sick baby. The girl waiting on the few tables of the scanty restaurant had nothing and was in danger of losing her infant. Lucia, on the other hand, had everything. She could just walk away from the whole thing, call Carlos, and hide away somewhere to wait for him. She could save herself and her daughter.

"Mom," Alicia said nervously as they reached the Blazer. "Let's call Dad and get out of here, please. Let's not get mixed up in any of that stuff."

She did not reply. She drove back to their motel and parked the Blazer across from their room. She checked the rear seat to make sure none of the guns had been touched. "Let's go inside and call your father."

"Carlos, it's me," she said from her cell, once inside their room. She had decided to use her cell. She guessed as she began talking to her husband that she needed to know that their cell phones could reach each other. She had decided they could not stay at the motel.

"Where are you, Lucia? Where are you exactly?" he asked.

She described her whereabouts to her husband. There was another reason she had used her cell instead of the phone in the room—she didn't trust the woman at the hotel's reception. She gave her an uncomfortable feeling. It seemed like these people were all connected, like some kind of a sect. The help at the hotel, the people at the restaurant: Were they all part of the same thing? But she hit a brick wall when it came to the young waitress. She seemed like such a helpless little thing facing that ogre of a man who ran the place. She could not say no to her. She was not sure why.

Then she heard her husband complain that he still had to live as if he were in Cuba. Here he went again, she thought, going into one of his typical, grumbling monologues about Castro. Nothing had changed, she thought, except when she heard him say "we'll get you out." She was going to ask him who was "we" but stopped herself. Something was up. His words went through her mind again like a flash, and this time she found them different. Living as if they were in Cuba meant you had to watch what you said. Use doubletalk to communicate. Yes, her husband had said he was still in Miami, but she knew better. She could see him now, traveling north on the Florida Turnpike, probably armed to the teeth. No, she could not leave. She had to stay put.

"All right, you want to take a shower before we go try to find that girl's house?"

"Mom, you're gonna go to her house? Why don't we just get out of here right now?"

"Let's go to the pharmacy and buy her some medications. She needs help."

"Let's just get out of here."

"We can't."

"Why not?"

"Because your father's coming to get us. Come on then, let's go."

Lucia pulled her cell phone from the chord and put it in her front pocket. She was still carrying her .45 in the back of her waist, strapped under her belt.

They got inside the Blazer and she drove through the main street in town, looking for the pharmacy that the waitress had mentioned. She saw the unlit sign on the opposite side of the road as she passed it and had to turn around and come back. She parked the Blazer off the road and went inside with Alicia.

"This is a pharmacy?" Alicia whispered in astonishment as they entered.

Lucia spoke in Spanish and stopped at the door. "This is not Miami, honey. And if you think this is bad, be thankful we never made it to Cuba. The pharmacies down there are empty shelves."

"I wish we were there instead of here."

"Act like an adult, Alicia."

Lucia walked up to the counter. The place actually seemed relatively modern and reminded her of some old mom-and-pop store from the sixties. There were no greeting cards for sale, no small tokens for gifts or scented candles, only medicine shelves all the way around.

A short woman wearing glasses came to the rear counter and spoke to her with a heavy Mexican accent. "*Señora?*"

"What do you have for a fever? It's for a baby."

"If it's for a baby you're better off with an analgesic like Tylenol or Tempra. How old is the baby?"

"A few months."

"Oh, then I'll get you some baby Tylenol. It has a smaller dosage."

"Don't worry about that," Lucia said, trying to sound professional. "I'll break them up to bring the dosage down. There are other things I need too."

"All right," the woman said, turning away.

She came back with a bottle of capsules.

"What else did you need?"

"Do you have any ice? I think I'm gonna need a couple of packs. I see you have those small blankets," Lucia said, pointing to one of the shelves. I'll take one of those. Also, a thermometer, and"—she took her time to say it, wondering how the woman would react—"a stethoscope. I need a stethoscope."

Lucia was thinking about her credibility. No one was going to think much of her if she did not walk into that house wearing a stethoscope—not that she had any idea on how to use one. She paid for all her supplies as she listened to the woman ramble on. "Another ten minutes, you would have missed us. I know it's a Monday but I usually close by 7:00. I figure nothing's going to happen after 7:00 and if it does, that's why they got hospitals."

"Not many of them around here," Lucia said daringly.

195

The woman did not answer. She gave her change and put the supplies in a brown bag. Then as if she had been thinking it over, she spoke. "Well, this is the countryside. People want the countryside to be like the big cities. And that can't be. We have to live with what we have. If people want modern hospitals and clinics they can always go live in one of the big cities like Guadalajara or even Mexico City. Here, we're small. We gotta do with what we have."

Lucia concluded she was harmless, perhaps proud but incapable of hurting anyone. If she had to bet, she was just as afraid of being mugged or kidnapped as Lucia was. This only confirmed her worst fears. The area was infected by smugglers and kidnappers. She closed the front door of the store, and immediately after she noticed the shade being pulled down behind the middle glass. Then she looked inside the bag and examined the supplies she had purchased. Everything seemed to be an antique for some reason. Perhaps they had been sitting on the shelf for ages. The thermometer was a regular one, inappropriate for a baby and she hesitated. But no, it would have to do. She could not afford to waste any more time. Her daughter did have a point.

"Mom, why did you have to get this?" Alicia asked her in the car, pulling the stethoscope out of the shopping bag. "You're nuts. You don't even know how to use it."

"Leave it alone. Anybody can use a stethoscope. Besides, that's not why I bought it. Don't you see?"

"No, I don't see anything. I don't see why you have to spend the little money we have to buy something totally useless."

"Because back there at that restaurant there is a young mother in fear of losing her baby and she needs hope right now, more than anything else. So I'm doing all I can for her, which is to portray myself as the doctor she thinks I am, even though I am far from being one, and treat her daughter as best I can and make her feel good. It's the least I can do."

"Yeah, but you're putting us in danger, Mom."

"Alicia, stop! Stop that right now! Haven't you learned anything from this experience? Haven't you seen how fragile life can be, how fortunate we are to live where we live? Doesn't the fact that someone needs our help mean anything to you?"

"I just don't want us to waste any time."

"Stop it! Stop it right now!" Lucia drove away and she headed back toward the restaurant. Then she saw a dirt road off the main road, just like the man had described, and she turned onto it. It was bumpy and made the Blazer shake up and down, reminiscent of their previous arduous trip after their escape.

It was getting dark, so she slowed down. There were no houses on either side of the road, so when she spotted the first one she was sure that was it. She stopped and stuck her head out the driver's window. In the dim light of the evening she could still tell the colors apart. No, this was not it. It was not green. She moved down the road and then she saw it. It was more like a shack, built with thin wood and a flimsy roof of zinc tiles that immediately brought her back memories of her childhood in Cuba. She remembered houses like this one in the countryside she visited as a young girl. She came to a full stop when she became convinced of the color. Then she turned the Blazer onto the dirt path that led up to the house.

"Let's go," she said to her daughter.

Alicia got out of the car hesitatingly, still doubting her mother. But Lucia walked as if she did not have a worry in the world, carrying the brown paper bag with medicines she had bought at the pharmacy. She had hung the stethoscope around her neck to make herself look more professional. She knocked on the wooden front door. Despite the hour, she did not see any sign of light inside, and total silence followed.

Then suddenly a short woman answered the door.

"I am the doctor that the waitress sent to examine the baby," she said in Spanish.

The woman looked humbly at her, in apparent surprise. "You are a doctor?"

"Yes."

"I did not know you were coming. Norma did not say. Please wait, let me get the baby."

It was then that Lucia came to realize that she had not even learned the waitress's name. Norma, that must be it.

"The boss at the restaurant won't let her come," Lucia said.

The woman rushed back from one of the rooms, carrying a baby wrapped up in a white sheet.

"Oh, that evil man. My poor daughter has the misfortune of having to work for him. And to think that he's the father. He won't even lift a finger to help his own daughter. *Ay, doctora*, please come inside."

A scene began to unfold in Lucia's mind, one that perhaps would have been unlikely the target of attention by any other woman who found herself in her present circumstances. But such was the strength of her character. She noticed the misery in the flimsy surroundings and felt the pain that the young woman whose name she had just learned was experiencing. She could see the face of the grotesque man at the restaurant, ignoring her handshake and giving her sketchy directions, almost unwilling, and felt repugnance at the thought of his abuse over his young employee—the mother of his baby, no less.

She followed the short woman into a narrow room with a small crib where the woman placed the baby.

"Let me see," Lucia said. She touched the baby's forehead

with the palm of her hand and felt the heat. What alarmed her most was the lack of reaction in the poor child, no crying or cringing, even after she funneled the thermometer through her lips.

"How long has the baby been running a fever?"

"It's been about three days, *doctora*."

The woman sobbed as Lucia placed the stethoscope on the baby's chest. Lucia had never before used one but had seen it done so many times that she felt confident she could find what she was looking for. Then she realized she did not know what she needed to check—the heartbeat, breathing? She listened attentively and felt the light, fast thumping of the baby's heartbeat, but she reasoned that what she needed to listen to was in the airwaves to see if there was congestion. She moved the stethoscope to other areas of the chest, and as she did she decided that the heartbeat was indeed way too fast. What did that mean?

She signaled the woman to turn the baby around and then began to examine the baby's back. She could not tell at first but eventually heard the crackling breathing of the small lungs and knew that there was real danger. She pulled the instrument off her ears.

"We gotta get this baby to a hospital," she said intuitively to the woman. "I'm almost sure she has pneumonia."

"But how, *doctora*? How? We have no money, no way to travel anywhere. Can you do something?"

Lucia reached inside the bag and grabbed the bottle of baby aspirins she had purchased at the pharmacy.

"Can you get some water, please?" she said to the woman as she reached for the baby. "Go get me some water in a glass. We'll have to dissolve the medication in water and feed it to the baby with a spoon. Go ahead, get me some water."

She followed the woman into another room and split one of the pills into a half on a table and then crunched it into powder. She mixed it with the water and slowly fed it to the baby while the woman held her.

There was no tub in the house, so she asked the woman to bring hand towels with wet cold water. She washed the baby's body with the towels and kept repeating the procedure over and over. Alicia kept standing behind her, amazed by her mother's abilities that she never knew she had.

"Her temperature is down to one hundred. Oh, excuse me, thirty-eight," Lucia said, converting Fahrenheit into Celsius faster than she could ever have imagined possible.

The mild-mannered woman before her seemed innocent enough, but she could repeat what she'd just heard to someone who might find it suspicious. If Lucia was a doctor from Cuba as she had claimed, she was definitely using the wrong rector scale.

"Is that still not too high, *doctora?*"

"Yes, it's still high, but it's gone down. We've gotten it down four degrees almost. That means that what we're doing is working, but she needs more than this. She needs other medications that I don't carry with me. We have to get help."

"But *doctora*, what can I do?"

"Where's the nearest hospital?"

"Oh, I don't know *doctora*. I wouldn't even know how to get to a hospital. There's a clinic in town."

Lucia stood quiet for a moment. She watched the woman holding the child and thought about what she was going to do. She decided she would work a little more on the child to get her temperature down to normal. Maybe she could.

It was close to midnight when she and Alicia left the humble house. There was still no sign of Norma, but the baby's temperature was under control and Lucia could see that Alicia needed sleep. She told the woman where she was staying and to call on her if she needed her help through the night.

They drove back to the motel and parked in front of the room. She put Alicia to bed first and waited a few minutes before going back to the car to bring the guns in. She placed them underneath her bed, except for the .45, which she placed under her pillow. She lay in bed and realized how tired she was. It was not more than a minute before she was asleep in the dark room with Alicia lying on the next bed.

She woke up to the touch of the cold steel barrel of an M-16 pressed tightly against her neck. The pressure made it difficult to breathe, and she actually swiveled her head back and forth, trying to shake it off in her sleep until it got so tight that it woke her up.

"Wake up, you lousy warmonger. Isn't that what Castro calls you Yankee lovers? You think you could fool us with your theatrics last night? So, you're a doctor, ah? A doctor from Cuba? What's your specialty? Killing young Mexicans with a double shot to the head?"

The man was standing next to her bed, looking down at her as he pointed the weapon at her neck. He had long, frizzled black hair and big gaping teeth that Lucia kept looking at as she began to realize her precarious situation. They had found her. She instinctively tried to move her head sideways to check on Alicia, but the man shoved the barrel so hard into her neck that it made it impossible for her to move.

"Don't you move, you little *jinetera* or I'll blow your brains out."

It struck her as odd that the man spoke with a Cuban accent, had even called her *jinetera*, a Cuban slang word meaning whore, but she tossed the thought aside. Although she could not move her head, she could see it was daylight. Had she been sleeping that long?

"So you thought you could just walk away and leave, ah? You think we're not for real, is that it? And what about your husband? What kind of a man is he that he abandons his wife and daughter in a kidnapping and doesn't move a finger to get them back? You're married to that scumbag? Anyway, get up! Slowly now. I got you right under the barrel, remember. One false move and you're history. Rodolfo! Get over here! Come on!"

She began getting up as he pulled the gun's barrel back slightly, waving at her with his other hand. She got as far as sitting on the bed when another man entered the room.

"Yeah, I'm here," the other man said.

He was short and chubby and was carrying a long weapon slung across his shoulder. Lucia tried to look at him but the man stuck the gun to the side of her neck.

"Where's my daughter?" Lucia asked, alarmed.

"Don't worry about your daughter," he said. "Worry about yourself. Not that it's gonna do you any good. You're worth nothing right now. You're probably worth more dead than alive. Look around," he said to Rodolfo. "There's gotta be guns in the room. Come on! Move!"

The man called Rodolfo put one knee on the floor to peek under the bed. Lucia's heart seemed to skip a beat. She had not thought of it last night. Hiding guns under the bed was as bad as hiding cash under the mattress. That was the first place to look.

"We got a stash of guns here, Beto," Rodolfo said, looking up from his kneeling position on the floor.

"I knew it. How stupid. It had to be a woman. Listen up!" he yelled, addressing Lucia. "You're gonna get up slowly and walk toward me. Then you're gonna sit down on this chair," he said, pointing to the makeup seat in front of the mirror. "You come slowly now, come on!"

Lucia quietly followed his directions. Her agitation was

due mainly to not knowing where her daughter was and how she had not heard them when they picked her up, if they picked her up.

"Where's my daughter?" she repeated—and then out of nowhere the words came as they had before when the others had held her in captivity. She cried, "You ugly looking creature. You have teeth like a monkey."

"Shut up! Sit down and shut up! Or do you want me to make your face any worse? It looks pretty bad right now."

She was going to respond when she heard the shuffling of feet and saw Alicia coming into the room, followed by a man who held her by the neck. Her arms were bound, and they had tied a red bandana around her mouth to gag her. Lucia felt a tremendous relief when seeing her but saw the terror in her daughter's eyes.

The man who brought her made her stop, and he dragged a chair next to Lucia. He forced Alicia to sit. Then he untied the bandana and pulled it out of her mouth. Alicia broke down.

"Alicia, calm down honey. It'll be all right," Lucia said.

"Like hell it will be all right," the man called Beto said. "Now, tie her up!" he yelled to the one who had brought Alicia in.

The man positioned himself behind Lucia and pulled her arms behind her back. He slipped plastic zip-tie handcuffs around her wrists, which he adjusted and then checked to make sure they were tight enough. Beto lowered his gun. Rodolfo had gone around the bed to retrieve the guns and was placing them on the floor behind him one by one. He also retrieved an ammunition box and loose bullets from under the bed.

"All right, Rodolfo, get the others! Come on!"

Beto took a moment, watching the guns stacked on the floor next to the bed.

"I've got to admit you got some guts, you lousy whore. You know that? You got some guts!"

"Asshole!" she said.

"And you got a mouth too. So far you've been lucky nobody has shut it for you, but I tell you something—I'm gonna put you in your place, you bitch."

The move was unexpected. He struck Lucia with his open hand on the side of her mouth. It was not a very hard blow but it tore open her upper lip. The impact thrust Lucia's head to the side and brought back the jaw pain like a bolt of lightning. She felt the blood spill out of the corner of her mouth and again felt that anger that she could not control.

"This is how you have to prove your manhood, scum. You have to hit a woman while she's tied because you're too afraid to handle her. What a poor excuse for a man. Get my hands untied and see."

"Shut up! Shut up!" He slid the gun sling across his back to give himself more balance and swung at her with his right hand. This time he struck her on the right cheek with much more impact. The punch knocked Lucia off the chair, sending her to the floor and the chair flipping behind her. She lost consciousness as she fell but regained it right away. The first thought that came to her mind as she came to was the gun. She had watched Rodolfo stash the two M-14s and the ammunition from under the bed and then walk away. He had missed her .45, which was hidden under the pillow. If she could only get hold of it. She felt a sharp pain on the left side of her face and slowly sat up on the floor.

"Beto, stop it! What are you doing?"

Rodolfo came hurriedly back into the room, followed by several other people. To her amazement, Lucia saw Norma, the waitress, walking behind him, her hands tied behind her back and the short woman Lucia had been with the night before at the house. She came in behind Norma, carrying her baby in her arms. Then two other armed men followed behind the women. Rodolfo pointed the women to the other bed in the room and had them sit down on opposite sides.

"Is everybody here now?" Beto asked.

"Yeah, that's all of them," Rodolfo said.

"So, *doctora*, aren't you surprised to see your patient here?" Beto asked. "See what you've done now? You made two other people hostages. No, I take that back, three. We have that baby here."

"You worthless piece of shit!" Lucia yelled out at him.

"Do you want me to spill your brains out right here now? Wouldn't you rather wait to see? Maybe we won't kill you."

"Let those women and the baby go. They have nothing to do with anything. That baby needs medical attention."

"Yeah, I'll say. She needs real medical attention and not a fake doctor. Lady," he said, addressing himself to the woman carrying the baby, "did you know this woman is not a doctor? Did you know that? And she's treating your baby as if she knew what she was doing. Good thing you picked up on it. She would have probably killed your baby."

The woman said nothing. She merely stared his way and then toward Lucia.

"Put that baby down," Beto said. "Go ahead, put him or her, whatever it is, on the bed. Come on."

"Sir, the baby is very warm again ... I ..."

"Put him down, I said. Put him down right now. Rodolfo, tie her up."

"No, *señor*, leave the baby with me. I'll do whatever you want. The baby is very ill. She needs someone to hold her."

"Shut up, old fool. I don't care if the baby lives or dies. Don't you see it doesn't matter?"

"Leave them alone, pig!" Lucia yelled from the floor.

Beto seemed to lose his senses. He walked toward Lucia and pulled her up. He slapped her on each side of the face, making her head swing from side to side, and then pushed her toward the bed and kicked her from behind. She landed on the bed, face down, and she rolled slowly to face him. Alicia's hysterical screams filled the room.

"Shut up, you little whore!" Beto yelled to Alicia. "And you, this is the last time I'll say it. One more word out of you and I'll shoot you, you got that? No, better yet, I'll kill this ugly bitch," he said, and stuck the M-16's barrel on Alicia's neck.

Alicia was drowning in tears, her eyes bulging from the effort not to speak, afraid to make Beto madder. For the first time, Lucia fought her instincts. She found herself in an interesting position, she thought. Unknowingly, Beto had delivered her near the spot where she had hidden her .45, precisely where she would have wanted to be. She thought of ways to reach the gun, but when she tried to move her wrists, she felt the tight grip of the plastic handcuffs binding her. She could not move her hands. She continued to think. Beto looked at her again, and seeing that she was quiet, he went about setting order with the others in the room.

"Rodolfo, make that baby quiet down. Do something."

"What am I gonna do? What the heck do I know about babies?"

Rodolfo had snatched the small bundle made up of a blanket wrapped around the infant from the woman, who remained sobbing at the edge of the bed. The baby was crying hysterically, and he laid it on the bed near the old woman.

"Now you don't move, you hear?" he said to her.

Lucia, meanwhile, had dragged herself to the headboard of the bed and slowly sat up. Beto gave her a glance. He noticed her bloody mouth and the swollen cheek and did not care. Of what danger could she be? He turned to the others and began barking orders about what they must do, who they must call. Lucia squeezed her tied hands under the pillow cautiously, trying not to show any movement, until her fingers felt the butt of the gun. She was thinking rationally about how she would go about shooting Beto. She wanted him dead more than any of the others, but it would be a real feat if she could accomplish it. Gosh, her hands were tied behind her back, which meant she would first have to get a firm hold of the gun and then swivel her body sideways and fire without looking at her target. It was pretty farfetched—not to mention the consequences it could bring to her and the other hostages in the room. But she did not think about that. It had to be done.

She concentrated on Beto and his movements. Actually, he presented an easy target. He had a big bulky midsection and moved quite clumsily, as if his body were too heavy for him to carry, and he seemed to linger in the same spot despite his awkward movements. She drew an invisible line from her position to his with her eyes and tried to figure the angle. She concluded it had to be about forty-five degrees, which meant she would have to aim, tilting the gun upward.

She looked at the other men in the room and waited. Rodolfo walked around the bed toward the others in the back to fetch a string handcuff to tie the old woman. This was the moment, she thought. Beto's back was facing her. Her two hands got a firm hold of the butt of the .45, and she pulled it from under the pillow. And then, very deliberately and with tremendous serenity, she rolled herself sideways, twisting her head back to see her target. She sloped the gun upward a bit and pressed the trigger. She struck him on the shoulder, and he froze. She moved the gun down a bit, and a second later fired it again. This time she got him in the center of his back. No doubt the bullet would penetrate his heart. The thing to do now was to create mayhem and confusion among the others and hit another if lucky.

She rolled on the bed and dropped to the floor, firing

aimlessly toward the other men, who had yet not realized the full extent of what had happened. One the bullets grazed Rodolfo. The others traveled above their heads.

"Alicia, get down!" she yelled from the floor. "Take his knife and drag yourself to me. You ladies, get down on the floor, fast!"

"Mom, where? What knife?"

"The one he's got on his waist, Alicia! Get it fast!" She was lying on the floor, sore from the fall and still holding the .45 with both hands. There was a burst of gunfire from the other men and it went above her head, shattering the window behind her. The men had finally reacted.

"Alicia, hurry!"

She heard her sobs getting closer as she dragged herself on her elbows. Another burst of gunfire missed Alicia's feet by inches. She dragged herself next to her mother on the floor, protected by the bed behind them.

"Cut the strings from my hands, fast!"

"Mom, my hands are tied. I can't!"

"Try, Alicia! Scrape the blade hard on the string. Come on!"

Alicia did as she was told, grabbing the knife's handle with both hands and running it up and down against the string handcuffs as if it were a saw. Another burst of gunfire went above their heads, smashing a hole in the wall above them.

"Keep trying, Alicia! Hurry!"

Lucia felt the blade cutting into her skin as Alicia began losing her coordination and missing her mark. Lucia pulled her hands away from each other as hard as she could, but still the strings did not give way. She overheard the men yelling outside the door of the room.

"We gotta get in and finish them! They're down!"

"Don't forget that lady's armed," said another. "And she

is near that pile of guns and ammunition that you put there, Rodolfo. You dumb ass!"

"How's Beto doing?" the other one yelled. "Can you see him?"

"Forget about Beto!" Rodolfo said. "Beto is gone!"

Lucia pulled her hands apart until the plastic strings seemed to eat against the skin. Then she heard a pop and her hands were free. She wasted no time. She rolled under the bed to reach for one of the M-16s lying on the other side. She yanked the fire mode selector, placed it on a three-burst fire, and quickly reclined the end of the gun on the edge of the bed and fired toward the room's front door.

The bullets tore through the open frame, leaving a trace of smoke behind them. She did not hit anything but sure scared the living daylights out of the men outside.

She heard them scream. "She's got the guns! Look out! Fire, fire!"

Lucia had pushed Alicia face-down toward the floor and then dragged herself over her to the end of the bed. She could not see the men, so it was hard to get a target, but she was able to get a glimpse of one by looking over the end of the box matrix.

There they were, gathered at each side of the door with their guns pointing toward them—really inexperienced, she thought. She was able to get a target by squeezing the gun under the bed and dragging herself forward. It could be a trap, she thought. Once she fired, she would have to roll to the other side, but she quickly shot at each side of the door frame, splintering the wood in the middle. She dragged herself to the side, near where the old woman was lying, perspiring heavily and crying. Then there was total silence.

"Don't worry," she whispered to the old woman," we'll get out of here soon."

"Mom, are you there?" Alicia was asking from the other side of the bed. "Are you all right?"

"I'm all right, Alicia."

"Mom," she said, sobbing. "Please, can we get out of here?"

"Stay still, honey. Be quiet."

Lucia quickly dragged herself to the edge of the bed. There was no one outside. Whoever had survived her attack had probably got others to help him. That was not hard to do in these parts, where kidnappers and robbers ran freely, subduing the locals and forcing them to cooperate. Here she was, she thought, alone, protecting an elderly woman, a young mother and her baby, and her own daughter. She had her hands full.

Chapter Eight

The Dodge Ram drove into the town of Ojinaga, near the US–Mexican border, late in the afternoon. The driver did not stop to see the "*zocalo*," or town square, or to buy some piece of local earthenware so sought by the tourists who came here.

Having just crossed the checkpoint at the border, his eyes were concentrating on the highway signs. It had been a twenty minute inspection at the checkpoint but no more thorough than anybody else's. Carlos had worked on hiding his arsenal of weapons and ammunition by putting everything apart and then sticking the parts inside the door panels, under the engine's manifold and on the inside of the axels. He had just left Route 67 on the US side and looked anxiously for any trace of highway 18, which would lead him towards Ciudad Camargo, near Federal Highway 45 D, where he would go south toward Zacatecas. He stopped off the road as soon as he saw a slope on the side. He had to be careful and made believe one of the tires in the truck had gone flat. He was replacing it but in the process he placed the ammunition and weapon parts inside the cabin where later he assembled them together again. He began to get edgy when he did not see a sign. The area had been plagued by drug wars, and mayhem and death were being brought upon the population on a daily basis, not much less than in Ciudad Juarez, located about five hours' drive from here. He was going to pull over into a local shop to ask when his companion traveler told him to keep going.

"I see it ahead," the passenger said. "Keep going. We only stop for gas after this."

Carlos had not traveled alone after all. Right before reaching Tallahassee, Steve Hartzman called him and told him where he would wait for him. He met him at a rest stop off Highway 10 where he dropped off his car. Carlos did not believe him at first. He understood perfectly what it meant to the middle-aged agent. He was putting his job on the line, his many years of service, his future, his retirement, his family, his life. That was a lot to ask from a man. But Carlos had not asked for anything. He was going it alone until Hartzman called again, perhaps dared by Carlos's own recklessness, but beyond that by his own integrity as a man. Steve Hartzman was nobody to play with, and Carlos was just about to learn a big lesson on government accountability. So much for his theory of government treason and cowardice at the Bay of Pigs. Here was someone who meant what he said and did what he promised. And there was no doubt that despite Carlos's apt hiding of the guns, he would have never crossed the border had it not been for Steve's influence. Once he showed his badge to the other agents, they let them through without questions.

Steve was not about to let Carlos enter Mexico by himself on a crazy rescue mission that would most likely lead to his death and that of his family. He could not sit by and let it happen. He had to act. He quickly informed his superiors of the fateful events that were taking place. That much he had to do, with the understanding that he would be going. Unofficially, that was the response he got. No government agent could participate in such madness. If he went, he went against a direct order, and he was on his own. There was no telling what action the agency would take against him once he got back—if he got back.

"I see it," Carlos acknowledged. "You know, you expect the signs to be as frequently posted as in the States, but I guess they're not. They rely more on common drivers' knowledge around here. I just don't want to make a mistake and take the wrong road. Every minute counts."

"You won't get on the wrong road. There are no major highways other than 18."

Carlos felt the vibration of his cell phone lying next to him on the seat and picked up before it could ring. "Lucia?"

"Carlos." Lucia's voice was on the other side. It sounded weak, like a whisper, and that alarmed him. It was a sign she did not want to be heard.

"Lucia, what's happening? Where are you?"

"It looks like we're at a standoff here. We're inside a room at the motel, but we can't get out. I think there are armed men outside."

"Is Alicia with you?"

"Yeah. They also brought two women and a baby who are now with us. I fought them off the best way I could and got rid of one, but I think more will come and they will probably surround this place and try to take us by force. Either that or they'll try to starve us out. I'm thinking whether we should make an effort to get away."

Carlos sorted through the information she gave him. He was still a long way from Zacatecas, and depending on road conditions and whether he and Steve ran into any trouble, he would probably not reach Rio Grande until tonight. He hesitated on how to counsel his wife. "Do you know how many men you got outside?"

"No idea. I think I may have hit at least one when I fired at them. There's the body of another in the room that I got to before, which would mean there are at least two outside.

I think I could make a run through the back window, but then where would I go? I'd have to face them to get to the car and leave."

"Don't!" Carlos said. "Stay put. It's too dangerous to go outside. I'm on my way."

"But I'm afraid it's a trap. These guys multiply like rabbits. They're all over the place. What if more come and surround us and try to take us? I can't hold them off for very long."

"You can, Lucia," he said, reassuring her. "What kind of a weapon you have there?"

"I've got two M-16s, a .45, and a couple of grenades. That can last me for a while, but not if they're smart and attack me from front and back. Then what do I do?"

Carlos hesitated. He wanted to tell her to take the initiative, go out, and give them hell while they were still weak from her previous assault, but he couldn't work the guts to send his wife into a firing line. He turned to Steve, who kept staring his way, hungry for news.

"Steve, how long you figure until we hit that town?"

"Not till tonight at least."

"Lucia, it looks like you're gonna have to hold them off till I get there. I've got a few hours to go. You can do it, babe."

"If it was just me and Alicia maybe I'd make a run for it. But we have a sick baby with us too. Maybe I should hit them while I still can and then make our getaway."

Carlos knew that was the right plan but couldn't tell her to do it. He just could not work up the nerve. Right now he would have given anything to be able to be with Lucia. If he only had wings, he would fly to her.

He tried to summon the most reassuring voice he could in the softest tone he'd ever used. "Lucia, do what you think is best, honey. Be real careful in whatever you do. Don't expose yourself. Please."

"I love you, Carlos," she said sweetly. "Don't get yourself

into an accident trying to rush here. We'll make it. I'll talk to you later."

He heard silence at the other end after she disconnected. Carlos turned to Steve. "She's trapped inside a motel room with Alicia and two other women who have a baby with them. The kidnappers are outside. I'm afraid that if they decide to break in they might kill them after what Lucia has done to them."

"Take it easy with the speed, Carlos," Steve said. "We don't want to get stopped by some Mexican police. How many of them are out there? Did she tell you?"

"She's not sure. She knows they're outside but can't tell how many, maybe two. We've gotta get there, Steve. Those guys are not waiting, and if they get hold of her again, I'm afraid they won't take her as a captive. They'll kill her. At this point, revenge for what she's done to them is what they'll want. Ransom is not an option now."

"I wouldn't say that, Carlos. These guys are not professionals. No, they'll settle for money."

"That was before Lucia wasted a few of them."

Steve stared at him and Carlos gazed back. He had to tell him, although he had reservations about discussing murder with law enforcement, sooner or later he would find out, so he might as well level with him. After all, they were partners in this very dangerous venture and this was wild country anyway.

"What exactly did she do?"

"She put one of them away, she told me. And something tells me she had to go through the ones who took her and Alicia captive at first. How else would she and my daughter have gotten away? I know my wife, Steve. She's a sweetheart, but she's got the determination of a mule, and you can't really judge her. I mean, what can you do in a situation like that if you're not prepared to kill? It's kill or be killed."

* * *

"Untie Norma," Lucia said to the old woman who was sitting at the end of the bed, hands across her face as if she did not want to face reality. "Untie her now. And hold the baby. Try to get her to stop crying. I've got more aspirin in my bag that I can give her to bring down the fever. I'm sure she's running one."

Lucia dragged herself under the second bed and then peered towards the front door. Everything was quiet out there. There were no windows in the front of the room, and she knew she could not be seen. But to get a look outside, she would have to expose herself among the remains of the front door, now with the frame obliterated and parts of it blown off. She did not think it was a good idea to parade herself in front of it. She moved slowly forward on the floor with her gun pointing ahead as she thought of what to do. When she was near the door, she stopped and listened. Not a sound. Then she decided she would take a peek out.

She reached for the door handle and noticed it was unlocked. Right at the moment she was going to turn it, she realized she didn't have to. Her previous shots at the men had carved a big gash on each side of the door frame. The top portion of the door was gone so she would have to remain in a slouched position. The left frame was ripped into shreds but had a ragged hole in the area of the lock, about half an inch wide and she could see through it. She saw her car parked directly outside, and with some difficulty she saw portions of the parking lot. A small Dodge was parked a couple of spots from hers, but otherwise the whole lot seemed empty. She noticed the green van parked on the other side, its back facing her door. She could not see whether anyone was inside, but the vehicle bore all the suspicious signs of having been used by kidnappers. It was a van with no side windows and with all-terrain tires that seemed oversized. Lucia took a few seconds inspecting the van. If there was someone inside, she had decided she would come out and give him hell.

"Yes! There he is!" she yelled.

"What is it, Mom?" Alicia asked from the bed.

"Nothing, honey. One of them is out there. I think it's the last one, so I'm gonna go out and try to clear him out. He's still alone. He's sitting inside, probably waiting for others to come help him. I gotta get out there before anybody else gets here. But we gotta see about the baby. How is she?"

She turned toward the woman. The baby was lying next to her, but she had not picked her up and merely kept patting her belly to comfort her.

"How's her temperature?" Alicia asked her in Spanish. "Is she hot?"

The old woman just shook her head and pouted. She was obviously in a state of despair and was unresponsive. Lucia turned to Norma, who was sitting a few feet from her and noticed she was not faring much better. Throughout the entire ordeal she had just sat there quietly, not saying a word, her hands still tied behind her back.

"Florencia, that's your name, no?" Lucia said to the old woman.

The woman nodded.

"Go untie Norma. We need her to help us. Alicia," she said, turning to her daughter. "Get the bottle of aspirin from my bag and bring me a glass of water from the bathroom. Do not walk. That man outside might see you. Crawl. Come on!"

She made her way back to the bed and felt the baby's forehead and realized it was very warm. Holding her weapon in her right hand she moved slowly over the bed and retrieved the thermometer from her bag on the other side of the room. She squeezed it into the baby's mouth. The child quieted down but kept grunting. She knew her temperature would be high.

Alicia came by her side and handed her a glass of water and the aspirins. Lucia wasted no time. She ripped a corner of her own blouse and wrapped one of the pills inside. She bit on the knot made by the cloth, cracking the pill inside and kept biting into it until she ground it into small particles. She poured the contents into the cup of water and stirred it with her finger.

"What's her temperature, Mom?"

"It's a hundred and four. It's high." She began feeding the mixture to the baby through her partially open lips.

"Florencia," she called out to the old woman, "there are towels in the bathroom. Get one wet with cold water and bring it here to wash the baby."

The old woman had untied Norma, but she hardly reacted. She seemed to have gone into a trance and kept sitting still at the edge of the bed. The old woman crouched and moved slowly to the bathroom. Lucia finished feeding the baby the aspirin water in drops that fell from her wet fingers.

"This should bring her temperature down," she said in a low voice. "Now, Florencia, you wash the baby with the towel slowly. Go ahead. I'm gonna be stepping outside."

"Mom, are you crazy? Where are you going?"

"Your father's coming," Lucia said. "I gotta do something about that man outside. We need to meet him half way."

"Mom, no, why don't you call Dad? Tell him about it. Don't go outside."

"It's all right. You stay put. Stay on this side of the room. No one can see you here from the outside."

She went near the bed again and opened the ammunition box. She took one of the two grenades that Rodolfo had so clumsily missed. It had been a long time since she had touched one, but she knew how to use them. She wasn't sure if she would need it but somehow she felt the need to carry one. This was war.

She scurried toward the door, keeping her body against the wall and away from the half torn door. When she reached it, she already knew what she was going to do.

She quickly pulled the door open and jumped out behind the car with her automatic weapon pointing forward. But she immediately knew she had misjudged the situation, and badly. The men she had thought she killed were standing to the right side of the parking lot, where she could not see them from where she stood at the door.

They immediately separated from each other and took a military stance, weapons in hand. They fired before she did, and the shots hit the Blazer on the hood and driver-side window. She crouched under the rear end of the car and moved to reach the front of the vehicle. A barrage of bullets hit the Blazer, the impact rocking it. The sound was deafening, and she realized she had to return fire. She could not wait. She raised herself enough to peer through the passenger window. There was no time to aim, and when she saw them, she was ready. She fired one round at the one on the left and then quickly fired at the other one.

The blazing heat of a bullet nicked the top of her left shoulder. She knew both men were dead, but she perceived movement coming from the van parked across from the Blazer.

"Don't come out!" she yelled out to him in Spanish. "If you do I'll blow you away." *That has to be Rodolfo*, she thought, and looking to her left lapel she realized now why she had brought a grenade.

She did not stop to think. She needed to destroy him fast, but better yet, she needed to destroy his means of communication and travel. Incinerate him, annihilate him, make him totally disappear. She grabbed the pineapple-shaped device, yanked the safety lever off, and tossed it under the van. The grenade rolled the short distance between the cars and disappeared under the back of the van. She saw Rodolfo with his back toward her. He had heard the shots and was opening the door, trying to get out while using his cell phone. She fired a warning shot that whistled past him, enough to keep him inside. She could barely see him, but the seconds were ticking and it was time to go for cover. She dived into the back of the Blazer and held her ears.

The explosion shook the Blazer, and the wall of her room rattled behind her. She looked to see the damage and saw the entire van engulfed in a ring of fire. He had not had time to get out. She could see him through the rear window, spread horizontally on the seat where he had been lying to avoid being detected but was now hopelessly trapped.

A moment later she realized she had to duck. Debris from the van had been catapulted into the air by the explosion, and she bent down in the rear of the Blazer, crouching behind its fender. A torn piece of the van's door passed nearby Then she felt the pain in her left shoulder for the first time. Her shirt was bloodied, and she took a moment to examine her wound. It was superficial. Miraculously, the bullet had only grazed her.

She stood up and looked around. The van was destroyed, merely a carcass burning up and spurting a cloud of black smoke that rose high over the roof of the building. Toward her right the men she had killed lay a few feet from each other, each in a pool of blood that kept growing by the second.

Then there was the small Dodge with no one inside, and the Blazer. Now was the time to leave, she thought. But when she looked at the Blazer, she realized the men had seen to it that she could not use it. The tires were blown and the windows shattered. The whole body had been ripped by bullet holes and fluid oozed from the front of the engine. It was perhaps not even safe to be near it, she thought. It could explode. She moved aside, cautiously looking everywhere. If there was any way to get out of here, she would need a car.

She went to the front office of the motel, where she had checked in the night before. The small receiving window was covered by a blind. She took a step back and kicked hard on the door while holding her M-16 with both hands in front of her.

"Open the door!" she yelled out in Spanish. "Open up!"

She waited. No response. She yelled out again, and hearing nothing she shot toward the lock and then kicked the door hard again, breaking it open. The room was small, with a desk and small bed. The woman who had received her yesterday was sitting on it, and Lucia pointed her gun at the her.

"*Señora*, please don't kill me. I didn't do nothing. I'm just trying to make a living. Please."

"I'm not gonna kill you. But you sure have a change of attitude from yesterday. Tell me, who owns that car in the parking lot?"

"That is Rafael's car. The owner of the restaurant down the road."

"Really? What's it doing here?"

"He lives here, *señora*. He stays here a lot."

"Where are the keys?"

"I don't know."

"All right, take me to his room, come on! Let's find the keys."

The woman grabbed a set of keys from a board behind the desk that held a dozen clips with key chains attached to them, apparently for all the rooms in the motel. Lucia grabbed them from her.

"Are they the keys for his room?"

"Yes."

"All right, come on with me. Let's go."

"*Señora*, is it safe to go outside?" The woman hesitated but was flanked by Lucia, who grabbed her by the arm and brought her out.

"You obviously know more about the crowd you tend to than anybody else around here. You run the perfect business for it, and don't tell me you have not seen any violence before. Where is Rafael now?"

"He's not here right now," the woman said fleetingly.

"How do you know?"

By then they had reached the room right behind the Dodge. Not too far from them lay the bodies of the men Lucia had killed, and on the other side of the parking lot the van was still burning. Lucia had three keys in the key ring, and she had to try all of them before the door finally popped open.

"He's not here during the day," the woman answered.

Lucia motioned with her rifle for her to go in.

"What's his car doing here then?"

"He leaves it here. He walks to work."

"Then you must know where the keys are. Let's go," she said, urging her to go in. "Go inside and look for the keys."

"*Señora*," she replied hesitantly.

"Yes?"

"I'm afraid."

"Really? And why is that? I thought you were friends."

Lucia knew she was being needlessly cruel. But she was by now pretty sure that the reason the thugs had caught up to her were because of that man from the restaurant—Rafael. And she had a pretty good idea that the motel's hostess was involved with him.

"Kind of friends, but—"

"Was it him who brought these guys here to get us?"

The woman evaded her eyes. They were standing in front of the door to the room, the door ajar, when a voice yelled out from two doors down.

"Mom, are you there? Are you all right?"

It was Alicia, yelling out at the top of her lungs.

"I'm fine, Alicia. Sit tight. All right," she said to the woman. "You go inside first. You know Rafael. You know where you keep his things, so find the keys for the car. Come on."

She waved her in using the barrel of her gun to remind her that she was armed and that she would not hesitate to use her weapon. The woman began to sob and cautiously pushed the door in. Lucia stood to the side, with her weapon held forward. The woman went in first, and Lucia waited until she was inside the room to follow her. It was a smaller room than hers, with a single bed and one single window in the back. Clothes were neatly folded on top of a chair, which somehow got Lucia's attention. They appeared to have just been washed.

The woman moved toward the highboy dresser and opened the top drawer. She went through its contents but did not find the keys. Then she moved to the third drawer and did the same.

"Open the second drawer," Lucia said. She stood behind her but toward the wall where she could get a good view of the outside. She knew the shots and the explosion would draw reinforcements for the gang. She had seen Rodolfo on the phone right before he had been emblazed by the fire. Who knows whom he might have called? She was sure it was only a matter of time before more men would show up. She had to hurry.

"All right, what do you have there?" She approached. She went through the contents of the drawer with her left hand, still holding her weapon, which she kept slung across her shoulder and close to the hostess. She went through some clothes, socks and T-shirts, until she ran across a yellow wire key chain with a leather pouch attached to it. She could see they were Dodge keys and knew right away they were the ones for the car outside. She decided to go through all the drawers, to see if Rafael kept any weapons. In the bottom drawer she found a pistol with loose ammunition that she stuck in her waistband. She took a good look around the room to see if she would spot anything of interest, but she didn't give herself too much time.

"Let's go," she said to the hostess.

"Where are we going, *señora?*"

"If there's gonna be an ambush, you'll be the first one to get shot. We're going to my room."

They walked cautiously outside and knocked on the second door next to the room to let them know they were coming. They went inside the room through the door opening. Alicia had pulled the bottom half of the door open and it had come off the hinges.

Alicia rushed toward her mother as soon as she saw her with her arms flinging, sobbing.

"Mom, are you all right?"

"I'm fine, honey. How's the baby, Florencia?"

She entered the room with the hostess walking next to her. Florencia seemed surprised at the sight of the hostess in the room. She was holding the baby in her arms.

"I think the fever is down, *señora*, but I can't really tell. Will you feel her?"

Lucia felt the baby's forehead. "She's still warm. But not as warm as before."

Then Norma, who had up until now showed little emotion, left her place at the bed and came toward Lucia. She hugged her tenderly and laid her head on her shoulder, the tears finally coming out. "*Señora*, I'm sorry I got you involved in all this. It was all my fault. But I was just looking for help for my baby. I was afraid I was losing her."

"You won't lose her, Norma. Tell me something, who is this woman," Lucia said, pointing to the hostess.

"She's Rafael's mistress," Florencia said, interrupting them as she gently swung the baby in her arms. "She takes care of him, washes his clothes, and keeps his room. And then he goes on and does what he wants, like abusing my daughter."

"Probably involved with all these thugs too," Lucia said.

"Oh, sure. He's the big shot in town. He's protected by the drug people."

"Florencia, you, the baby, and Norma get ready to leave with us. We're going. But first I need to bind this woman. I don't want her running to Rafael the minute we leave."

"I won't," the hostess said. "I promise."

"Yeah, right. Like you promised a lot of other things."

"Mom," Alicia said, approaching her, "you're taking them with us?"

"Sure, Alicia, we can't leave them behind. They'd be dead the next day. We've got to save that baby."

"But Mom—"

"Alicia," she said, ignoring her comment. "Get one of those string handcuffs and tie this woman up. Tie her feet too. We don't need her running around after we're gone. I'm sure Rafael will find her after he gets back."

"I'll do it," Norma interjected, suddenly flowing with energy. "I'll be glad to do it."

Lucia grabbed the ammunition box from the side of the bed and went outside to put it in the trunk of the Dodge. She came back for the other M-16 and put that in the trunk also. She got the car's engine running and then came back into the room one last time. Before leaving, she tied a piece of cloth over the hostess's mouth and left her lying on the bed with hands and feet tied. Once she got the car into Highway 49 she decided it was time to call Carlos and let him know what she was up to.

* * *

Carlos had been quiet now for more than ten minutes, listening to Steve's account of his impressions about the Cuban dilemma. Had it been under normal circumstances, he would have surely engaged in what had proved to be Carlos's passionate lifetime theme. But he sat immobile behind the wheel, making as much speed as possible and thinking about what Lucia must be going through. Twice he had dialed her number and she had not picked up. He was growing more desperate by the second.

"How close are we to the juncture with Highway 45, Steve?"

"We're almost there. We'll be hitting it in five minutes. We're making terrific time. Well, like I was saying, I think our government bears some of the blame for not toppling Castro, but for a different reason than what you believe. I think it's the embargo. If the United States decided to simply forget its pride and do business with Cuba, Castro would be finished. Once the American goods began flowing in, the people would rebel. It's that simple."

"You know, you've got me wrong. I'm against the embargo for the same reason. I say let's open the gates. They want to buy American goods, do business with the United States? Go ahead. Give it to them. It's been bad policy not to trade with him since day one. But I'll tell you something, and the United States should know this by now—Castro will never let it happen. He needs the embargo. The embargo is what feeds his power. It's what keeps him alive, so the minute that the United States gets serious and makes a move to lift the sanctions, you'll see him striving to create chaos and discord so the relations don't ever go back to normal. It could be a simple incident, a ship that turned overboard for which the Americans will be blamed, and he will rile up all the people. The negotiations will be stopped. It's how he operates."

"Maybe. I don't see that happening if there's determination in the administration to carry it through. I think we know enough about him at this point to recognize his beguiling. We wouldn't fall."

Carlos gave him a look of ridicule. Despite the tension, he found room in his busy mind to engage in his passionate beliefs. How could Americans be so gullible? And then he ended as he did always when he said this to himself. He had served in the naval officer corps for four years, left as a lieutenant, and would have given his life for his adopted country if the need arose. He too was an American. But a first generation American, influenced heavily by the traumatic experiences of his youth and his fateful encounter with communism. Perhaps that had made him more skeptical, more unbelieving, and more prone to action.

"There it is!" Steve yelled, in a tone of voice Carlos had never yet heard him. "There's the sign for Ciudad Camargo. That means we're going to bump into Highway 45D at any minute now. One thing about this road, Carlos. You must go slow. They've been having shootouts daily. We don't want any encounters. Go slow."

"On the contrary; we should get out of here as fast as we can."

"No. What you do in these situations is, you don't stir the mud. Don't give anybody any reason to think you're hiding something. We wanna mix with the other traffic. Go only as fast as they're going."

Carlos slowed the pickup and went at a slow pace through the center of town. What seemed like the main road was a single lane going through a commercial area where traces of the ferocious fighting could be seen.

"Just keep straight," Steve said. "A shootout could happen anywhere in this area, at any time. It does not have to be dark, so keep going. Highway 45D is coming up. Once we hit that, we go south toward Torreón."

Carlos felt the phone vibrate at that moment and did not even look at the screen. He put the phone on his ear. "Hello."

"Carlos, it's me! I'm on my way! I'm on Highway 49, just left Rio Grande!"

"Are you all right? Is Alicia all right?"

"Alicia's fine. I got a little scrape by a bullet on the shoulder and my face is swollen, but I'm fine. I switched cars, Carlos. I'm in a Dodge, don't know the model, but it's blue. I'm gonna try to move as far up as possible. Come nighttime, these people are going to come after me."

"Listen, Lucia, stay on that road all the way to the Federal Highway, which will be Highway 40D. I'm seeing it on the map here. You're not too far from there. Highway 40D will connect with 49, so we'll meet at some point. Just don't stop anywhere. This is real dangerous country."

"You don't have to worry about me stopping anywhere, Carlos. The only way I'm stopping is if some gang tries to shoot me down."

"Stay on course, honey. Nothing will happen. Where did you get that car?"

"I took it from some creepy guy who deserves to have his gut spilled out. He paid a small price for all the misery he's created for some of the people around here. I stole it."

"Yeah, but he may come after you now, Lucia. Be careful."

"He won't know of the theft until the evening. I saw to

that. By then I should be far enough. What's my next town I'm coming up to?"

"You'll be crossing some small farming towns like Juan Aldama, Atotonico, and Cuencame until you get to Torreón. By then I think we should be running into each other. Lucia, I can't wait to see you."

"I can't wait to see you either, Carlos. Can we make a pledge to each other right here, right now? You remember how our mothers used to do that in the old days? They would make pledges about something they wanted and keep it. It was something silly sometimes, like not getting a haircut or not eating a particular food. But I want us to make a pledge to each other. Let's neither one of us travel ever without the other, you swear?"

"I swear, my Lucia, and I never wanted you to travel alone," he replied, suddenly leaning forward against the wheel.

"Lucia, I've got to go. We got trouble!"

Carlos had not even seen the truck coming. He had been too involved in Lucia's conversation to realize something was amiss. But then out of the corner of his eye he noticed Steve pull out his pistol from under his jacket and knew they had problems. He had never seen Steve in an aggressive mood, and the fact that the man actually had a gun in his hands made him seem like a real lawman.

"Slow down, Carlos," he said. "That truck is gonna try to run us over."

"How do you know?"

"I know."

Suddenly Steve was leaning out the passenger window, and with impeccable accuracy he aimed his gun toward the oncoming truck. Carlos could not see the purpose of shooting at the vehicle. Then he heard the first pop of the gun, and then another and another. He saw the truck in the distance losing control and swerve aimlessly toward the middle of the road. Steve had shot both of its front tires. And then he saw the red flashes made by the weapons being fired from above the truck's cabin.

"Duck!" Steve yelled. "Duck and drive!"

Carlos hit the dashboard as he heard the shattering of the pickup's windshield. Steve kept firing through the broken windshield. The popping sounds were similar to the cheap fireworks shows Carlos would stage at his home on the Fourth of July. *Now,* he thought, *that's how the FBI intended to guard our borders. No wonder we're in so much trouble.*

Carlos had never been in a shootout, but perhaps due to his familiarity with guns, he was able to handle it coolly. He peeked through the surface of the dashboard. There were no other cars coming that he could see. The truck must have been operating alone. He pulled the pickup off the road and quickly reached out into the back of the seat without taking his foot off the brake.

"Carlos! What are you doing? They're right in back of us. It's an army of them. Keep going. Drive!"

"You drive, Steve. Go ahead!"

Carlos took his foot off and rolled himself to face the rear. He had retrieved his M-16 and shattered the rear window with the barrel as he prepared to fire. The truck began to roll as Steve took the wheel. They took a barrage of fire, badly aimed but dangerously close.

Carlos took aim at the truck and released a burst of fire from his weapon. He hit the cabin and the open driver's window. But that was not enough. Steve was right. There was probably an army of them inside who would spring out at any moment. He had to hurry.

He took his time looking for the gas tank and then spotted it. He let out another burst of three consecutive shots. There was a crackling sound and then the rupturing of metal.

He saw the scarlet-red fire rising up and the black smoke that followed it. The rear of the truck was lifted by the explosion and then turned on its side like a wounded animal.

"This is how you fight wars, FBI," he yelled at Steve. "Not with toy pistols. You ought to talk to your boss about hiring some of the old Cubans for the border operations. They know what to do."

"My boss doesn't even want *me* here. Come on, let's go! Let's get out of here while we still can."

Steve moved aside, and Carlos got behind the wheel. He shifted the pickup into drive and stepped on the gas. He made deep tracks on the sand off the shoulder before hitting the road. Steve was leaning on the seat, still shooting the last few rounds of his pistol at the remnants of the truck.

"What the heck are you shooting at? We finished them."

"No we didn't. We disabled them. Hey, don't miss our exit! Follow that sign toward Federal Highway 45. That'll take us south. What did Lucia say? What road is she on?"

"She's coming up north on Route 49. Look it up on the map. I think we could meet her midway through. I mean if we make it. At this rate, I don't know."

There was broken glass all over the dashboard, even on their clothes. Half of the windshield was gone, and it happened to be on the driver's side; loose fragments were hanging off the window frames, tottering from the force of the wind. Despite that, Carlos kept the truck at eighty.

"Carlos, watch the glass and your eyes. Slow down."

"Not now, Steve. We've got to make it before nighttime, right? That's when it gets really wild around here, no?"

"Yes."

"So how did you know about the truck? What made you think it was going to hit us."

"You get a feel for these things. He was on war mode.

I could see the driver pulling his gun using these." Steve showed his binoculars, which Carlos had not seen before now.

"Speaking of guns," Carlos said. "I got something for you. Stop using that ridiculous pistol if you don't want to get blown away by some AK-47. Here."

Carlos took his hand off his M-16 for a moment to reach behind the seat. He grabbed the barrel of another rifle from the back and struggled to pull it out. Steve grabbed it from him and slowly placed it vertically against the floor next to him, checking its parts.

"What did you bring with you? An arsenal?"

"No. Just enough to blast my way into this place and rescue my family. I'm not gonna come with a toy pistol like you did. That's ludicrous."

"Remember one thing. We're not here to join this war. Our mission is to get in and out as soon as possible. Find your family and go. We confronted those guys back there because we had no choice, but let's not get into any shooting spree. If we lose the truck in one of these shootouts, we're dead. Let's try to keep a low profile and do what we have to do. If we have the choice, we run away rather than fight."

"Yeah, yeah," Carlos said, eying him slyly. "The FBI really has it on rescue operations."

* * *

Lucia was already at the junction of Highway 40D and highway 49 by late afternoon, after skirting the towns of Cuencamé and Tierra Blanca. She did not have a map but had been receiving detailed instructions from Carlos. Luckily she had not encountered any trouble but was worried about nightfall. The fact that all the passengers in the car were women was a concern, so she had asked everyone to lie down on the seat to keep them from being seen. Every car that came close meant a threat to her, especially those in the opposite direction and even more the heavy vehicles like trucks and SUVs.

"How's the baby's temperature, Florencia?" she asked the old woman who was lying in the back behind her with the baby in her arms.

"She's warm, *doctora*. Still a little warm."

"Give her some water. There are some water bottles up here. Here," she said, passing one back. "We have to stop somewhere and dissolve some aspirin for her. Let me just get on this big highway and get near those two towns my husband mentioned. I feel more secure there. Here," she said. "Take this thermometer and put it in her mouth, not in her underarm, you hear me?"

"Yes, *doctora*. I know."

Although Lucia had told her several times, the old woman still could not break away from her old habit of using the armpits to take the temperature. It was a practice doctors had given up decades ago, yet it prevailed in some of the Spanish countries.

"*Doctora*," the woman asked somberly. "Is it true what those men said, that you're not a real doctor?"

"I am not a real doctor, Florencia. My daughter and I were on a trip to Cuba and they kidnapped us in Mexico City and brought us here. We're Cubans but do not live on the island. We live in the United States. I'm sorry I had to lie to Norma about our identity, but we were doing it to protect ourselves. We had just stopped at Rio Grande to get some rest and then go north. Then Norma started asking us all these questions, other people were listening, and I played it safe. I figure they would not want to hurt a doctor who's doing charity work, so I used that line. Little did I know I was going to be called right there and then to look after your sick child. I guess fate brought us together that way."

"Thanks to the Virgin of Guadalupe, *doctora*. I don't know what would have happened if you had not come along."

"Mom, shouldn't you check with Dad? Where are we?"

"I know we're passing Torreón. Then we're supposed to pick up on highway 49D, which is like an extension of 40. But I don't know. I don't see it."

She wasn't aware of the row of houses that they passed and some of the high rooftops in the distance. She was trying to dial Carlos again.

"I know Gomez Palacio should be to our left," she murmured. "But I'm not sure. At least it looks pretty metropolitan around here. Maybe peaceful, do you know, Norma or Florencia?"

"Ay, *doctora*, we don't know. This is the first time we are out of Rio Grande in our lives."

Lucia traded looks with her daughter, crouched in the small foot space in front of the front passenger seat. Her face was swollen from sobbing, but she was alert. She shook her head in dismay at her mother, indicating how little she thought of Florencia and her daughter. There was a trace of contempt in her attitude, which Lucia did not appreciate.

"Alicia, they are very poor people, honey," she said to her daughter in English. "Try to be compassionate. You're lucky, but not everyone is."

"Mom, what are you going to do with them?"

"For the time being, they're with us. We can't just leave them behind. They're victims like we are."

"But Mom—"

"Stop it, Alicia. I won't have any of that. I am not going to leave these people behind so that that ugly creature back there can abuse them."

Her phone vibrated and she picked it up.

"Lucia, what road are you on?" Carlos asked.

"I just hit 49D. Seems like I passed by Torreón, a town?"

"You're good. That's right. Just keep coming up north. We're not far from each other at this point. Another two hours maybe and we'll meet. You're going to pass another town, and then you'll come into Córdoba, which is probably where we'll meet. Just don't stop anywhere, Lucia."

"Carlos, I have to gas up. I only have half a tank at this point."

"Okay. Well, do that now before it gets too dark. See if you can find something in that area."

"Wait, Carlos, wait! Something's happening. I see a road block ahead. Oh, my God! What do I do?"

It was less than a mile ahead. Being on the phone had distracted her, and she had been caught off guard. Cars were on both sides of the road, cordoning off the highway on each lane, but not quite closing the entire road, leaving a space smack in the middle. Her first thoughts were whether she could fit her car through that opening and then she looked at the vehicles to see if they were police.

"Carlos, what if it's the police? Do I stop?"

"Tell me what kind of cars they are, Lucia," she heard another voice say from Carlos's phone. "I'm Steve Hartzman, FBI. I'm with Carlos. Tell me what kind of cars you see."

"They're small. I see a Toyota, a Ford sedan, I think. I see an SUV."

"What does the SUV look like?"

"Don't know. Just like a regular car."

"Don't stop!" Steve's voice suddenly went up in volume.

She handed the phone to her daughter. She agreed. These guys weren't police. They had gathered a group of cars from the oncoming lane and had them line up on the other side.

These people were stopping traffic, just hassling or robbing, surely armed.

She got to work immediately. She opened the driver's window and locked the barrel of her M-16 against the door frame. She grabbed the midsection of the weapon with her left hand and held onto the wheel with her right. Then she remembered she had another grenade and let go of the wheel for a second to pull it from under the seat. She was driving straight into that opening in the middle of the road where the front ends of two small cars faced each other.

A man walked toward her car, raising both hands as a sign for her to stop. She decided not to hurt him but opened fire against the vehicles on both sides, riddling them with bullets. The man threw himself on the pavement and rolled to the side. She saw one of the end cars move out of the lineup—why, she did not know, probably to avoid being shot or to give chase. It was the SUV. She decided he would be the target of her grenade.

"Everyone down!" she told the women in Spanish. "They're going to be firing at us. Stay down!"

As she neared the lineup, she braced for gunfire and fired her weapon more intensively as she got closer, hitting all the windows and as many tires as she could. As she went through the opening, she quickly pulled the pin off the grenade and tossed it at the moving SUV, which was now moving straight ahead in the same direction she was going. By pure luck, the grenade did not bounce off the car's window frame and back into her car. It slipped inside through the passenger's open window, less than an inch from the bottom of the frame. The driver had apparently left it open to spray Lucia's vehicle with fire as it passed, but he ended up juggling his gun in shock as he felt the weird object land quietly by his feet. He knew he was dead.

Lucia accelerated her engine and bent her head down.

All hell would break loose, she figured. Again she had underestimated herself. The car she had hit with the grenade was the only one that could have presented a real danger to her in pursuit. The midsize Dodge she was driving could have given any of the other cars in the lineup a run for their money—although their occupants could perhaps have reached her with their weapons.

She did not hear anything for a few seconds and thought the grenade had not detonated, but as she lifted her head to regain control of the wheel she heard the loudest boom of her life behind her. It was a roar that seemed to travel over the road, under her car, and forward, like a moving earthquake. It shook the Dodge as the explosion went full blast. She took a glimpse through the rearview mirror and caught sight of a mushroom cloud of smoke that lifted itself into the sky and then widened, making the other cars invisible.

"That car must have been carrying some heavy firepower for it to explode like that. Oh, my Lord!" She couldn't even make herself be heard.

Everyone inside her car was screaming frantically, even the old woman who had up to now seemed to be the most stable of them all.

Alicia had buried her face under arms, looking like a bundle of clothes on the floor.

"Everybody calm down!" Lucia yelled in Spanish. "We're fine. We'll be fine. We got them. They won't be coming after us. Alicia! Alicia! Hand me the phone!"

Alicia was unresponsive. All Lucia could make out of her was her back section, bent forward and down onto the floor, shaking.

She grabbed the cell phone from the passenger seat herself. "Hello, are you still there?" she said into the phone.

"I'm here," Steve Hartzman said from the other end. "What happened?"

"I went past the line. I think I hit the SUV pretty hard with a grenade, and it exploded like an atom bomb. I'm far away from them and it looks like some of the other cars may have caught on fire. I'm trying to get away from them."

There was silence at the other end for a moment as Steve digested the news. "Just keep driving as fast as you can and don't look back. Drive at least half an hour before you think about stopping for gas. It's too dangerous right now. I know you're worried about that but you'll be all right. We're not that far away anymore. If you think you're running out of gas, then get off the road and find some shade. We'll find you. Here's Carlos."

"Lucia, are you all right?"

"I'm surviving, Carlos. How far away do you think you are from me?"

"Two hours at the most. What happened?"

"I was lucky. I hit the SUV with a grenade. So far no one has come after us, but I can't imagine they won't. It's only a matter of time before they find me."

"I'm proud of you, Lucia. Just hold on a little longer, honey. We're coming. How's the gas situation?"

"I'm running low. Soon I'll have to decide what to do. I can't just keep on driving and run out of gas."

"You're bound to hit a station off the highway. There are some small towns off the highway coming up. There have to be some stations around."

"Carlos, you know what the violence is like down here? Shootings are rampart. Yes, there are gas stations but they're closed, especially now that it's getting late. I don't know."

"Don't lose faith honey. We're almost there. Don't lose it, babe."

"I don't know, Carlos. I don't know. I need to get off the phone. I'll call you." She had lied to him. She was about to break down but couldn't let him see her. Was there an end to this nightmare? She gazed at Alicia who hadn't moved from her position and then at the women in the back seat. Everyone was sobbing in the car.

"How's the baby?" she asked Florencia.

The woman was shaking from fear and placed her feeble hand on the child's forehead. "Not as warm as before, *señora*."

"That's good," she said, looking ahead.

She spotted two vehicles off the road, parked at a horseshoe entrance to a shabby-looking store with a gas pump in the middle. It reminded her of her own driveway at home. She began to slow down.

Alicia sat up. "Mom, what's happening? Are we stopping?"

"Stay down, Alicia. Everybody, stay down. Yes, I'm gonna stop. I'm going to try to gas up."

She parked next to one of the cars. They were both American model SUVs, one a-late seventies model, the other one probably from early two thousands. There did not appear to be anyone inside.

"All right," she said. "I'm gonna go inside for a moment. You all wait here until I get back."

"Mom, I need to go to the bathroom. I really need to go."

"Hold it a little, Alicia. Let me check the place out first."

She felt for her .45, which she was carrying on her waist, under her beltline. She knew already what she was going to do. She was growing more daring by the minute, but she put all hesitation aside. Extreme situations called for extreme measures.

She opened the mesh screen door to the store. She felt the cool air inside and wondered where it was coming from since there did not appear to be any air conditioning. One man was standing by the counter, talking to another who was sitting behind it.

"We're not open for business, *señora*," the man sitting behind the counter said.

"Who owns the Ford Explorer outside?" she asked, ignoring the man's comment.

"It's my car," the other man standing said, smiling to her. "Why? You need a ride somewhere, *señora*?"

"Does it have gas?"

"Of course it's got gas," the man said, with an obvious Mexican accent. "I just filled the tank."

"Good, let me see the keys."

The man frowned, confused by her abruptness but still believing that he may have gotten lucky. The woman before him looked like she had been in an accident. The left side of her face was swollen and there were black and blue spots around her mouth. But she was incredibly attractive, and judging by her accent, she was probably some high-class whore from Mexico City, lost in these parts, or perhaps even an actress. Who knew?

"They're right here," he said, pulling them out of his front pocket.

"I take it that the other car out there is yours?" she said to the other man.

"That's mine, yes. Why do you want to know, *señora*? Are you lost?"

"No. I'm not lost. Give me the keys." As she said it, she grabbed them from the other man, who stood perplexed for a moment before reacting. It was too late. She pointed her .45 at his temple as she dangled his keys with her other hand, waiting for the other man to hand her his keys too. He complied.

"You guys want to stay alive, right? All right, this is what you'll do. You, sir," she said, pointing to the one standing up. "Get behind the counter and stay there with your friend until help arrives. No one goes outside, understood? Anyone who goes out there will have his brains blown out, you hear me?"

She saw the fear in their eyes and knew she had them. She did not even back off to leave the store. She walked out as if she had just made a normal purchase. Outside she moved quickly. She got the Explorer started and moved Alicia and the others inside. She carried her M-16s and ammunition box to the trunk of the Explorer and then very coolly shot all four of the Dodge's tires with her .45. She then turned to the other vehicle belonging to the man inside and did the same. She got behind the wheel of the Explorer and made off into the highway at normal speed. After a mile or so she tossed the two sets of keys out into the sandy banks off the road. Then she called Carlos.

Chapter Nine

Somewhere in the region of the small town of Ceballos, located to the west of Highway 49D, where the road begins to border the well-known Reserva de Biosfera, an arid and desert-like region, Lucia caught sight of the Dodge Ram speeding toward her.

"Is that you? Because if it isn't I'm about to start shooting. You look like you're about to run me down."

"Yes, it's me, Lucia. I'm here. We're finally all gonna be together. Pull over."

Even after hearing him, she made a point of checking the pickup's windshield to make sure it was smashed, as Carlos had told her. The way things had gone, you couldn't trust your own shadow, and she was determined to keep her daughter alive, and now the two women and the baby who rode in the back. She pulled the Explorer off the road and into the sandy ground where cactus and *nopales* grew sporadically throughout the terrain. She jumped out of her car as the pick up made a U-turn and ran around the front of the truck to the driver's door. Carlos ran toward her and the two embraced like college kids. She wrapped her legs around his waist, and he held her by her armpits to bring her lips to his.

"I love you so much, Carlos," she managed to say between sobs and the discomfort of her swollen jaw.

"Lucia, you're the light of my life, honey. I would go to the end of the world for you."

They kissed again and again and then she laid her head on his shoulder as if the two were alone.

"You're hurt," he said. "There's blood on your shoulder. Let me look at it."

"No, leave it, Carlos. Leave it until we get home. I want to stay like this forever. Now that I have you, I can relax. I can finally relax."

"I can't believe you got that SUV, Lucia. That is just unbelievable."

"I stole it. You didn't know I was a thief? Don't ever let me in one of your supermarkets. I'll steal everything."

"You'd be stealing from yourself."

"I can't help it. I am a psychopath."

"Dad! Dad!" Alicia ran toward him, yelling. She could not find a spot to hug him because her mother was clinging onto him, so she reached out to him from the side, kissing his cheek, struggling to get between them.

"How are you, honey? Are you all right?"

"I'm sorry, Dad. I'm sorry for causing all these problems."

"There's nothing to be sorry about, honey, nothing. None of this is your fault. It's fine. We're going home. Some day you'll see Cuba, not now though. It's not the time."

"I know, Dad. I know. You were so right."

"Who are they inside the car, Lucia?" Carlos said, looking toward the old woman who had opened one of the back doors of the SUV.

"You know, I told you. The two women and the baby. They've been through so much too."

"What are we going to do about them, Dad?" Alicia asked.

"What can we do? Take them home, right, Lucia?"

"Of course. We can't leave them behind. They're dead here."

"Excuse me," Steve said from behind them.

He had quietly exited the pickup and waited patiently for their excitement to abate. He understood the significance of the moment.

"Oh, Lucia. This is Steve Hartzman. He's a detective with the FBI."

Lucia put her feet on the ground and turned, keeping a hold on Carlos's hand. "Nice meeting you. What are you doing in Mexico?"

"Trying to get you and your daughter back."

"Well, thank you for coming. I appreciate it."

"I hate to break up this romantic moment, but we have to get going. Now what's this about the two women and the baby? We can't take them with us. Not even in our dreams. It's against the law."

"Mom, I've been telling you," Alicia echoed him.

"What are you proposing we do with them then?"

"We turn them over to the Mexican authorities."

"Mexican authorities? What Mexican authorities? I have yet to see one police car anywhere in Mexico. There's nobody. I mean *nobody*."

"There is, Lucia. You just happen to have been the victim of a kidnapping, so naturally they're not going to take you near any police or military area. You have been in seclusion."

"Not exactly. We've been out for more than a day. We did not see one single uniform in the town of Rio Grande, nothing on any roads either. We could have used some, believe me. But nothing. There has been nothing."

"Well, we could talk about it all day, but I can assure you they're out there. The Mexican government is putting up a brave fight against these drug lords. So my idea is that we must head out to the nearest military post and hand these people over. We can't take them. First of all, they won't be allowed to cross. Secondly, if we try that would be smuggling, which is against the law and I would never allow that to happen."

Lucia and Carlos traded looks. They could communicate in many ways, not necessarily with words, and the harmony was high between them; their affinity was awesome, almost supernatural. You could say Alicia was an off-product of their union. She did not have their hearts.

"We're not taking them anywhere, Steve," Carlos replied. "Sorry if it puts you in a bad position, but that was a risk you took when you decided to help me and come on this trip. Anything goes down here. Those women and that baby are as good as dead if we leave them down here. I'm bringing them home with me."

"Carlos, which car are we taking?" Lucia said, ignoring any further comments by Steve.

"Well, now, that's a good question. The pickup just about had it. One side of the windshield is gone and it's got a couple of bullet holes. I think it's a marked car, so if we take it up north again it might just get spotted. Steve, do you agree?"

"I agree. You don't want that pickup anywhere near Ciudad Camargo. Besides, it's got no room. The SUV is our only choice."

"But it's a marked car too," Lucia said. "Don't be surprised if a group of them are after us, following that car. Remember, it is not mine."

"So you think we should go back in the pickup?" Carlos asked.

Lucia let go off Carlos's hand and looked around. True, the pickup was a mess and there was no room for so many people in it. Steve was right. They should all go in the SUV.

Then she turned toward the two women who had by now gotten out of the Ford and stood shyly by the rear door watching them, with Florencia holding the baby, perhaps wondering what they were going to do about them. Lucia waved for Carlos and Steve to follow.

"Come on, guys, meet Florencia, Norma, and the cutest baby you ever saw."

Carlos spoke to the two women in Spanish, telling them not to worry. They'd be coming with them. Then he asked to see the baby. Lucia put her hand on her forehead and noticed it was warm.

"She's still running a fever. We've got to do something about that."

"Yeah, I think we ought to be going," Carlos replied. "Steve, what do we do with the pickup?"

Steve looked around. There were no trees nearby, and the biggest object was a hill that looked miles away. The landscape was bare.

"I'm gonna run the pickup off the road and make it look like there was an accident. This could throw them off a bit. Pick me up after I crash."

Carlos took the wheel of the Explorer, and Lucia sat next to him in the front seat. They watched as Steve took the southern lane of the highway. He gained some speed and then swerved abruptly off the road. The vehicle went through the sandy banks off the road and traveled a few yards, running by inertia until it stopped. Steve turned off the engine but left the keys in the ignition and then slowly walked back to the road, doing his best not to leave any tracks.

"Are you all right?" Carlos asked in jest. "Looks like you crashed pretty badly."

"Only a couple of broken bones," Steve joked.

"All right. Get in. We've gotta go."

"Let's go. Back the same way we came."

"I like the way this baby rolls," Carlos said, reaching eighty in a few seconds. "It moves like a brand new car."

"Slow down, Carlos. We can't afford to be stopped by any federals."

"They're nowhere to be found, like Lucia said. All that stuff about the army fighting the cartels is an exaggeration. It's happening, yes, but only in certain areas."

"I wouldn't say that. They'll be around when you least expect them."

"And that's my point. They're not where they're needed."

"I've yet to see a federal, Steve," Lucia said.

"They're around, believe me, and if we get stopped, we're in for it, so take it easy. I have to get behind the wheel anyway. You've been at it too long."

"Look, we'll do it this way. We've got almost a full tank of gas. We'll be at Camargo by nightfall. Maybe if we get lucky we can find some gas station open and then you can take over. If not, we might have to camp out somewhere in town. We can't take the chance of running out of gas."

"Agreed. Except that things may get a little loud even in Camargo at night. That's when the gangs come out."

"We'll find a good place. The main thing is we're on our way back and we got Lucia and Alicia. We also picked up three passengers on the way."

Carlos looked at Lucia and winked.

"We've gotta talk about that," Steve said somberly. "We can't transport illegals across the border, Carlos. We have to find them a place."

Carlos glanced at Lucia, who had taken the baby from Florencia. She smiled at him in one of those gestures the two shared privately, and only they knew what it meant.

* * *

It was almost daybreak when they reached the foot of the

international bridge at Ojinaga. Steve sat behind the wheel. He had anticipated a great debate among the passengers regarding the fate of the two Mexican women and the baby, so he stopped in sight of the checkpoint.

"All right, Carlos, the guns and ammunition, whatever is left of them, I can explain to the border patrol, but the women and the child are out of my league. I'd have to hand them over."

"Who says?" Carlos answered.

"No way," Lucia said with a groggy voice. "They're coming home with us."

"Lucia, you don't understand. That is smuggling, and it constitutes a federal crime, for which there are severe penalties. We can't transport people across the border if they do not have legal immigrant status in the United States. As it is, I'm going to have a hard time getting you and your daughter through. You have no papers with you, nothing to prove you're American citizens. How do you think the border patrol is going to react when they see two Mexican nationals, I mean three, in this car with us? What do you think they'll conclude, huh?"

"Steve, you can handle it," Carlos said. "You're FBI, aren't you? As far as me and Lucia, what can they do to us? Deport us? Where to? Cuba? Come on, Steve, there's a thousand ways you could get these people through. I'm not a lawyer and don't know anything about these things, but isn't it true that when you need a witness for an investigation you can get them a visa?"

"Well, there's a process for that, Carlos, but it doesn't happen at the border. It's done normally by a prosecutor and takes time to complete. Besides, what investigation would that be that I'd need these people for?"

"Ours, Steve. There was a kidnapping here. A few people may have been killed, and look, my wife is shot on the shoulder and she has a broken jaw, and I don't think your department has a clue about how this happened. You mean to tell me that we're just gonna back to Miami and forget this ever happened? You're not going to try to find out who set this up? What about investigating that guy Cardona? I can't believe you're thinking about scrapping all that."

"I'm not, I'm not. Still, I have no justification for using these women and the baby."

"You have all the justification in the world," Lucia said. "Norma was a slave to this man Rafael at Rio Grande. She had his baby, who he would not even acknowledge, not even feed. These people were living in extreme poverty, to the point where this baby was dying for lack of an aspirin ..."

"Lucia, with all due respect, you've just described more than 50 percent of the population of Mexico. That's got nothing to do with your kidnapping, and I can't by far make a case out of that."

"Mr. Hartzman, how do you think this gang found us at the hotel? It was Rafael who sent them, and he meant to dispose of us, these two women, and the baby too. They found me through them because I went to their house that night to try to help the baby."

"Still," Steve said. "Of what use would these women be to me in a kidnapping investigation? What do they know? Have you asked them? They are victims, yes, but they would be of no use to me until someone can prove that this Rafael person is somehow connected to the people who kidnapped you, which I doubt will ever happen. No, I'm turning them over to the border patrol—not as witnesses but as victims of this country's poor choices that have caused the misery their inhabitants are now experiencing."

Florencia and Norma had sat there quietly, staring ahead, without giving a hint that they had a clue about what the stuffy detective was discussing yet looking very much the victims of treason. Lucia sat up on her seat and asked them to open the door.

"That's enough. We're walking to the border patrol by ourselves. Alicia, get out of the car from the other side. Carlos, come on."

The two women went first, and then Lucia, carrying the baby in her arms, followed by Alicia, who caught up with them by going around the front of the Explorer. Lucia turned back once to look at Carlos who had not moved from his position.

"You know, Steve," he said. "You once ridiculed me because I brought up the subject of the Bay of Pigs as an example of how faltering the American government had been in their policy toward Cuba. I may sound like a lunatic to you, but this situation is not much different. I gotta give you a lot of credit, Steve; you took a risk with your job and joined me in this venture to save my family, but you have to have some integrity, man. You can't just turn your back on people that you have begun to save and walk out on them. It's just wrong. I don't know what will happen to my daughter and wife out there. Like you said, they have no papers, no proof of identity, and neither do those two Mexican women. But I sure as hell am gonna try to get through, even if I'm shoved back and have to cross the border illegally. I'll get my family through."

He stuck the .45 under his belt in the front of his pants and jumped out of the SUV, walking fast to catch up with the women.

* * *

Carlos drove the black Mercedes on the outer lane of the Palmetto Expressway. Mr. Peña sat by his side. The car was doing well over seventy.

"I'm anxious to get there Carlos, but I wanna get there alive. Can't you slow down?"

Carlos laughed. "Tell me something, Peña. In all the time you've been hanging around with me, when have you gotten into an accident? Have we ever? Ah?"

"Doesn't mean it couldn't happen. Be careful. There's no need for more problems."

He suddenly changed lanes and took the exit for S. W. Fortieth Street. There was traffic built up on the ramp so he squeezed through the right edge of the road to reach the stop sign.

"Carlos, you're gonna kill us," Peña yelled. "Slow down!"

"Calm down. You should see how they drive in Mexico. This is nothing." He made a right turn onto Fortieth Street and took the fast lane, moving at a fast pace until they reached *La Carrreta* on the opposite side of the road. He made a left turn and found a spot as a car was pulling out from the short strip in front of the restaurant, something he usually did not do. He always used the rear parking lot. The two got out and headed for the counter mobbed with customers in this early evening.

"We'll have two espressos," Carlos said to one of the young attendants. "And a *guarapo*."

"A cigar for me," Peña added.

She turned around and grabbed a pack of cigars from the back.

"Here, Peña," she said, "pick what you want." He looked carefully at the pack, pulling some of them out and slowly putting them back until he found one he liked. He lit it up and turned around to exhale a cloud of blue smoke. Then he turned again, ignoring the small cup of steaming hot espresso the girl had placed on the counter.

He was looking inside the restaurant, going one table at

a time but he stopped all of a sudden. He'd heard a voice he recognized. Then he saw him. He was standing at the end of the walkway, past the restaurant door, talking to someone. He bit on his cigar and walked hurriedly toward him. Carlos did not realize it at first.

"Peña, where are you going?"

Then he saw him too and his blood boiled with anger, but he controlled it. He was more concerned about Peña making a foolish mistake than taking his revenge on Cardona. Before leaving for the restaurant, they had agreed to meet with some of Steve's agents. The service was hot on Cardona's trail, but they did not want to make any waves. After some back and forth arguing, they agreed to have Carlos point him out to them. Carlos was sure that if Cardona was still in Miami, he would show his face at *La Carreta*, the high-quality Cuban restaurant he and Peña visited daily. It was inevitable, Carlos had said. To stay in the kind of business he was in, he would need to show his face in public. The agents doubted him. They had searched for the elusive Cardona and had found no sign of him. The only problem was, Carlos said, that Peña would be with him and he could not trust Peña anymore when it came to Cardona. There was a certain tinge in the old man's eyes, something he had never seen in him before but that he knew. Peña wanted revenge. He felt responsible to some extent for what had happened to Lucia and Alicia because he had recommended Cardona's services to Carlos. He had cajoled Carlos to use him for his family's trip, and even though Carlos had assured him a thousand times that it was not his fault, Peña felt guilty about it.

"Peña, hold it! Where're you going?"

He caught up with the old man just as he broke free of a small crowd that had exited the restaurant through the main door.

"That son of a bitch," Cardona said. "I've been looking for him day and night."

"Stop. Don't do anything foolish, Peña. That's what the agents are for. Besides, that's not him."

"Oh, yes it is," Peña said. "I'd recognize his faggot face no matter what wig he wore."

The man they were speaking of had done a remarkable job with his disguise, if he was in fact Cardona. He had jet-black curly hair and wore a short-sleeve flowered shirt and pleated pants. You could have taken him for an early retiree or a vacationer from the north, out for a stroll, but unmistakably like the astute peddler that Peña had known for years—and for some strange reason, immediately recognizable to Carlos too. Why? Carlos did not know. There was something about him that gave him away. If the FBI had not picked up on him it was due to pure incompetence. The man they wanted had been here all the time.

"Hey, you piece of crap!" Peña yelled at him. "You think I don't know who you are?"

The man he addressed seemed genuinely startled at first but seconds later became pale. Peña did not wait for him to answer, nor for the other man he was speaking with to move out of the way. He took a swing at him that Carlos knew was a dropper. Carlos was right behind him but couldn't stop him. Peña caught the odd-looking man right on the side of the jaw. It was a beautiful punch, never mind that it came from a man who was about to reach eighty. The unsuspecting Cardona did not make a sound. He dropped like a tower of bricks. He fell first on his buttocks, and then his upper body dropped slowly backward, as if sleep had suddenly caught up with him. He lay flat on the floor, unconscious.

"Peña, get back! Stop!"

Carlos grabbed Peña by both shoulders and pulled him back. The man Cardona had been talking to had stealthily disappeared. Some of the waitresses, hearing the commotion, had come outside. The patrons standing at the counter were on tiptoes to get a glimpse of what had happened. There were usually one or two officers hanging around the counter, taking a break. A patrol car was parked by the front of the restaurant nearly all day. The patrolmen were usually well-known among patrons and on a first-name basis with some of the customers, Peña being one of them. Two officers who were having their coffee around the counter corner rushed over when they were alerted to the scuffle by Carlos's high pitched voice. They hastily walked over to the end of the walkway.

"What happened?" one of them asked.

"Ah, just a brawl," Carlos said. "Got out of hand."

"A brawl? That man looks like he's dead, Carlos."

Carlos was looking at Cardona on the floor too, wishing and praying that he would make a move, utter a sound. Cardona slowly opened his eyes with some trepidation, and as he did, he swept the shiny knee-high boots of one of the officers, kneeling over the wounded man and clicking his radio mike on with his left hand. The other officer, who had come to stand behind them, asked Carlos to step back.

"Mr. Peña, step back over here. Give them some room. What happened?"

Just as he said that, Carlos heard Cardona cough slightly. He shook his head, and in a spring-like motion he sat up and looked around.

"Are you all right?" one officer asked.

He looked at him dazed and cracked a smile.

"Yeah, I feel all right." He turned and began walking to the back of the restaurant with the officer following behind him.

"Sir, wait, what happened?"

Peña had made a move to walk forward but Carlos

quickly blocked his path. The other officer, standing behind them, patted him on the shoulder.

"Come on, Peña, let's go back here and talk it over, ah?"

"There's nothing to talk about," Peña said. "A creep gets what's coming to him."

"Peña, sit down, come on. Tell me what happened." He pointed to one of the two mosaic tables located in an island to the left of the door of the entrance to the restaurant, just before the parking pavement lot began, and waved for him to sit down. But their path was blocked by two tall suited men who discreetly showed them their badges.

"FBI," one said. "Where did your partner go with that man?" One of the agents asked the patrolman.

"My partner is right around the corner. Why?"

"Officer, this is federal business."

They turned and hastily made the corner. The trooper sat next to Peña but seemed aloof, not quite satisfied with the exchange.

"I'll be right back," he said, getting up. "Peña, don't move."

"I guess you're officially under arrest. Don't worry. These other guys won't let them take you. We got the FBI behind us now," Carlos said. "You sure downed that man, Peña. What the heck came over you?"

"I've been wanting to do this for a long time. I've been coming around here while you were gone, looking for him, but he wasn't around. He's been in hiding. Today was the first day I saw him since your wife and daughter left. I've been coming every day looking for him. Believe me."

"The minute I saw him I knew it was him."

The two agents came around the corner of the building with Cardona in the middle. They were holding him by his arms. They had removed his wig and his hair looked cropped but definitely made him seem more like himself. The two officers were behind them. The group stopped by the table where Carlos and Peña were sitting.

"This is the guy that hit him," one of the officers said.

"Good going, Mr. Peña," one of the two agents said.

"We gotta give this man his rights. He was assaulted," the officer insisted, pointing to Cardona.

"It's out of your jurisdiction, officer. We'll read this man his rights. He's being arrested for conspiracy, kidnapping, fraud, and various other charges. We'll handle his rights."

He and his partner turned from them and walked away, carrying Cardona by his arms. They passed through the crowd that had gathered by the restaurant's counter and total silence reigned among them for a few minutes. The two patrolmen were still standing near them when Carlos got up to leave.

"Let's go, Peña. I've gotta stop at the market."

"Wait a minute," one officer said. "Mr. Peña, I hope you don't—"

"Listen, son, you know that uniform you're wearing? I respect that. If it wasn't for that, I wouldn't be talking to you the way I am now. But do you know something? I'm really astounded by the way you fellows conducted yourselves today. You've known me for years. You've been seeing me in this place daily for probably ten years now, and all I got to say is, what's wrong with you? I could be your grandfather."

He didn't wait for their apology. He walked ahead of Carlos and opened the door to the Mercedes, then sat on the passenger side while Carlos chitchatted with the patrolmen for a few seconds.

"Let's go home. Lucia is waiting for us. She's making a shrimp in sauce, Cuban style, with *congrís* and *yuca*. She doesn't often cook like that. It's a special occasion, as you know. Lucia can sometimes cook just as good as she can do other things."

Carlos smirked and Peña let out a laugh. Only Carlos knew what he was referring to. He picked up his phone as he got behind the wheel and pressed on the number for his new market.

"Estrellita," he said into the phone. "I need to replace Guillermo's pickup. I need to buy him a car. Do you think he'd want another pickup?"

"Probably. If I was you, I'd just get him something similar to what he had. He'll be happy with that."

"No. The poor guy was in love with that pickup, and I lost it for him. I wanna get him a better car that he can take back and forth to Mexico. That's what he'd want. You know what you do? Send him over to the car dealer on Eighth Street that my friend Fred runs and have him pick what he wants."

"Are you sure that's what you wanna do, Carlos? He could take advantage, you know."

"He won't."

"All right," she said complacently. "Nick wants to talk to you. He's been calling you."

"Nick always wants to talk to me, Estrellita. I'm going to have a late lunch with Lucia and then I'll be over, okay?"

"Okay," she replied.

Carlos disconnected and turned to Peña.

"Thanks for looking after the business as you have while I was gone, Peña."

"I did nothing, Carlos. I just watched that woman and Nick run the place. She's some woman, that Estrellita."

"They don't make them like her anymore," Carlos said. "Sometimes I think she should be the manager and not Nick. Speaking of Nick."

He picked up his cell again. "Yeah, Nick, what's up?"

"When will you be back here?"

"Later. You're not the only store."

"I hate to tell you, but we've got problems with the freezers again."

"You can handle it, Nick."

"A burned compressor," he went on.

"Okay, Nick, call for service." Carlos put the phone down and concentrated on the driving.

"If I might say so, Carlos, Nick is a baby."

"That's putting it mildly. What I wanna know, Peña, is where that punch came from. I didn't know you had it in you."

"Nothing to be proud of, Carlos."

They had reached Carlos's driveway, and Peña let out a long breath after they came to a stop. He always did when they reached a point successfully, as if it were a miracle he had survived Carlos's aggressive driving.

They went inside, and as soon as they passed the foyer Lucia greeted them. She put her arms around Carlos and kissed him. "I'm so happy to be home, Carlos. You have no idea."

He picked her up and carried her in his arms as if they were newlyweds. She had band-aids on one side of her face which was still swollen. They went into the living room, and he let her down easy on the sofa. Alicia was sitting at the end holding Norma's baby in front of their large-screen TV. The two Mexican women were sitting comfortably on loveseats, watching the screen. They stood as soon as they saw Carlos enter the room.

"Sit down," he said to them in Spanish. "You're home."

"Thank you, *Señor* Garcia. You have no idea how grateful we are for what you've done."

"I've done nothing, Florencia. If it wasn't for that man, Steve Hartzman, none of us would be here because the border patrol would not have let us in. But you and Norma especially owe him your entire future. I'm still trying to figure out how he was able to pull it off for you. He got you into the States because you're witnesses to a federal crime. I understand that there's some paperwork that has to be done. Lucia will be taking you to see a lawyer with all your documentation so you can begin to be processed. We've gotta get you to be permanent residents."

"Thank you."

"What made Steve change his mind back there?" Lucia asked. "At first he seemed that he was all discipline, you know, doing things by the book and that's it. I really thought we were going to fight it out with the agents by ourselves, which would have been no match, of course. We'd all probably be in jail right now. But then he suddenly jumped in and saved us. What made him do that?"

"You know, honey. I've been thinking about it a lot. There are people who just go around showing they're tough, and then when the situation heats up they're all as squishy as a bleeding heart. I kind of think Steve is like that."

"I like the way you say that, Carlos," she said holding his hand. "But I don't really think that's it. I think it's a calculated decision, something that leads them to do what may look to us as a charitable act when in fact it is nothing more than a logical conclusion they made. Steve sorted things out in his head that morning. He realized he could not leave Mexico without Florencia and Norma, that they would be vital to his investigation later on and his pitch to make good with his job. They were in fact a prize for him. What agency can say that they are holding witnesses who have actually seen the gangs shooting someone? As far as the legal immigration aspect of it, he knew it could have been easily worked out. When the Feds need you, they will get you. There's a thousand ways that Norma and Florencia can be made legal in this country. They know that."

"And now they're part of our family," Carlos said in Spanish.

The women both said thank you and stood up from their chairs, looking humble.

"It's okay," Carlos said. "Relax. Look, even Alicia has come around. Now she's watching your baby. That's a lot considering it's coming from a capricious teenager."

Alicia looked up and laughed. But it was a laugh of deception. She had been saddened like no other member of the group. Her biggest disappointment after all she had been through with her mother was that she did not get to see her parents' homeland.

"Dad," she said. "Do you think we'll get to see Cuba someday?"

"I'm sure you will, honey. It might be too late for me."

"But, Dad, that's not how I wanted it. I wanted you and Mom to be there. I wanna go with the two of you and share the excitement. What will happen to that island? When will things change?"

"No one knows that, honey," he said, caressing Lucia's hair. "Life holds no promises, but some things will always remain. You know, after all that's happened to our island—the cruel executions, the unprecedented exodus of people leaving by the thousands, the dire economic conditions—despite all that, some things will never change, like the tall palm trees breezed by the tropical winds, the long coconut trees with their pregnant-looking trunks, twisting themselves and growing near the surface of the ocean, the beautiful crystalline beach water. Those things will always be there."

There were tears in Alicia's eyes. It was a final perception of the truth. Her father was right. Maybe things would never change in the regime, but the beauty of that mystic island, so loved and missed by so many, would never leave. It would continue to overwhelm the hearts of those who had once called it home, and however far from it fate may have lodged them, however long they may have lived apart from it, they would always remember it nostalgically as the great treasure they once knew and lost. Carlos Garcia was one among those men and women.

About the Author

Erálides E. Cabrera is an attorney-author who resides and practices law in New Jersey. He was born in Cuba and immigrated to the United States as a child. He has written numerous fiction books, love stories, and mystery tales. He is a graduate of Fordham University and Brooklyn Law School. Mr. Cabrera's writing style is vivid and detailed, and his stories usually have an unexpected twist ending.